THE GIRL IN GREEN

STACi LAYNE WiLSON

THE GIRL IN GREEN

The Girl in Green
by
Staci Layne Wilson

Copyright © 2026 by Staci Layne Wilson

Published by Sinister Smile Press, a division of Crystal Lake Publishing
P.O. Box 637
Newberg, OR 97132

Cover art by Reza
Cover design/interior design by Steven Pajak

Trade Paperback ISBN: 978-1-968532-43-7

www.sinistersmilepress.com

Rain patters against the windows of Bob's Book Nook, creating a gentle backdrop to the otherwise quiet store. Los Feliz Boulevard shimmers outside, lined with pine trees and ubiquitous Southern California palms. Traffic crawls by, headlights cutting through the gloom.

Janet sits behind the counter, her young, unlined face reflecting both plainness and a subtle prettiness that seems to shift depending on the light. She's donning a Bob's apron with her name embroidered over the right breast pocket, but her peasant skirt and white poet shirt give her a bohemian look that matches the cluttered charm of the used bookstore. She wears only two pieces of jewelry—a simple necklace and a wristwatch—practical items for a practical job.

The cash register stands guard on the desk, surrounded by scattered papers, crumpled receipts, and a push-button phone with numbers worn faint from years of use. A small, tarnished bell sits nearby, ready to call for help should Janet step away from her post.

The chime above the door rings as a female customer and her child prepare to leave. The woman wears a spaghetti-strap floral sundress and sandals despite the drizzle. Beside her walks a small figure, a girl of about ten, barefoot, in jeans and a forest green hoodie pulled up over her head. The child clutches a hardcover book tightly under one arm, hiding it. Their faces stay turned away, shadows beneath fabric, anonymous in their departure.

"Thanks! Come again," Janet calls out with practiced cheerfulness, lifting her hand in a friendly wave as they exit into the gray afternoon.

The phone rings almost immediately, its shrill sound cutting through the quiet that follows the door chime. Janet picks it up, tucking a strand of hair behind her ear.

"Bob's Book Nook. This is Janet. How may I help you?" Her voice shifts into customer-service mode, professional and pleasant.

She nods as she listens to the inquiry on the other end, her free hand absently straightening papers on the counter.

"Yes, we have an extensive mystery section," she confirms. "The Sins of the Fathers? Yep. We've got two or three copies." A pause as she listens. "At six. M'hm. 'Bye."

The doorbell sounds again as Janet puts down the receiver. She looks up to see a bald man in his fifties entering, his raincoat dusted with fine droplets that catch the light from overhead. The deluge has picked up outside; she can hear it drumming steadily against the storefront windows now.

"Hello. Welcome to Bob's," she greets him with the same rehearsed warmth she offers all customers, her smile automatic after two years of gainful employment.

"Thanks," he mumbles in return, his voice barely audible as he hunches his shoulders slightly and makes his way to the bargain bin at the front of the store. His shoes leave faint damp impressions on the hardwood floor as he shambles toward the collection of discounted titles.

Janet goes back to shuffling through papers while keeping

one eye on the customer. The gentle rustle of pages being flipped breaks the silence as the man browses through the markdowns.

After a few moments, he approaches the counter, his expression unreadable under the harsh fluorescent lighting. His gaze darts briefly toward the door before settling somewhere just below Janet's chin, avoiding direct eye contact.

The young clerk draws in a breath and holds it... There's something about this man that makes her feel uneasy.

"Do you have *Firestarter*... the new Stephen King?" he asks.

Janet sighs, smiles apologetically, and shakes her head. "No, I'm sorry. We don't. We only carry used books here, and that one just came out. Maybe next week...? You never know."

The man nods, accepting the information without complaint, his shoulders relaxing slightly. "Okay. Where's your horror section?" His voice is soft, almost gentle, at odds with his imposing presence.

Janet points toward the back of the store, to a dim corner nearly hidden from view where the overhead light flickers intermittently. "All the way to the back, far left. Just past the mystery novels," she adds, her finger tracing the path through the cramped aisles.

"Thanks," he says, and heads in that direction. Janet watches him go, the unease in her stomach not quite fading as he disappears between the towering shelves.

East Hollywood is pretty in its own worn way, but it's rundown and fraying at the edges, with peeling paint and cracked sidewalks that tell stories of better days. Janet has heard about other stores in this tree-lined street being robbed... at gunpoint. The whispered accounts from neighboring shopkeepers still make her stomach clench. Tales of trembling hands raising cash drawers toward concealed faces, of new-fangled security cameras that captured everything and helped no one.

The phone rings again, and Janet picks it up, her professional tone lilting. "Bob's Book Nook. This is Janet. How may I help you?"

Her demeanor changes instantly. A saucy, closed smile blooms across her face, and a faint blush colors her cheeks. "Oh, hi," she says, her voice softening into something more intimate.

She listens for a moment, her blush deepening. "Ooh. That's so bad." She giggles, twirling the phone cord around her finger.

In the horror section, the bald man pretends to browse the spines of aging paperbacks, but his head is tilted slightly, surreptitiously eavesdropping on Janet's side of the conversation. His fingers trace over the embossed letters on the book covers, never lingering long enough to suggest genuine interest, while his ears strain to catch every word.

"Mmm. About eight?" Janet's voice carries through the empty store, bouncing off the high ceilings and wooden shelves. There is a beat of silence before she gasps playfully, "Eight inches? Stop!" Her tone is mock-scandalized, barely containing her delight.

Her laughter echoes off the bookshelves as the store's sole customer rolls his eyes, a mixture of disgust and world-weariness crossing his features. He reaches for a book and pulls it from the shelf with more force than necessary, disturbing a thin film of dust that dances in the late afternoon light. He examines the cover—a garish illustration of grand guignol horror, all dripping blood and contorted faces—before tucking it under his arm with a soft huff of disapproval, as if Janet's conversation were somehow more offensive than the grotesque imagery in his hands.

"I've got to hang up now," Janet says, her voice lowered but still audible. "There's a customer in the store." She pauses, listening. "Shh! I'll see you tonight. 'Bye."

The plastic click of the receiver being returned to its cradle coincides with the man's approach to the counter. He places his selection before her, avoiding her eyes.

Janet opens the book, checking for the penciled price on the inside cover. "$1" is marked in the upper right corner in fading graphite.

"Excellent choice," she says, as though she's read it herself, though they both know it's merely a line she repeats a dozen times each day.

"I hope it's nice and gory," he replies, a hint of something sadistic in his tone.

Janet chuckles politely. "It's one or the other. That'll be a dollar, plus four cents tax." She glances out the window at the increasingly heavy rainfall. "Would you like a bag?"

The man follows her gaze to the wet world outside and nods. "Yes, please."

He reaches into his pants pocket and pulls out a rolled dollar bill and a nickel, handing them to her. Janet carefully flattens it against the counter, presses a few buttons on the ancient register, and the drawer springs open with a metallic ding.

"Keep the change," he says.

She places the book in a small paper bag, tucking the receipt inside before handing it to him.

"Enjoy. And have a nice day," she says with detached professional courtesy.

The horror fan's eyes flicker over her with a subtle leer. "You too," he says, and after a beat adds, "And a nice night."

He winks before turning away, the bell announcing his departure as Janet's smile falters. Her cheeks color slightly—not from flirtation this time but from the embarrassment of knowing the customer has overheard her personal phone conversation. She chides herself, then shrugs—that's probably the most action baldie had gotten in a year of Sundays.

Outside, the rain continues to fall, drumming a steady rhythm against the storefront windows. Inside, Janet is alone again with only the musty smell of old books and the soft ticking of the wall clock for company. She straightens a stack of paperbacks, completely unaware that others will be the architects of her fate, setting in motion a chain of events from which she cannot escape.

Dusk settles over the convenience store parking lot. The rain has stopped, but signs of the downpour remain in puddles reflecting neon signs and the glistening sheen across the blacktop. Janet pulls her VW Bug into a parking space, the headlights briefly lighting up a faded advertisement for slushies before she cuts the engine. She's still in her work apron, looking slightly disheveled after a long day among the dust and must.

She reaches behind the driver's seat for her fringed leather purse, the worn hippie accessory a quiet reminder of more hopeful high school days. Her movements are automatic, routine, the motions of someone who isn't truly present in the moment, someone already thinking about getting home, pouring wine, kicking off shoes, spending time with her boyfriend. The leather strap catches on her watch, and she tugs it free with impatience. Inside the purse, her wallet rests between crumpled receipts and a paperback with a permanently bent spine, its pages dog-eared from countless lunch breaks spent escaping into fiction.

Outside the convenience store's glass entrance, three teenage boys loiter with the idleness of youth with nowhere better to be. Two clutch skateboards like shields while the third leans against a mountain bike, its frame as battered as their collective attitude. They watch Janet with wolfish interest as she exits her car, not bothering to lock it; a small-town habit that might eventually cost her.

As Janet approaches the entrance, the skinniest of the three—a scrawny, unwashed specimen with an unlit cigarette dangling from his lips—steps forward to intercept her. His face bears the particular blend of cockiness and insecurity unique to teenage boys trying to look dangerous.

"Hey, lady," he calls out, his voice cracking slightly.

Janet stops, her body language instantly shifting from tired to alert. She meets his gaze with the wariness of a young woman who understands what it means to be alone after dark.

The boy lights his cigarette with theatrical flair, taking a deep drag before blowing a cloud of smoke that drifts between them. His confidence grows with each movement, shoulders squaring as if the nicotine has instantly transformed him into something more substantial than he is.

"Buy us a bottle? You can keep the change." He pulls a few bills from his pocket, holding them out like a peace offering. The money, probably no more than six dollars, is folded and refolded, worn at the edges from being handled too many times.

Janet shakes her head without hesitation. "I don't think so." Her voice is flat, unimpressed.

"Please?" The boy tries again, softening his approach. His eyes widen slightly, attempting a look of innocence that falls far short.

Janet shakes her head more firmly this time, making it clear the conversation is over. She shifts her weight, ready to move past him toward the store entrance.

The rejection transforms his expression. The pretense of politeness slips, showing the petulance beneath. His jaw tightens, nostrils flaring with indignation. He takes the cigarette from his mouth and spits on the ground, the glob of saliva landing inches from Janet's shoes. The sound is deliberately wet and offensive in the quiet parking lot.

"Bitch," he mutters, flicking his still-burning cigarette at her feet. The ember traces a brief orange arc through the darkness before scattering sparks across the asphalt.

His friends snicker their approval as he rejoins them, stuffing the rejected bills back into his pocket. Their collective gaze follows Janet as she hurries into the store, a small animal fleeing larger predators.

Inside, Janet glances back through the glass doors, her eyes darting to her vulnerable, unlocked Bug sitting unprotected in the lot. The possibility of vandalism flickers across her face before she forces herself to focus on the task at hand.

The convenience store is a monument to low expectations. Harsh fluorescent lighting, linoleum floors worn to a dull patina, shelves stocked with off-brand merchandise. Janet makes her selections quickly: a family-sized bag of generic potato chips, an assortment of individually wrapped snack cakes with too-bright frosting, and a bottle of cheap red wine.

At the counter, an East Indian clerk watches her approach with the bland expression of someone who has seen too many faces in one day to register another. He scans her items listlessly.

"Eight dollars and seventy-six cents please, miss," he announces, his accent lilting over the numbers.

Janet takes out her wallet from her purse, counts out the bills, and pays him. The transaction happens without conversation or eye contact, one more forgettable interaction in a day full of them.

"Thank you," she says absently as he bags her groceries in a plain brown sack.

Her departure is as quick as her entrance. She rushes past the teenage boys, eyes fixed straight ahead, clutching her bag of modest indulgences. The boys have already moved on to other potential targets, her existence forgotten as soon as she's out of sight.

By the time Janet arrives home, night has fully claimed the sky. Her small, modest house sits dark and quiet as she approaches, juggling her purse, the grocery bag, and a closed umbrella. She fumbles with her keys, unlocks the door, and steps into darkness.

The flick of a light switch transforms the blackness into the warm glow of home. Janet's living space is modest but thoughtful, a reflection of a young woman who has created her own sanctuary with limited means. Houseplants crowd every available surface, their green leaves bringing life to the small rooms. Unframed posters, mostly art prints and a few band advertisements, are tacked directly to the walls. The bookcases overflow with paperbacks, a pleasant hazard of working in a bookstore with employee discounts.

Janet moves to the kitchen and sets down her purchases. She turns on another light, revealing a cozy if cramped cooking space. Through a door in the kitchen, the darkness of her small backyard presses against a window pane.

She unpacks her modest feast with care, arranging the items on the counter. From a nearby cabinet, she retrieves two wineglasses. The second glass sits empty and waiting as she uncorks the wine bottle and pours a generous measure into the first.

A glance at her wristwatch tells her it's 6:50 p.m. Time enough to relax before her boyfriend arrives. She selects one of the snack cakes, balances it atop her wineglass, and carries both to the sofa. The television sits across from her, a small set with rabbit-ear antennae, an artifact picked up secondhand.

Janet settles onto the cushions, places her improvised dinner on the coffee table, and reaches for the remote control. The television springs to life, bathing her in its blue glow as a male newscaster's voice fills the silence.

"And in entertainment news, it's been reported but not

confirmed that John Lennon will go on his first tour in five years..."

She takes a sip of wine, allowing herself to unwind after the workday. But just as her shoulders begin to relax, a sound interrupts her solitude—a soft, muffled cry coming from somewhere outside. She pauses, listening intently, but the sound doesn't repeat immediately. Perhaps she imagined it. Her attention goes back to the television.

"We've got more used vehicles than you can shake a stick shift at!" blares a commercial. "Come on down to Cal's Car Bazaar..."

There it is again. A mournful cry, more distinct this time. Janet mutes the television, the faint glow still illuminating her concerned expression as she rises to investigate. She sets her wineglass down carefully next to the untouched snack cake and moves toward the kitchen, her bare feet silent against the cool tile floor.

The wind picks up outside, whistling through small gaps in the weatherstripping. The back door rattles slightly in its frame as Janet approaches, casting eerie shadows across the darkened kitchen. She hears the cry once more, clearer now that she's closer, but still indistinct. Is it "help" or "meow"? It's impossible to tell, but something small seems to be in trouble. Janet hesitates, her hand hovering over the doorknob as another gust of wind sends a flutter down her spine.

Caution wars with curiosity as Janet cracks open the door and peers into the darkness. The wind rushes in, cool against her face, but the night is dry. Every scent carried on the crisp air smells fresh and renewed.

She listens for a moment, hears nothing, and begins to close the door.

The cry comes again, stopping her mid-swing.

"Kitty, kitty?" she calls tentatively. Getting no response, she steps outside.

Janet's backyard is small and fenced in, creating a modest private space in the suburbs. A metal storage shed squats in one corner, its aluminum sides gleaming dully in the darkness, while a weathered wooden gate stands at the far end of the sodden lawn. She flicks on the porch light, illuminating patches of wet grass and shadows that seem to shift in the uncertain light, dancing and receding with each subtle movement of the clouds overhead.

She slides her feet into the flip flops she keeps by the back door and steps outside. "Here, kitty-kitty," she calls again, her voice soft and coaxing, barely louder than the whisper of wind through the neighboring yards.

She waits, listening to the night sounds. Distant traffic humming along the main road three blocks over, the rustle of trees swaying gently in the aftermath of the storm, the rhythmic drip of water from saturated leaves falling onto the already damp earth below.

"Help..." comes a small voice from the darkness, unmistakably human this time.

Janet freezes, then moves forward cautiously. "Who's there? Are you okay?"

"I'm here..." The voice is small, vulnerable.

Janet tilts her head, trying to locate the source of the sound. Her eyes scan the yard, finally settling on the storage shed. In the shadows behind it, she glimpses something pale—a bare foot, small and dirty, belonging to a child. Hiding. Scared.

She steps closer, peering into the darkness. "Hello?"

A loud sniffle reaches her ears, followed by soft sobs. As her eyes adjust to the dim light, the form becomes clearer. A blond girl of about ten sits on the ground, hugging her knees. One of her hands is tightly clenched into a fist. She's barefoot despite the cool night air, wearing jeans and a long-sleeved western shirt. Her long hair hangs damp and stringy in two tattered, very short braids.

Janet rushes forward, protective instinct overcoming caution as she kneels in the mud beside the child. "Oh, honey. Are you okay? Are you lost?"

The girl looks up, her eyes red-rimmed as though from crying, though strangely, there are no tears on her cheeks. "I need help..." she says, her voice small and plaintive.

Janet leans closer, scanning for injuries, her hands gently touching the girl's knees. "Are you hurt?"

The moment stretches between them—a single heartbeat of concern from Janet, of intention from the girl. Something flickers behind those red-rimmed eyes—something cold and deliberate that doesn't belong on a child's face. Then, with the lightning quickness of a striking snake, the child's fist opens. The switchblade appears as if by dark magic, its blade ejecting with a metallic snick before plunging deep into Janet's exposed neck.

Blood doesn't immediately appear, just the sensation of pressure, of wrongness, as the razored edge finds the jugular vein. There's a curious moment of disconnect where Janet's brain hasn't yet registered what's happened. The girl leaps to her feet in the same moment that Janet rises, her hands flying to her throat in desperate, useless protection. Her fingers meet warm wetness beginning to pulse between them, her body understanding what her mind still struggles to accept.

The stab has rendered Janet mute, her ability to scream severed along with her vein. Only strangled gasps and wet gurgles emerge as her eyes widen with the shock of betrayal and the sudden knowledge of her own mortality.

She pulls her hands away from her neck as though to confirm what's happening, and in that moment, the arterial spray erupts, a pulsing red geyser that coats the little girl and splatters against the metal shed. Janet stares at her gore-stained palms with an expression of absolute disbelief, as though unable to comprehend that the blood covering her belongs inside her body.

Her knees buckle first, then her consciousness begins to fade. She crumples slowly, gracefully, to the wet grass, sliding down into a heap in the mud. Her eyes remain open, fixed on nothing, as the last of her blood pumps out onto the sodden earth.

Thunder cracks overhead like nature's exclamation point, and rain begins to fall again, sudden and heavy. It washes over the scene, thinning the blood on the little girl's face into pale pink rivulets that drip from her chin.

The youngster stands over her victim, studying the body with an expression that mixes curiosity and satisfaction, the look of someone who has just completed a successful experiment. There is no remorse in her eyes, no horror at what she's done. Instead, there's only a detached interest, as though she's wondering what will happen next. Her head tilts slightly to one side, rain plastering her hair against her pale cheeks as she observes the corpse with detachment. Blood has stained her small hands, yet she makes no move to wipe it away, seemingly unbothered by the evidence of violence clinging to her skin.

In the distance, lightning flashes, briefly illuminating her face with stark white light that catches the empty hollows and vivid green of her eyes.

CHAPTER 3

Amy shuts Janet's gate behind her, casting a final glance at the dark yard where her victim lies cooling in the mud. Rain continues to fall, helping to wash away evidence as effectively as any accomplice. The alley behind the house stretches before her, empty and silent except for the patter of droplets hitting concrete and the occasional distant rumble of thunder.

Water beads on her skin, slicking her blond hair to her scalp. Her clothes cling to her small frame, the fabric darkened by a mixture of rain and gore that becomes indistinguishable in the night. She doesn't run, for running would attract attention, but walks with purpose toward her destination.

Parked nearby, hugging the wall beside a cluster of trash cans, sits an old beater car with fogged windows. The condensation on the glass suggests someone has been waiting inside for some time, breath gradually obscuring the view out or in. Amy approaches without hesitation, her pale feet splashing through puddles with childish abandon that contradicts the adult satisfaction in her expression.

At her approach, the car wheezes reluctantly to life, its engine protesting like an arthritic old man forced from a comfortable chair. Headlights cut through the rain-mist, carving twin pathways of visibility in the dark alley. The driver pulls away from the wall, and the passenger door swings open, a silent invitation.

Amy hops inside, her small body disappearing into the dimness of the car's interior. She pulls the door shut, but it doesn't catch—a mechanical failing that mirrors the dysfunctional relationship inside the vehicle. With a child's impatience, she yanks the door open again and slams it with determined force. This time, the latch catches with a satisfying click.

The car lurches forward, suspension groaning beneath them. Its taillights glow like malevolent red eyes, smeared streaks of crimson against the rain-slicked darkness. The vehicle vanishes around a corner, swallowed by the night, carrying its deadly cargo away from the scene of Janet's murder, leaving behind only tire tracks that the rain will soon erase, as if trying to wash away all evidence of what just happened.

Inside the car, Beth grips the steering wheel with white-knuckled intensity. At twenty-six, she appears both youthful and prematurely aged, her face bearing the particular weariness unique to those who've lived hard lives without enough resources. She wears the same floral sundress and sandals from their earlier visit to Bob's Book Nook, now speckled with raindrops. Her purse sits between her and Amy, a buffer zone in the confined space.

A thin sheen of cold sweat gives Beth's skin an unhealthy gloss under the occasional passing streetlight. Her eyes dart frequently to the rearview mirror, though no one follows them. As she turns slowly out of the alley, she reaches into the backseat with one hand and grabs Amy's forest green hoodie.

"You're soaked to the bone. Put this on, baby," Beth says, her voice strained despite her attempt at maternal normality. She keeps her eyes fixed on the road ahead, unable to look directly at what her daughter might have done. Her knuckles whiten as she grips the thin, plastic steering wheel and runs her thumbs over the grooves, a nervous tic she's developed over years of crisis management.

Amy complies without comment, peeling off her wet western shirt to reveal snowy skin, goose bumps rising in the chilly air. She pulls the hoodie over her head, her face momentarily hidden by the fabric, giving Beth a fleeting reprieve from the weight of their shared circumstance. When Amy emerges, her expression is unreadable, a mask of stoicism hiding whatever turmoil churns underneath. She's wet, but no longer bloody. The rain has sluiced away the most damning evidence, leaving only the faintest rust-colored stains in her fingernails that neither mentions.

With businesslike efficiency, Amy reaches into the front pocket of her jeans and produces a few crumpled bills. "Thirty-eight bucks," she announces flatly, holding out the victim's money.

Beth takes it and shoves it quickly into her purse, as though touching it for too long might transfer some psychic stain. "That's all?" The disappointment in her voice is evident. Disappointment not in the act itself, but in its meager financial yield.

Amy's head dips slightly, perhaps the closest thing to shame or regret she's capable of feeling. Not for taking a life, but for failing to make it sufficiently profitable.

"I got a Moon Pie too. Wanna split it?"

The Budget Motor Inn appears on the horizon like a neon-lit purgatory. Its sign flickers erratically, illuminating sad promises of "Low Weekly Rates," "Sparkling Pool," and "Color TV" that seem more like mockery than amenities. Below these empty assurances, the words "No Vacancy" buzz in red, though it's clear from the nearly empty parking lot that rooms are available.

Beth guides the decrepit vehicle into a space near the office, the engine sputtering to silence as she turns the key. The exhaust pipe coughs a final puff of smoke before going quiet. She engages the parking brake with a metallic groan that sounds like the car itself is in pain.

The vast expanse of cracked concrete stretching before them is littered with tired old sedans and a couple of vintage motorcycles. Vehicles that, like their owners, have seen better days. The motel itself is a two-story campus of beige stucco buildings so old they appear to be slowly melting into the ground. No one lingers outside; all curtains remain drawn, each room a sealed box containing private desperation.

Beth and Amy step out of the car, the child clutching the hardcover book she stole from Bob's Book Nook, a seemingly innocent souvenir from a day marked by death. When Amy shuts her door, it bounces open again, the latch failing to catch.

"You have to slam it, honey. Hard!" Beth instructs, her voice carrying the edge of someone always fighting against things that don't work properly.

Amy slams the door with all the strength her ten-year-old body can muster. The metal creaks in protest, but the latch finally catches, securing the door until the next time it decides to misbehave.

Beth slams her own door with mundane force and slings her purse over her shoulder. She moves around the front of the car to her daughter and hands her a room key attached to a large plastic tag—the kind designed to be too bulky to lose or steal, though it rarely prevents either.

"You go to the room. I'll be right up," Beth says, her tone softening. She hugs her bare arms against a shiver that seems more about nerves than temperature.

"I expect to see you in the bathtub when I come in," she adds, the instruction serving multiple purposes: to wash away any remaining evidence, to warm up after being in the rain, and to establish some semblance of normal parental concern.

Amy nods, her small, smooth face serious. "Yes, ma'am," she responds with unexpected politeness, a jarring contrast to the violence she's capable of.

They separate, Amy climbing the rickety exterior stairway to their second-floor room while Beth heads toward the clerk's office, her sandals slapping against the wet concrete. The distance between them grows, but the invisible cord connecting mother and daughter—a bond forged in blood, necessity, and shared secrets—remains taut.

In the motel office, the clerk, Tami, sits behind a podium that serves as both check-in desk and barrier between herself and the world. She's in her forties, with the weathered appearance of someone who's lived twice that many years. Her fingernails are painted black but chipped, and she picks at them idly, perhaps wishing they were as easy to repair as they are to damage.

Tami's hair, a startling combination of black, white, and hot pink, stands up in a deliberately stiff faux-hawk, a remnant of punk sensibilities that have softened with age. A silver stud gleams in her nose, multiple rings line her ears, and she wears a black bowling shirt with her name embroidered on the front pocket, transforming a uniform into something approaching personal style.

The bell above the door chimes as Beth enters, the sound pulling Tami's attention from her nails. Her face settles into an expression of exasperation as she recognizes Beth, her pockmarked skin contorting into familiar lines of disapproval.

"Beth," she says, her tone somewhere between greeting and accusation. "You here to settle up, or ship out?"

Beth approaches the podium with a smile that doesn't reach her hooded hazel eyes, a submissive expression she reserves for those who hold temporary power over her. She reaches into her purse and takes out the bills that Amy stole from the bookstore lady, smoothing them carefully before speaking.

"I don't have it all yet, but here's thirty-eight dollars toward what we owe," she explains, her voice soft and placating. "And next week, I promise, I'll be early."

Tami takes the bills with a snort of disbelief, her fingers adorned with several cheap silver-plated rings, closing around the money as though it might try to escape. She stashes them in a nearby cash register that appears to be a relic from the Great Depression, its metal keys worn smooth from decades of use.

"Yeah, sure," Tami responds, making no effort to hide her skepticism.

"I will. You'll see," Beth insists with forced brightness.

Tami dismisses her with another snort, turning her attention back to her battered fingernails, the conversation clearly over.

Beth gives a polite nod of farewell, maintaining her deferential posture until she turns away. The moment her back is to Tami, her obsequious smile transforms into a lip-curl of contempt, revealing the true nature of her feelings. The mask slips only when it's safe to do so, a survival skill honed through years of necessity.

She exits the office without another word, the bell announcing her departure with a tinny jingle that seems to mock her retreat. Outside, the night air feels cleaner in some way, free from the stifling atmosphere of judgment and dependency. Beth inhales deeply, filling her lungs with the cool evening breeze that carries the faint scent of rain. She pauses for a moment, allowing her face to relax into its natural lines, shoulders dropping slightly as the tension bleeds away. With a resigned sigh that forms a small cloud floating on air, she straightens her worn jean jacket and climbs the concrete stairs to join her daughter, each step taking her further from one obligation and closer to another.

In the darkness behind the motel, unseen by human eyes, a cockroach scurries across the pavement, a silent witness to the arrival of predators more dangerous than itself. The insect pauses, antennae waving as though sensing something amiss in the night air, before disappearing into a crack in the concrete.

Beth enters the motel room, the door swinging shut behind her with a soft click. The space is lit by the yellow glow of a cheap lamp and the flickering blue light of the television set, which hums with static as the picture rolls endlessly. The room is a study in decay—patchy carpet worn thin in high-traffic areas, water stains forming abstract patterns on the crumbling ceiling, and the faint smell of mildew that no amount of cheap, by-the-barrel industrial cleaner can fully banish.

Two twin beds stand against the wall opposite the TV. Between them hangs an amateurish painting of a ship being tossed on a stormy sea, the kind of generic motel art that's meant to be ignored but somehow draws the eye with its unintentional melancholy. Beside the front door, a bright red fire extinguisher provides the only splash of color in the otherwise dingy room. Next to it, a window with drawn curtains hides the night beyond.

Opposite the front door, beyond the beds, is the bathroom. The door is shut, and no sound emerges from behind it.

Beth kicks off her sandals with a sigh of relief, wiggling her toes against the neglected carpet that scratches pleasantly against her aching soles. She peels off her jacket and sundress with careless efficiency, the fabric sliding over her head in one smooth motion, revealing ratty underwear but no bra. The last one she had had shredded to uselessness months ago, another casualty of her nomadic life. The underwear follows, kicked carelessly aside with her big toe, landing in a small heap as she stands naked in the center of the room, exposed but unself-conscious in her momentary solitude, goose bumps rising on her skin in the room's tepid air.

She opens the dresser drawer, its runners protesting with a metallic squeal that echoes in the quiet space, and pulls out a long robe that's on its last seams but offers comfort in its familiar softness. The once-vibrant blue has faded to a washed-out periwinkle, frayed at the cuffs and collar. She slips it on, the cool fabric settling against her skin like an old friend, tying the belt at her waist with a double knot. From another drawer comes a pair of mismatched socks, which she puts on while sitting on the edge of her bed, the mattress sagging with her weight with an audible creak of weary springs.

In the quiet of the room, the absence of sound from the bathroom becomes noticeable. No running water, no splashing, no childish humming, nothing to indicate that Amy is following her mother's instructions to take a bath.

"Amy?" Beth calls, her voice carrying a note of tired inquiry rather than concern.

Silence answers her.

"Baby, are you taking a bath?" She tries again, louder this time.

Nothing.

Beth rises from the bed, her movements quickening as the first threads of worry begin to weave through her mind. She crosses to the bathroom door, her socked feet silent on the worn carpet.

She knocks, the sound sharp in the quiet room. "Amy?"

All remains quiet.

She rattles the knob. It's locked.

"Amy Andrea Elder. You open this door right now!" The worry in her voice has hardened into command, threaded through with genuine fear.

A single splash sounds from within, but no verbal response follows.

Beth rattles the knob harder, her patience evaporating. She pushes against the flimsy hollow door, applying her shoulder with increasing force until, with a sudden WHOOSH, it gives way. Beth stumbles forward, catching herself against the sink to prevent a fall.

Amy's clothes litter the dull linoleum floor in disarray. Her new book, the one about sideshow freaks, sits on the closed toilet lid, perched atop a folded white towel. The shower curtain is drawn across the tub, an opaque barrier hiding whatever lies within.

The tub appears empty at first glance. No splashing water, no visible child. Beth's heart leaps into her throat as she steps forward and draws the curtain aside with a shaking hand, the plastic rings scraping loudly against the metal rod.

In the water lies Amy, completely submerged. Her face is serene beneath the surface, eyes closed, mouth slack. No air bubbles rise from her lips or nose. Her hair fans out around her pale face like seaweed. She looks like a drowned doll, unnaturally still and peaceful under the glassy water, which has gone eerily quiet.

Beth's face contorts with pure panic, blood draining from her cheeks. "Amy!!" she screams, her voice cracking with terror, her hand already plunging toward the water to grab her child. Her fingers break the surface, reaching desperately for Amy's shoulders.

Amy sits up suddenly, erupting from the water with a gleeful laugh that echoes off the bathroom tiles. Water cascades from her hair, her shoulders, her face. Droplets spray in all directions as she shakes her head, her eyes bright with mischief and satisfaction at her mother's obvious horror.

Beth gasps, her relief mingling with anger in equal measure. "You scared me half to death," she says, one hand pressed against her chest as though physically restraining her pounding heart.

Amy gives a sly smile but attempts to layer an air of contrition over her obvious enjoyment of the prank. "I'm sorry, Mom," she says with fake sincerity. "I was just seeing how long I could hold my breath. Like the men in the painting."

Beth stares at her, uncomprehending.

"On the wall by my bed," Amy explains, then adds with unsettling curiosity, "Do you think it hurts to drown?"

Beth doesn't engage with the morbid question. Instead, she grabs a washcloth from the sink and tosses it into the bathtub. "Use soap," she instructs flatly. "And wash your hair too."

"Okay," Amy agrees, then pauses. "But, Mom..."

Beth sighs, the sound heavy with exhaustion. "No, I don't think it hurts to drown."

Amy gives a single, satisfied nod, as though filing away this information for future reference. "Will you read to me tonight?" she asks, changing subjects with childlike quickness.

Beth shakes her head. "Honey, you know how to read. You need to practice. For when you go back to school."

Amy's face darkens as she crosses her arms over her chest, water dripping from her elbows. "I'm not going back to school, ever," she declares with absolute conviction. Then, her voice shifting to a wheedling tone: "Please? Please-please-please? Just one chapter."

Beth sighs again, her resistance crumbling under the burden of maternal guilt and simple fatigue. "Okay. One chapter. Now wash up."

She bends to pick up Amy's clothes from the floor. As she lifts the green hoodie, another wrapped snack cake, swiped from the bookstore clerk's house, falls from its pocket. Beth retrieves it without comment, adding it to the bundle of clothes in her arms.

"You got anything else for the laundry?" she asks.

Amy shakes her head and begins humming tunelessly while soaping her arms, already moving on from the conversation.

Beth turns to leave, but Amy's voice stops her. "Shut the door."

Later, Amy sits propped against the pillows of her bed, the one closest to the bathroom. Her wet hair is neatly combed, its champagne, shoulder-length strands catching the light from the bedside lamp. She wears a frilly, girly nightgown that creates a disconcerting contrast with what this child is capable of. On her feet are pastel green socks with lace trim, an incongruously innocent touch. Her face, scrubbed clean, has the cherubic quality that adults find so disarming.

She's eating the snack cake, peeling back the wrapper with meticulous care to avoid dropping crumbs on her clean nightgown. Her small fingers work with surprising precision, tearing the cellophane in a perfect line. The sweet, artificial scent of preservatives and sugar fills the space between them.

Beth sits at the edge of her own bed, facing Amy. The book rests in her lap, its lurid cover featuring sensational images of historical human oddities—conjoined twins, bearded ladies, and limbless wonders stare back from the glossy surface. She studies it for a moment before speaking, her thumb absently tracing the worn spine where the binding has begun to crack from repeated openings.

"'*Sideshow Freaks*, by Michael Sandoval,'" she reads from the cover.

Amy giggles, crumbs speckling her lips. "Silly. You don't have to read the cover."

Beth offers a wan smile in response, then opens the book and turns a few pages until she finds her place. Her reading is stilted, and she struggles with the unfamiliar monikers and medical terminology.

"'Jo-Jo the Dog-Faced Boy was born Fedor Jeftichew in St

Petersburg, Russia, in 1868,'" she begins, stumbling over the foreign name. "'When he was just five years old, his father put him to work in the circus. Jo-Jo was covered with long, silky hair from head to toe and was said to resemble a terrier. He inherited a rare disease called hypertrichosis from his father, who was said to resemble a poodle.'"

Amy laughs at this detail, the sound high and tinkling. "A poodle?"

"That's what it says," Beth confirms with a shrug.

"What kind of dog do I look like?" Amy asks, tilting her head in a manner that is both childish and calculating.

"A mutt," Beth responds flatly. "Now, do you want to hear this story or not?"

"I want to hear," Amy insists, settling deeper into her spot.

Beth continues reading, her voice gaining confidence as she progresses. "'Jo-Jo grew up in the sideshow circuit. As an adult, he stood five feet eight inches tall, had only four or five teeth, and spoke Russian, German, and English. For his performances, he dressed in a cavalryman's uniform, and he would bark at the audience. After being discovered by an American showman, Jo-Jo went to the United States. In 1884, Jo-Jo was working under the big top for P.T. Barnum.'"

Amy finishes her nosh and lies down, snuggling into her pillow with contentment. "Who's P.T. Barnum?" she asks.

Beth flips back a few pages, scanning the text for information. "I don't know, baby," she admits after finding nothing. "This is why you have to go to school, so you can teach me."

"Keep going," Amy urges, impatient for the story to continue.

Beth returns to the passage. "'Barnum's flyers said Jo-Jo was captured by a hunter in the wilds of central Russia. He toured the world, and he was made to perform as often as twenty-three times a day, and in 1886, he was making five hundred dollars a week: a fortune in those days.'"

Amy's eyes widen with materialistic wonder. "Wow! Five hundred dollars?! Have you ever seen that much money?"

Beth shakes her head, a hint of bitterness in her simple denial. "Nope."

Suddenly, a hard knock at the door shatters the moment. Beth closes the book with a snap, her body tensing as though bracing for impact. Her fingers curl protectively around the worn cover, knuckles braced. Amy sits up, more curious than alarmed, her head tilting slightly toward the sound like a bird catching the whisper of something interesting in the distance.

Beth presses an index finger to her lips. "Shh..."

But Amy, never one to follow instructions, calls out loudly: "Who is it?"

A tense silence follows, stretching between mother and daughter as they stare at the door. Beth's face is a study in apprehension, her mind clearly racing through possibilities, none of them good.

Silence hangs between them for a moment, stretched thin as a garrote wire. Beth remains frozen, her eyes fixed on the door as though it might burst open at any second. The television continues to roll with static, its monotonous white noise providing an eerie soundtrack to their tension.

A male voice, warm with a Southern drawl, finally breaks through.

"Amy Andrea Elder, why ain't you asleep?"

The relief that washes over Beth's face is palpable. Her shoulders drop several inches as she exhales. "Cecil."

Mother and daughter share a look.

Beth rises from the bed, setting the book aside on the nightstand between them. The volume lands beside a half-empty glass of water and a hair elastic. Small, ordinary items that seem incongruously normal given the evening's earlier events.

She opens the door, revealing Cecil Hickman, a man past his prime with the kind of wiry build that speaks of hard living rather than deliberate fitness. He's shopworn, but traces of former handsomeness linger in his sharp, angular features. His thinning hair is slicked back with more effort than success, his mustache is sparse, and he's dressed in slacks and a short-sleeved, button-down shirt sporting a noticeable stain on the front. His loafers, worn without socks, complete the picture of a man trying to maintain dignity despite limited capital. Cecil's forearms bear fading bruises, yellow-green islands on pale skin. He smiles at Beth, exposing a front tooth partially capped in silver. The cheap dental fix catches the harsh motel lighting.

He steps inside without waiting for an invitation, closing the gap between himself and Beth with the confidence of established intimacy. His kiss lands on her mouth, lingering just long enough to establish possession rather than affection. The faint scent of cheap aftershave and cigarettes surrounds him like a personal cloud.

Amy scrambles off her bed, face twisted in exaggerated disgust. "Oh, gross!" She makes a gagging sound and presses her palms against her eyes as if trying to erase what she's just witnessed.

Beth and Cecil break apart, sharing a knowing chuckle at the child's reaction. He makes himself comfortable on Beth's bed, the one nearest to the door, his weight causing the worn mattress to sag like a swaybacked horse. He grins at Amy, studying her with something between genuine fondness and cunning, his eyes narrowing slightly.

"Have you grown?" he asks, his accent drawing out the words like taffy. He glances sideways at Beth and adds, "She's so tall if she fell down she'd be halfway home."

Amy giggles, apparently charmed despite her earlier display of revulsion. "I am home!" she declares, gesturing at the shabby motel room as though it were a palace.

Cecil chucks her under the chin, a gesture somewhere between affectionate and condescending. "Why, so you are." He pauses, his expression shifting into a playful sternness. "What are you doing out of bed? Do you know what time it is, young lady?"

Amy grins at the attention, then crawls back under her covers with theatrical obedience.

Cecil rises and returns to Beth, who stands by the door looking suddenly tired, the momentary joy of his arrival already fading. She glances toward the window where rain spatters against the glass.

"Is it still raining out?" she asks, seeking mundane conversation.

"Off and on," he replies, then adds with a crude humor that seems habitual, "Who's the dumb sumbitch that said, 'It never rains in Southern California'?"

"Mind your mouth," Beth admonishes quietly, her eyes flicking toward Amy.

Cecil nods, catching her meaning. He turns toward Amy with an stage wink. "Oh, right. There's ladies present."

He removes an imaginary hat and bows toward the bed with amplified formality. "My deepest apologies, Lady Amy Andrea." His voice drops into a mock aristocratic tone. "Do you accept?"

Amy sits up straighter, crossing her arms across her chest in a posture of deliberate petulance. "I'll think about it," she declares, holding court from her threadbare throne.

Beth moves toward Amy's bed, her voice softening into maternal gentleness. "Lay down, baby. Go to sleep. I'm going to visit with your uncle Cecil for a bit."

Something flashes in Amy's eyes—a brief, cold flash that vanishes almost before it registers. "Noo-oo. Don't go. I can't sleep when I'm alone," she says peevishly.

Cecil dismisses her concerns with a wave of his hand. "Pshaw! A big girl like you? You can't fool us. You're slicker'n pig snot on a glass doorknob."

His colorful imagery makes him chuckle, but Amy's face flushes with genuine anger. She turns away, facing the wall, her small body rigid with barely contained rage.

Cecil grins at Beth, oblivious to or perhaps enjoying the child's displeasure. "Come on, darlin'."

Beth glances uncertainly between her daughter and Cecil, torn between conflicting loyalties. "Okay. But just for a few minutes."

She walks toward the door with Cecil following close behind. As she opens it, she calls back over her shoulder, "Amy, I'll be back in a half hour."

He raises an eyebrow at Beth, a silent communication that clearly says, "That's all?"

Beth ignores him, turning off the lights before pulling the door shut behind them. The room falls into darkness broken only by the faint glow of the powered-down television. Amy remains motionless on her bed, staring at the wall, her small hands clenched into fists under the covers.

In the sudden quiet, a tiny white, red-eyed mouse zips across the floor, emerging from a crack in the baseboard. It pauses, whiskers twitching as though sensing the atmosphere of the room, before continuing its journey toward the bathroom. The creature moves with darting purpose, its translucent ears catching what little light remains. It stops again briefly, standing on hind legs to sample the air, perhaps detecting the lingering scent of Cecil's cheap cologne or the stale beer on his breath from earlier. Finding nothing immediately threatening, the rodent resumes its midnight expedition, disappearing beneath the bathroom door with a flick of its hairless pink tail.

CHAPTER 6

Cecil's room is nearly identical to the one Amy and Beth share. The same ragged carpeting, the same water-stained ceiling, the same generic landscape paintings designed to blend in with the drear. The only differences are the queen-sized bed instead of twins and a small table with two chairs where Beth and Cecil now sit.

Cecil plays with the opening of Beth's robe, his fingers tracing lazy patterns along the edge where fabric meets skin. He leans over and kisses her neck, his lips lingering on her pulse point as if marking a target.

She doesn't respond to his advances, her mind elsewhere. Perhaps with Amy, perhaps with the dead woman in the storm-soaked backyard, perhaps with some version of herself that exists only in memory or imagination.

"What's wrong?" Cecil asks, finally noticing her lack of enthusiasm.

Beth sighs. "Nothing. Just a tough day. And I'm behind again. Made a payment at the front desk, but—"

Cecil interrupts before she can finish, unwilling to listen to problems he has no intention of solving. "I've got something that'll make you feel better."

He rises from his chair with the anticipatory energy of someone about to share a treasured secret. Moving to the dresser, he opens a drawer and pulls out a wad of tinfoil, handling it with the reverent care usually reserved for religious artifacts. He carries it to the small table and sits, gesturing for Beth to come closer.

She follows with obvious reluctance, her movements sluggish. "No…" she protests weakly, already knowing she'll give in. A little voice, wailing and howling, clawing at her innards, cries out in hunger.

He unwraps the foil with an almost dainty delicacy, revealing a few small, jagged rocks of crack cocaine nestled within like pale, toxic gems. Beside them lies a much-used glass pipe, its bowl blackened from repeated use, and a cheap plastic lighter with a nearly empty chamber.

"I've got to get back to Amy," Beth says, but she doesn't move. Her eyes stay fixed on the drugs, a hunger awakening in her pupil-widened gaze.

He arranges everything with the dexterity of ritual, placing a rock in the pipe and handing both it and the lighter to Beth. "Just one hit," he coaxes, his voice dropping to a wheedling tone reminiscent of Amy's earlier pleading. "Stay for a spell. Please? Please-please-please?"

Beth can't resist Cecil's wheedling any more than she can her daughter's. The parallel isn't lost on her, but she pushes the uncomfortable thought aside as she takes the pipe. The lighter flicks to life, the small flame dancing as it catches the edge of the rock. She inhales deeply, holding the smoke in her lungs until her eyes roll back in euphoria.

The high hits her with the force of a physical blow. Sharp, electric pleasure washes through her nervous system, temporarily erasing every worry, every fear, every memory of blood on small hands. For these fleeting moments, nothing exists but sensation, bright and overwhelming.

He takes the pipe from her slack fingers and takes his own hit, his cheeks hollowing as he sucks in the smoke. The sacrament of sharing the pipe creates a false intimacy between them, a bond formed not of genuine affection but of mutual chemical dependency.

Taking advantage of the short-term effects of the drug, Cecil guides Beth to his bed. Her movements are fluid now, resistance melted away by artificial bliss. She lies on her back, and he opens her robe with hungry hands, exposing her body to the room's cool air. His kisses trace a path from her neck to her breasts, leaving goose bumps in their wake. The cold makes her shiver, but the drug in her system transforms even this discomfort into a kind of pleasure, every sensation heightened and distorted.

A flash of maternal concern breaks through Beth's high. "I'd better not," she murmurs, her words slightly slurred. "Amy is sleeping right next door." Even in her chemically altered state, some primal instinct of protection remains intact, a thin thread of responsibility that hasn't quite dissolved in the flood of euphoria coursing through her veins.

Cecil isn't deterred. "Come on, honey girl," he drawls, his Southern accent thickening with desire. "I'm hotter than a two-dollar pistol."

Before she can object further, his mouth covers hers, silencing her protests with a kiss that tastes of chemicals and desperation. Beth yields, as she always does, her body responding even as her mind drifts elsewhere.

In the room next door, Amy lies facing the wall, her small body rigid with silent scorn. She hears every thump-thump of Cecil's bed against the shared wall, each sound feeding the cold fury building inside her. The TV's static provides an eerie soundtrack to her anger, casting blue-tinged shadows that dance over her still form.

Across her headboard slithers a thin green viper, its scaled body undulating with sinuous grace. It moves as Amy's thoughts move, predatory and patient. Its forked tongue flickers in the television's glow, tasting the acrid emotional current that fills the room. The serpent's eyes, obsidian and unblinking, reflect Amy's own unspoken desires, her willingness to strike when the moment presents itself. As the rhythmic thumping intensifies, the reptile coils tighter, muscles tensing beneath emerald scales, mirroring the knot of resentment twisting in the girl's stomach.

Amy turns to stare at the ceiling, her eyes wide open and fixed with an intensity no child should possess. Her hands clench and unclench, mimicking the action of gripping her switchblade. She imagines Cecil's neck under her fingers instead of the pilled cotton sheets, visualizes the arterial spray that would result from a well-placed cut. The fantasy brings a small smile to her thin lips.

Amy hears everything—every creak of the bedsprings, every muffled moan, every moment her mother chooses Cecil over her. The sounds feed something dark and hungry inside her, a monstrous shadow growing beneath her childish exterior.

In the space between heartbeats, between one ragged breath and the next, Amy makes a decision. Her small hand reaches between the box spring and mattress, fingers closing around the reassuring metal of her switchblade. She doesn't pull it out yet, just holds it, drawing comfort from its presence the way another child might clutch a teddy bear.

Cecil won't be part of their life much longer. Amy will see to that.

Outside the motel, rain begins to fall again, a gentle tap-tap against the windows that sounds almost like applause. In a puddle forming in the parking lot, the reflection of the neon "No/Vacancy" sign shivers and distorts, its red glow transformed into something that looks remarkably like blood spreading through water.

The aftermath of intimacy settles over Cecil's motel room like marijuana smoke, ephemeral yet clinging. They lie tangled in the sheet, their bodies cooling in the artificial chill of the room's struggling air conditioner. Cecil takes a long drag from his cigarette, the ember brightening briefly before fading, much like the high they'd both just experienced. The bedclothes are tangled around them, twisted evidence of passions now subsided. Neither speaks, letting the hollow silence fill the space between their sweat-dampened skin. Outside, the neon sign flickers through the thin curtains, painting their naked forms in alternating washes of garish red and shadow. She stares at the discolored ceiling, counting the yellowish blooms while he exhales a plume that spirals upward, dissipating against the same blank canvas of her contemplation.

"I'm about as useful as an ashtray on a motorcycle around here," he says, breaking the silence. His voice carries a restless dissatisfaction that seems permanently etched into his character. "I need to get back to Miami, get more product. I'm tellin' you, darlin', this is the next big thing."

Beth sighs, her eyes closed against realities she'd rather not see. The crack high is receding, leaving behind the familiar hollow sensation that makes her chest feel cavernous and empty. "It's pretty great," she admits, then pauses. "For a while."

"Nothing lasts forever," Cecil philosophizes, smoke leaking from the corners of his mouth as he speaks. He strokes her hair with unexpected gentleness, his fingers dragging through the tangled strands.

He takes another drag, the cigarette now burned halfway down. "Why don't you come with me? You and Amy?"

Beth's eyes remain closed, but a small furrow appears between her brows. "No... We need to stay here."

"Why?" he challenges, genuinely perplexed. "What kind of life have you got here?"

The question floats in the air between them, impossible to argue against. Beth has no roots here, no connections, nothing tying her to this particular nowhere except inertia and fear of the unknown.

"Well, she's going to go to school," Beth offers weakly, grasping for the trappings of normalcy. "I'm going to look for a job, and..."

Cecil shakes his head, his expression a mixture of pity and contempt for what he perceives as naiveté. "You are? What skills have *you* got?"

The question lands like a slap. Beth has no reply, her silence an answer in itself. What skills does she have? Survival, perhaps. The ability to look the other way when her daughter does unspeakable things. Hustling. These aren't qualifications that belong on résumés.

He chuckles, the sound lacking any real humor. "That's not much of a plan, Elizabeth." He takes a final drag before crushing the cigarette in the bedside ashtray. "Put hard work in one hand and bullshit in the other and see which one fills up first."

Beth sighs, the exhale carrying a multitude of disappointments. "I've got to get back to my daughter," she says, using Amy as both excuse and anchor—the one constant in her shifting, uncertain life.

Cecil waves his hand dismissively, already emotionally disengaged. "Yeah, yeah. Go back to your brat."

The words carry a subtle accusation, positioning Beth's maternal responsibilities as an inconvenience rather than a priority. His dismissal reveals the transactional nature of their relationship, sex and companionship exchanged for drugs and the temporary illusion of stability. Beth feels it in his tone, that familiar sting of being reduced to a function rather than a person. In these moments, the gap between them yawns wide—not just the physical space she'll create by leaving, but the emotional chasm that was always there, papered over with chemical highs and desperate need. This is the pattern they've established: brief connections followed by casual dismissals, neither willing to acknowledge the hollowness at the center of what they share.

She rises from the bed, her movements sluggish as she gathers her robe around her. She feels Cecil's eyes on her body, assessing and cataloging in the same way he might evaluate merchandise. She ties the belt with fingers that tremble slightly, either from the drug's aftereffects or from something deeper and more troubling.

As she moves toward the door, her mind drifts to Amy alone in their room, perhaps awake, perhaps listening. The thought sends a chill through her that has nothing to do with the air conditioning. There's something unsettling about leaving Amy alone for too long, and Beth knows all too well why.

She pauses at the door, hand on the knob, wondering if she should say something more to Cecil. A goodbye, a thank-you, something to acknowledge what's passed between them. But words seem inadequate and ultimately unnecessary. Their arrangement requires no pleasantries.

With a soft click, she leaves the room, stepping into the night air that feels surprisingly clean after the stale atmosphere inside. The walkway outside the room offers a view of the parking lot below, and Beth takes a moment to breathe deeply before heading back to face her daughter.

In their shared hovel, Amy remains awake, her small body absolutely still, like a predator waiting in tall grass. Her fingers still touch the switchblade tucked in her mattress, drawing comfort from its presence. When she hears her mother's key in the lock, she quickly withdraws her hand and feigns sleep, her breathing deliberately deep and regular.

Outside the motel, a lone coyote howls at the glowing, cloud-shrouded moon, its cry echoing through the night like a warning no one heeds. The mournful sound carries across the empty parking lot and fades into the darkness beyond the flickering neon sign, a primeval voice speaking to a world that has largely forgotten how to listen.

The coyote's call permeates the atmosphere, a lonesome echo that stirs something primitive within Amy. Even as she pretends to sleep, her mind is alert, attuned to the wild, untamed note in the animal's song—a ballad of survival and wile, of adaptability and resilience.

Like the coyote, Amy is a creature of the night. She moves with the same quiet purpose, her actions deliberate and calculated, her intentions hidden behind a guise of innocence. The coyote is known for its ability to thrive in a variety of environments, making do with what's available, always ready to seize any opportunity. Amy, too, has learned to adapt to her circumstances, to navigate the treacherous landscape of her life with a resourcefulness that belies her years. She is a survivor, her spirit unbroken despite the hardships she has faced.

The coyote is often solitary, and in this, Amy sees a reflection of her own isolation. She stands apart from her peers, her experiences setting her worlds away from the normalcy of childhood as it's commonly understood. Her bond with her mother, tenuous and strained, is complicated by the presence of Cecil and the shadowy secrets they keep.

But it's the coyote's reputation as a trickster that resonates most deeply with Amy. She understands the power of deception, the necessity of wearing masks to navigate a world that doesn't understand or value her true nature. She has learned to use her perceived vulnerability as a weapon, to lull others into underestimating her, just as the coyote uses its wiles to outsmart larger predators.

As the coyote's call fades into silence, Amy allows herself to drift into a fitful sleep, her dreams filled with visions of open skies and vast, unforgiving landscapes. In her dreams, she runs with the coyotes, her bare feet moving silently over the earth, her senses pulsing with the thrill of the chase. She is fierce and free, a creature of instinct and raw emotion, unburdened by the complexities of human relationships.

In the quiet moments before dawn, the motel room is a world unto itself. A small, self-contained universe where a mother and daughter orbit each other in a delicate dance of need and resentment, love and fear. The neon sign outside continues to flicker, casting an intermittent glow over Amy's peaceful face, betraying nothing of the tumultuous thoughts that swirl behind her closed eyelids.

Beth watches her daughter sleep, her own restlessness momentarily stilled by the sight of Amy's serene features. In the soft, red-tinged light, she can almost believe that her daughter is just a child —vulnerable, innocent, untouched by the darkness that seems to follow them wherever they go.

For now, the world outside the motel room can wait. The coyote's call has faded into the night, leaving behind a silence that is both comforting and ominous. Within these four walls, Beth and Amy are cocooned in their own private reality, a microcosm of their shared existence. Here, in the quiet before the day begins, they can pretend, if only for a moment, that they are safe, that they are loved, that they have a chance at a future unmarred by the scars of their past.

But as the first hints of morning light begin to seep through the thin curtains, the illusion starts to crumble, and the relentless demands of their life come creeping back in. The coyote may have fallen silent, but its spirit lingers in the air, a reminder of the wildness that resides within them both, a wildness that neither time nor circumstance can fully tame.

CHAPTER 7

Amy stands in the parking lot of an all-night diner, leaning against the front grill of a parked car. The metal still holds engine warmth, seeping through her jeans as she watches the people inside the restaurant. Her small body appears ordinary, just another truant preteen up past bedtime, but her eyes contain the wise intensity of a much older soul.

Through the large windows, the diner glows with honeyed light, giving off the sort of nourishing warmth that Amy has experienced only through glass barriers. She studies the scene like an anthropologist observing an exotic tribe, cataloging behaviors she might someday need to mimic.

A young couple sits at a corner booth, their fingers intertwined across the table as they sip from steaming mugs of hot chocolate topped with whipped cream. The boyfriend lifts a finger coated in white sweetness and places it against his girlfriend's lips. She licks it off, their eyes locked in the private language of intimacy. Amy watches, her face blank but absorbing every detail, filing it away for future reference.

Near the counter, an elderly gentleman sits alone, his weathered face lit by the glow of his newspaper. His mostly finished meal has been pushed to the side, a half-empty coffee cup still steaming beside it. He puffs contentedly on a fat cigar, the smoke creating a personal atmosphere around him. There's something peaceful in his solitude, a comfort with his own company that Amy finds foreign yet fascinating.

A group of forty-something women occupy a larger table, their hands moving animatedly as they talk over burgers and fries. Their laughter erupts periodically, bubbling up and spilling over like the carbonation in their soft drinks. A waitress approaches, refilling their water glasses quickly before moving on to her next task.

But it's the family in the center of the diner that truly captures Amy's attention. They form an ideal tableau of domestic harmony —a handsome young father, a pretty mother with patient eyes, a tween daughter who looks both bored and content in that particular way of adolescents, and a baby boy secured in a high chair. The mother spoons pureed food into the baby's mouth, wiping away the excess that dribbles down his chin. The father says something that makes the daughter roll her eyes, but a smile plays at her lips despite her feigned annoyance.

They are normal. They are whole. They are everything Amy isn't and doesn't have.

Her gaze sharpens, drinking in the scene with an intensity that would disturb anyone watching her. But no one is watching Amy. They never do until it's too late. Her expression shifts from curiosity to naked longing, then to something harder and colder. Envy crystallizes in her deep-set green eyes, transforming momentary vulnerability into something minacious. She is a spider sac brewing, a ball of black widows.

The family laughs together at some shared joke, their heads tilting toward each other in unconscious unity. The baby bangs a plastic spoon against the tray of his high chair, demanding attention that is immediately granted. They exist within a bubble of belonging that Amy can see but never penetrate.

Amy peels herself away from the car, her fingers lingering on the cooling metal as if reluctant to break contact with the last remaining warmth. The night air wraps around her, early October chill with teeth. She shoves her hands into the pockets of her too-thin hoodie and turns away from the diner's golden glow.

The parking lot's asphalt stretches before her, pockmarked with potholes filled with recent rainwater that reflect fractured moonlight. Her sneakers make soft scuffing sounds as she walks, the rhythm matching her shallow breathing. She doesn't look back at the family or the other diners. What's the point? They exist in a different universe than hers.

A semi-truck roars past on the nearby highway, its headlights briefly illuminating Amy's small figure before plunging her back into shadow. She follows the frontage road, keeping to its edge where weeds push through cracked concrete.

The motel squats low against the landscape, a sprawl of faded yellow doors and grimy windows. Amy approaches room 14, fishing the key from her pocket. The plastic number dangling from the keychain has been chewed at the corners—evidence of boredom or anxiety or both.

She unlocks, opens, and then shuts the door carefully behind her, ensuring the latch catches with barely a sound. Her key lands on the dresser with controlled gentleness as she tiptoes toward her bed, believing her absence has gone undetected.

"Amy, where have you been?" Beth's voice emerges from the darkness, heavy with sleeplessness and worry.

"Just walking," Amy replies, the excuse sliding from her tongue with ease. She begins to undress, her movements unhurried despite being caught. Her nightgown lies across the bed, a pale ghost in the dim light filtering through the curtains.

"Honey, I don't want you walking at night around here. It's

dangerous," Beth says, concern evident beneath her fatigue. "How many times have I told you that?"

Amy pulls the nightgown over her head, the fabric settling around her like a veil, whispering against her skin as it falls into place. "What? Are you worried the Hillside Stranglers are going to get to me?" she asks, referencing the serial killers who had so recently terrorized Los Angeles. "They've been caught, remember? Besides, their youngest victim was twelve. I'm only ten." She smooths the cotton against her thighs with small, deliberate movements, as though the precision of this routine could normalize the darkness of her words. A short, harsh chuckle escapes her, brittle and unsettling, like windshield glass about to shatter.

Beth's voice softens, vulnerable in the darkness. "That's not funny. I don't know what I'd do without you. You're my angel."

The irony of the statement dangles, unacknowledged but palpable. Amy approaches her mother's bed, leaning down to place a kiss on Beth's cheek, a gesture that seems both genuine and affected.

"I'm sorry, Mom," she whispers, though what exactly she's sorry for remains uncertain.

Morning brings a shift in routine. The pool area of the Budget Motor Inn becomes a playground for children whose parents are either working, sleeping, or simply uninterested in their whereabouts. The water is tinged green with algae, a breeding ground for mosquitoes and bacteria, though the children are blissfully unconcerned. The smell is swampy, fetid. The outdoor lounge furniture has long surrendered to the elements, fabric faded from years of exposure and metal frames spotted with rust.

No adults supervise the area—certainly no lifeguard patrols these tepid waters. A couple of children sit at the pool's edge, their bare feet dangling in the questionable liquid as they chat about things that seem important only in the insular world of childhood.

Amy stands facing a Hispanic girl of similar age, their hands moving in the synchronized patterns of the clapping game "Say Say Oh Playmate." The sing-song recitation flows between them, a ritual of normalcy that Amy performs with surprising accuracy for someone so disconnected from ordinary childhood rituals.

"Say, say, oh playmate, come out and play with me, and bring your dollies three. Climb up my apple tree," they chant together, their voices rising and falling in cadence. "Slide down my rain barrel, into my cellar door, and we'll be jolly friends forever more more more more more."

Their hands continue the pattern as they move to the second verse. "Say, say, oh playmate, I cannot play with you. My dolly's got the flu, boo hoo hoo hoo hoo hoo. Ain't got no rain barrel, ain't got no cellar door, but we'll be jolly friends forever more more more more more."

The innocent game creates an illusion of the mundane, as though Amy is just another child engaging in age-appropriate play. For a moment, she almost seems to believe it herself, absorbed in the rhythm and rhyme that connects her temporarily to the girl across from her. Their clapping hands create a hypnotic pattern, and Amy finds herself smiling genuinely for the first time in days.

The illusion shatters when a uniformed truant officer steps into the pool yard, his presence as jarring as a hundred-decibel alarm. "Why aren't you kids in school?" he demands, his voice carrying the weight of adult authority. His polished badge catches the sunlight, sending a warning flash across the ruptured concrete.

The children scatter like startled birds, each fleeing in a different direction without a word. The game is instantly forgotten, solidarity abandoned in favor of self-preservation. Sneakers squeak against pavement and small bodies duck through fence gaps and behind buildings, the makeshift playground emptying in seconds as if a hurricane had swept through.

Amy races back to the motel room, her heart pounding not from exertion but from the surge of adrenaline that comes with near-capture. She jams the key in the lock, slams the door behind her, and immediately re-locks it, her breath coming in quick gasps.

Beth looks up from the television, where an old black-and-white movie plays. Concern flickers across her face at Amy's obvious distress. "What's gotten into you?"

"The truant officer is back," Amy explains, her voice tight with what appears to be genuine fear. Her eyes well with tears that materialize on command. "I don't want to be put in a foster home..."

"Don't be silly, baby. They can't do that," Beth assures her, though uncertainty shadows her words.

"Uh-huh. They can! They told me," Amy insists, the tears now threatening to spill.

Beth opens her arms in invitation, and Amy steps into her embrace. She hugs her daughter tightly, stroking her hair with gentle soothing motions, but Amy's arms remain stiffly at her sides, not reciprocating the gesture. Her body is tense, almost wooden against Beth's warmth. The physical connection flows in only one direction, like water against an impenetrable dam, Beth's motherly love washing over Amy without finding purchase or return.

"Nobody's taking you from me," Beth promises fiercely. "I fought too hard to keep you, and that's always going to be so."

Amy steps back, sniffling dramatically, then shuts off her tears as abruptly as turning off a faucet. She sits on her bed, the sudden shift in her emotional state jarring but unnoticed by Beth, whose attention has already begun to drift back to the television.

"Tell me about my dad," Amy demands with deliberate abruptness.

Beth sighs, recognizing the familiar request. "Again? Honey, I've told you..."

"So? Tell me again!" Amy snaps, her voice sharp with command that seems misplaced coming from her petite frame.

Beth surrenders without further resistance, reaching for a can of generic beer from the mini-fridge. She pops the tab and takes a swallow before beginning the oft-repeated tale.

"Your father was the most handsome boy in school. An A+ student and rich too. His family is from old money, and..."

Amy interrupts eagerly, reciting her lines in this well-rehearsed performance. "Did he take you on nice dates? Did you dress up, and eat steak and lobster?"

"Yes, of course. He was so romantic," Beth continues automatically.

"But..." Amy prompts, knowing every beat of this fictional narrative.

"But his family didn't approve of me. When I got pregnant with you, they told me to give you away. Or get rid of you."

"But you wouldn't do it."

"No. Never," Beth confirms, the only truth in an ocean of fabrication.

"And he wanted to marry you, didn't he?"

"He did. But of course, his family sent him away to college in England, and I never saw him again."

Before Amy can continue the familiar script, Beth's attention is caught by something on the television screen. It's a photograph of the clerk from Bob's Book Nook, her smiling face preserved in a moment of life that no longer exists. Beth turns up the volume, and both mother and daughter watch with rapt attention as the news unfolds.

"Breaking news. The victim has been identified as Janet Marina, a bookstore clerk," the newscaster announces over the grainy image. "She lived not far from where she worked, in Los Feliz."

The studio anchor appears on screen. "Tina Flores is on the scene where the body was discovered. Tina?"

The scene shifts to a field reporter standing in front of Janet's modest home, now transformed into a crime scene. Yellow police tape flutters in the breeze, creating a macabre border around what was once a sanctuary.

"I'm here in front of the home of Janet Marina, a twenty-three-year-old woman who was found dead in her backyard last night by her boyfriend, Thomas Gardiner," Flores reports with professional solemnity. "Gardiner was questioned and released. He is not a suspect. We talked with some of Ms. Marina's neighbors, who expressed shock at this senseless murder."

The camera cuts to a bone-thin woman, her face pinched with distress. "She was a quiet, kind person... I can't imagine who'd want to kill her."

Amy watches without expression, her features arranged in perfect neutrality as the consequences of her actions play out on screen. Only the slight tightening of her fingers on the bedspread betrays any reaction at all.

The broadcast continues with another neighbor, a father holding a small child against his hip. "I'm afraid to let my kids play outside," he says, glancing down at his daughter with protective anxiety.

Back to Flores, who adds the detail that both Beth and Amy have been waiting for. "The police have not released details on the murder, and when asked, detectives declined to comment on whether or not this could be the work of the so-called 'Bonnie Rotten and Kid Vicious' robbery-homicides that have struck fear into Los Angeles County residents for the past six months."

A police flyer fills the screen, showing crude sketches of two suspects: a slender, twenty-something woman, and a child wearing a dark hoodie. The reporter's voice continues over the image: "Based on the description of an eyewitness in regard to the second murder in what is believed to be four in total, the woman has a thin build and dark hair, and the young boy, approximately nine years old, was seen wearing a dark green hooded sweatshirt—"

"Why do they think I'm a boy?" Amy whines suddenly, her voice rising with indignation. "I don't look like a boy!"

Beth turns off the television, plunging the room into sudden silence. The moment stretches, Beth not acknowledging Amy's wish for proper credit, Amy not trying to disguise it.

Outside their window, a crow lands on the railing, its black eyes fathomless pools, reflecting nothing as it watches the room's occupants through the thin curtain. The bird tilts its head, studying the pair with an intelligence that seems almost supernatural, its feathers gleaming like oil in the fading afternoon light. The glossy black plumage catches the sun's dying rays, creating an iridescent shimmer of purples and blues across its wings. Its beak, sharp and polished as slate, opens slightly as if considering whether to speak the secrets it has observed.

For a moment, the world beyond their hideaway falls away—the police reports, the sketches, the manhunt—and there is only this: the heavy silence between killer and accomplice, punctuated by the soft sound of their breathing in the stuffy room. The crow remains motionless except for an occasional ruffle of its wing feathers, its patient, knowing gaze bearing witness to their unspoken pact, as if it understands the blood-soaked bond that ties the woman and the girl together.

The creature seems to be weighing them, judging them perhaps, with eyes that reflect nothing yet somehow see everything.

The motel room feels smaller with Cecil's presence. Amy bounces on the bed with requisite enthusiasm, her small body launching into the air again and again, the springs protesting.

Cecil and Beth sit at the small table by the window, curtains drawn against the night, cutting off the outside world from witnessing their plans. The overhead light casts harsh shadows, making everyone look slightly ghoulish.

Amy's unicorn tee and corduroy pants are a kid's costume, at odds with the purposeful glint in her eyes. Beth wears a loose dress and sandals, her feet already anticipating the long drive ahead. Cecil's jeans, Western shirt, and cowboy boots complete his carefully cultivated image. A man who fashions himself a modern outlaw. Near the door, their meager possessions wait: a single suitcase and paper grocery bags overflowing with hastily packed thrift store clothes.

"What made you change your mind, darlin'?" he asks, his voice carrying a note of triumph.

Beth's answer comes too quickly, rehearsed. "Nothing. I was just thinking about what you said. You're right, Cecil. I'm not going to find a job, and the truancy officer was here again, looking for Amy." She pauses, adding as an afterthought, "And I like you."

She places her hand on Cecil's as Amy continues jumping on the bed.

"Gross!" Amy calls out, not pausing her bouncing.

He squeezes Beth's hand, a proprietorial gesture that doesn't escape Amy's notice. "How's that old jalopy of yours running? We'll be driving through Arizona, New Mexico, Texas, Louisiana, Alabama, and Georgia." His face brightens with off-color humor. "Gonna be hotter than a billy goat's asshole in a pepper patch."

Beth rolls her eyes. "Language."

He winks at Amy, who finds herself giggling despite her disdain for him.

"When you wanna head out?" Cecil asks, glancing meaningfully at the packed bags. "Looks like you're in a hurry."

"Well, yeah..." Beth fidgets slightly. "Remember I told you, I owe Tami money. And I haven't got the rest."

He crosses his scrawny arms, smiling with smug satisfaction. "Hm. I don't know if I should be associating with the criminal element."

Amy stops jumping immediately, her protective instincts flaring. She crosses to her mother and wraps her arms around her shoulders. "My mom's not a criminal," she declares, her voice sharp with conviction.

Cecil grins, showing his silver tooth. "You tell it, missy. Your mama's a good lady." He pauses for effect. "Now me, on the other hand. I was born in trouble. When I was a kid, I was so bad I'd whup my own ass twice a week."

Amy laughs, her posture relaxing slightly. "You're funny."

He reaches out without warning and tugs Amy's long hair

playfully, but just enough to hurt. She winces, the pain registering in her eyes before she can cover it.

"So are you," Cecil says irritably, the words hanging between them like a threat.

Behind Amy, on the windowsill, a grungy brown rat scurries by, skittering and chittering. Its long, naked tail drags behind it like a dirty rope as it pauses to twitch its whiskers, beady eyes glinting in the dim light before it disappears into a shadowy corner with an ominous scratching sound.

Amy's heart races, an electric thrill surging through her as she watches the rat vanish into the corner. The creature's small frame moves with an agility she admires. It doesn't hesitate, darting for cover at the slightest sound, a survivor in its own right.

She shifts closer to the edge of the bed, curiosity igniting her imagination. Like that rat, she senses danger lurking in every corner of her life—Tami's threats, Cecil's temper, and even her mother's anxious glances. Instinct guides her; it tells her when to stand firm and when to hide. Cecil's laughter echoes in the background, but it feels muffled now. The air thickens with unspoken truths. She feels a kinship with the rat, both caught in a world too big and hostile to navigate alone.

The scurry of claws against the floorboards repels her, yet she leans forward as if to catch a glimpse of something that belongs only to her. Freedom, maybe? The rat returns briefly, its tiny nose twitching as it sniffs out potential threats before darting away again.

Beth's dilapidated Chevy creeps along the highway, nearly alone on the road, headlights cutting through the humid night mist. Inside, Cecil drives with one hand draped casually over the wheel. Amy sits in the passenger seat, while Beth dozes in the back, her head lolling with each bump in the road.

Amy fiddles with the radio, twisting knobs and pressing buttons, trying to coax some sound from the ancient device.

"Ain't no antenna on this heap, girl," Cecil informs her with an odd satisfaction, his voice carrying a hint of smugness at her futile efforts. "You can forget about the radio. Thing's been dead longer than most'a the roadkill we passed."

Amy sighs audibly, turning it off with more force than necessary. The plastic knob makes a threatening crack under her fingers. She crosses her arms and pouts, a picture of childish sullenness. She bunches up her green hoodie—the same one she wore during Janet's murder, still bearing an almost imperceptible dark stain near the cuff—against the window and lays her head on it, watching the occasional headlights from oncoming cars flash across her face like interrogation lamps.

Cecil reaches out suddenly, flicking her bare arm with his finger.

"Ouch! Stop it," Amy protests, rubbing the spot.

He flicks her again, harder. "Stop what?"

He returns both hands to the wheel, his face a mask of innocence. "Just trying to make you laugh is all. Here's some advice for you." He glances over at her.

Amy keeps her head against the window, her expression closed off.

"Words to live by. You ready?" Cecil continues, undeterred by her silence. "'Make your smile change the world but don't let the world change your smile.'"

He returns his attention to the road, but his thoughts remain on Amy. "You're gonna smile, any minute now. I know it."

Without warning, his hand shoots out, and he tickles Amy's side. She giggles involuntarily, her body betraying her.

"Stop it! Stop," Amy demands, then adds with venom, "You bastard!"

The curse word awakens Beth, who sits up abruptly in the back seat. "Amy! What did you say?"

"Nothing, Mom. I'm sorry," Amy responds instantly, her voice transforming into that of a victimized little girl. "I'm trying to sleep, and Cecil keeps bothering me."

"Am not," he counters.

"Are so!" Amy fires back, turning her body away from him, facing the passenger window.

Beth leans forward from the back seat, her voice weary. "This is going to be a long night."

"I know what you need," Cecil announces. "A beer. Bet there's a 7-Eleven around here somewhere." He glances at Amy. "Keep your eyes open, Amy."

Amy sits up, suddenly engaged. "Do I get a beer too?"

"No!" Cecil and Beth respond in unison.

"I was only kidding," Amy says, rolling her eyes. "Beer is gross."

Beth narrows her eyes. "How would you know, young lady?"

"I've tasted it before," Amy admits.

"When?" Beth presses.

"Never mind," Amy deflects. "I'm bored. Wanna play 'I Spy'?"

"Lord, no," Cecil groans.

"How about I read to you?" Beth offers. "From your book?"

Amy brightens. "Okay."

Beth rummages in the dark backseat until her fingers find the worn paperback. Beth clicks on the car's overhead interior light, casting a yellow glow over the pages as she finds her place.

"'Born February 5, 1908, in Brighton, England, Daisy and Violet Hilton were born conjoined at the buttocks,'" Beth reads, her voice slightly stilted. "'The infants were abandoned by their mother, and adopted by a midwife who charged people two pence to look at the girls. For an extra fee, one could lift up their dresses and pinch the flesh that bonded them.'"

"I wish I had a twin," Amy interjects, her voice wistful.

Beth continues reading. "'Eventually, they were performing in sideshows and even on vaudeville with a young Bob Hope. The magician Harry Houdini was a fan of theirs. Doctors wanted to cut them in two, but Daisy and Violet were adamant. They said no: "We'll be together always." Daisy and Violet shared a bed, and even a lover...'"

"What the hell's that?" Cecil interrupts, disgust flaring in his voice.

"My book. On sideshow freaks. Real ones," Amy explains, a note of defiance creeping into her tone.

"It's educational," Beth adds weakly.

Cecil snorts, his contempt unmistakable. "It's sickening is what it is."

Beth shuts the book without argument, unwilling to fight this particular battle. Amy closes her eyes and scrunches herself against the car door, shutting out both adults.

"I gotta piss so bad my eyeballs is floatin'," Cecil announces.

Beth turns the overhead light off, plunging the car back into darkness as they continue down the lonely road, hurtling through the night toward an uncertain future.

The convenience store gleams under harsh fluorescent lights, a beacon of artificial life in the dead of night. Outside, the parking lot sits empty except for Beth's car, stationed near the entrance like a getaway vehicle, which, in a sense, it is. Inside, the fluorescent brightness creates strange shadows, transforming ordinary objects into potential weapons, ordinary people into looming threats.

Cecil emerges from the bathroom at the back of the store, zipping his pants with the casual indifference of someone for whom public restrooms are a necessary evil rather than a source of shame. He moves toward the exit, passing by the register where a clerk in his early twenties stands, boredom etched into his pock-marked features. The young man doesn't look up from the tabloid spread before him, his posture suggesting a weariness of the grave-yard shift.

"Thanks, man," Cecil tosses casually over his shoulder, as he throws the key on the counter. "Thought I'd bust a kidney."

"Yeah," the clerk responds without enthusiasm, barely acknowledging Cecil's existence.

Cecil exits the store, returning to the car where he immediately slumps in the driver's seat, his head tilting back as fatigue overtakes him.

Inside the store, Beth and Amy navigate the aisles with efficiency, the hoodie pulled over Amy's blond bob, a familiar disguise that has now appeared in too many police sketches across multiple counties.

Amy clutches an assortment of snack cakes and candy bars—small, bright packages designed to deliver quick sugar highs. Beth, more practical, holds a six-pack of generic beer and a bunch of bananas, provisions for the long journey ahead. She glances at Amy's selection and shakes her head in silent disapproval.

Amy returns the sugary treats to the shelf with only minor reluctance. "Beef jerky?" she suggests instead, her voice pitched to achieve maximum persuasiveness.

Beth nods, the compromise acceptable. "Okay. Only one stick, though," she cautions. "We've got to watch our money until we settle in." The word "settle" resonates, a fantasy rather than a plan.

Beth approaches the clerk, who continues reading his tabloid. "Is there a motel around here?" she asks.

The clerk shrugs without looking up. "Not too near. Closer to San Diego, if you're headed south."

"Thanks," Beth replies.

As Beth and Amy approach the counter to pay, their attention simultaneously locks onto what the clerk has been reading. The tabloid lies open to a two-page spread featuring rough sketches of a woman and child. Sketches that, despite their artistic limitations, bear unmistakable resemblances to Beth and Amy. Above the illustrations, a sensational headline screams in bold type: "IS 'KID VICIOUS' THE ANTICHRIST? REAL LIFE DAMIEN

CREATES HELL ON EARTH, SAYS VATICAN. EXCLU-SIVE! PHOTOS!"

The clerk looks up, as if seeing his customers for the first time. His bored features shift subtly, eyes narrowing as they dart between the newsprint drawings and the faces before him. A flicker of possible recognition crosses his features, followed by something that might be fear or morbid curiosity. His fingers tense against the page, creating small creases in the paper as his thumb unconsciously presses against the corner of Amy's sketched face.

The clerk's expression downshifts to neutral, making it impossible to determine whether he's made the connection or simply lost interest. His eyes, previously animated, now reveal nothing behind their glassy surface.

Amy's hand moves to her back pocket, fingers brushing against the switchblade that has become an extension of herself. The metal feels cool against her fingertips, reassuring in its lethal potential. She's carried it so long now that its absence would feel like missing a limb.

The clerk seems oblivious to the danger as he rings up their modest purchases, entering each item with bored efficiency. "That'll be six fifty-nine," he announces in the flat monotone of someone who's repeated the same sort of phrase thousands of times.

Beth pays with crumpled bills, smoothing them against the counter before handing them over, and the man opens the register to make change. "That'll be three forty-one back," he says, counting out the money like an automaton.

Amy's eyes widen slightly as she notices the cash drawer full of bills, neatly arranged in their compartments. A familiar hunger ignites within her, hot and insistent, but she's learned that direct confrontation isn't always the best approach.

She crosses her legs suddenly, her face twisting into an expression of childish urgency, the performance beginning with the slippery ease of a veteran liar.

"Mom..." she says, her voice pitched slightly higher than normal. "I've got to tinkle."

Beth offers an apologetic smile to the clerk. "Do you mind?"

The young man sighs, clearly annoyed at having to let yet another of this family use the john. "I'm really not supposed to let anyone use it..."

Amy intensifies her performance, grimacing and fidgeting with theatrical desperation.

"Okay..." the clerk relents.

"Thank you, sir!" Amy chirps, all syrupy gratitude as she snatches the key from the counter and dashes toward the back of the store.

The man bags their items, his attention already drifting back to the next page of the tabloid as the bathroom door opens and closes.

A moment later, it opens again.

"Excuse me...!" Amy calls out, her voice carefully calibrated to grab attention. "Mister, there's something wrong with the toilet."

The clerk shakes his head in annoyance, casting a baleful glance at Beth before locking the cash register. The keys jingle from a chain attached to his belt loop as he moves toward the bathroom, irritation evident in every step.

Amy stands in the doorway of the tiny bathroom, looking sheepish. The toilet lid is closed, providing a prop for her deception.

He brushes past her with gruff authority, stooping to lift the lid, his back fully exposed to the child behind him.

With a swift, practiced motion, Amy whips out her switchblade, the metal gleaming wickedly under the fluorescent beam, as if taking a bow in a spotlight. She strikes with lethal intent, driving the blade into the clerk's lower back, her aim unerringly targeting the kidneys. The impact of steel on flesh produces a sickening, wet sound, a punctuation to the violence.

The clerk's shout of alarm is cut short as the searing pain radiates from the wound. He spins around automatically, his eyes wide with shock and agony, but the movement only exposes him further to Amy's onslaught. She shifts her hold on the knife, angling it upward, and launches a series of rapid, upward thrusts into his abdomen. Each brutal stab is executed with a force that belies her small stature, the switchblade slicing through tissue and ribs, ravaging the vital organs within.

The young man falls to his knees, hands clutching at his gut incredulously. Bile rises in his throat, and he vomits reflexively, his body attempting to purge the wrongness that has invaded it. Blood and stomach contents mix on the floor, creating a slick, foul puddle under him.

Beth appears in the doorway, drawn by the sounds of struggle. She gasps, though whether from horror at the act or fear of discovery is unclear. "Amy...!" The word contains volumes. Shock, desperation, resignation.

Amy ignores her mother, focused entirely on her victim. He's on his knees now, his throat level with her knife—a fatal coincidence of geometry. Amy delivers the coup de grâce, opening his throat with one clean slash.

The clerk's final breath escapes as a wet wheeze, and he crumples to the floor, sliding in his own fluids until he comes to rest in a growing pool of gore and puke.

Only then does Amy turn to face her mother. She holds the bloody blade with a trembling hand, her expression suddenly transforming into that of a frightened child. The veneer of rational efficiency that had guided her through the killing dissolves completely, leaving behind only vulnerability. Blood spatters her sleeve and drips from the blade onto the linoleum floor with soft, accusatory taps.

"Are you mad at me?" she asks, her voice small and uncertain, like a girl who's broken a household rule rather than taken a human life. Her eyes, wide and searching, plead for reassurance even as crimson evidence of her savagery clings to her fingertips.

Beth stays frozen, speechless, in the doorway.

"He was reading that story," Amy offers by way of explanation, the justification of a predator who believes herself hunted.

"I know, baby," Beth manages finally, her voice soft with a twisted form of understanding.

She takes the knife from Amy, moving to the sink to rinse the blade clean. The water runs red, then pink, then clear, evidence swirling down the drain. She turns to her daughter, maternal intuition reasserting itself.

"Your hands," she instructs. "Wash them. With soap. Come on..."

Amy skirts the corpse with ease, approaching the sink to cleanse herself of evidence.

"Hurry," Beth urges, glancing nervously toward the door. "Cecil could come in any minute. Then what?"

Amy nods grimly, accepting this practical concern without comment or remorse.

"Let me see," Beth says when Amy finishes washing. "Are you dirty anywhere else?"

Amy extends her arms for examination. The green sleeves look pristine, and her face shows no sign of telltale splatters. The precision of a bullfighter contained within a child's frame.

Beth takes her daughter's hand and pulls her quickly from the bathroom, leaving behind the cooling body of a young man whose only crime was reading a tabloid at work. As they approach the front of the store, Beth glances anxiously toward the car. Cecil remains slumped in the driver's seat, head tilted back, mercifully asleep.

Amy picks up the paper bag holding their purchases, then looks pointedly at the cash register before turning to her mother with unspoken question.

Beth shakes her head. "He locked it."

Amy glances toward the back of the store, where the clerk's body lies. "I'll get the keys," she offers, pragmatic as ever.

Before she can move, headlights sweep across the store windows as another car pulls into the lot.

Without hesitation, Amy grabs a handful of candy bars from a display and the incriminating tabloid from the counter, shoving both into their bag before hurrying out the door. Beth follows close behind, her desire to protect her daughter overriding any moral qualms.

Outside, they climb into the car just as another pair of customers steps out of their vehicle. The newcomers pay no attention to Beth and Amy, engaged in their own conversation as they enter the store, unaware they're walking into a crime scene.

Amy and Beth settle into their seats, adrenaline making their movements sharp and precise.

"Let's go," Amy says, her voice once again calm and controlled, as if she hasn't just committed murder.

Cecil stirs, blinking awake, unaware of the horror his companions have orchestrated while he slept. He turns the key in the ignition, and the car pulls away from the convenience store, carrying its deadly passengers into the night.

"What took you so damn long?" Cecil asks, as the convenience store gets smaller in the skewed rearview mirror.

"The clerk said there's a motel going south, toward San Diego," Beth replies. After a pause, she adds, "Amy, put on your seatbelt."

On the highway sometime later, it's still dark, but dawn is approaching. Everyone is awake but silent, each lost in their own thoughts. Suddenly, the steering wheel shudders, then steadies.

"Lordy," Cecil sighs. After a beat, he asks, "Where'd you say that motel is, Elizabeth?"

"I thought it was close. How far are we from San Diego?" Beth responds.

Cecil shrugs.

"Mom, I can't sleep. Would you read to me?" Amy asks.

Cecil interjects, "I don't want to hear anymore sick stories from that damn book."

Amy whines, "Whhhyy?"

He shoots the little girl a look. "Because I said so." He glances back to Beth. "She could start an argument in an empty house, that one."

"She's just tired. She's ten," Beth says, her voice softening in defense of her daughter. "Children get cranky; deal with it."

Cecil shakes his head dismissively, then mutters, "Little weisenheimer."

"Then tell me about my dad," Amy requests, her high voice cutting through the tension in the car. She shifts in her seat, suddenly alert despite her earlier complaints of fatigue.

Beth doesn't respond. Her gaze fixes on the darkened landscape rushing past the window, her reflection a pale ghost against the glass.

"Come on... one more time. Please? Please-please-please?" Amy persists.

"Yeah. Let's hear about Amy's father. This oughta be good," Cecil says with a harsh chuckle.

Beth shifts in her seat and, looking down, says, "I met your dad after I'd run away from home. I was hitchhiking."

"And he was driving a big semi-truck, right?" Amy asks.

"That's right. He was the most handsome, dashing man I'd ever seen. He was older than me by twelve years," Beth confirms.

"But it was love at first sight," Amy adds.

"You bet. I felt so grown up," Beth says.

"And...?" Amy prompts.

"And he was a long-haul trucker. I loved riding beside him, so high up I could see for miles and miles," Beth continues.

"How romantic. I'm crying over here," Cecil interrupts sarcastically. After a pause, he adds, "Amy, open me a beer, will ya?"

Amy folds her arms. "No. Drinking and driving is bad."

He shakes his head. "Well, you're about as useless as a screen door on a submarine." After a beat, he turns to Beth. "Elizabeth?"

Beth reaches into the paper sack, separates a can of beer from the soft plastic ring, opens the tab, and hands it to him.

Cecil takes it and swallows deeply, saying, "Thanks, darlin'." He looks pointedly at Amy, as if to say he got his beer anyway, *so there*.

Amy folds her arms and looks out the window. The trio drives in silence for a few moments.

"So... what happened to Amy's pa?" Cecil eventually asks.

Amy answers before Beth can. "He was drafted into the Vietnam War. He was killed in action, and he got a Purple Heart, a letter from the president, and everything."

"Oh, yeah?" Cecil replies, then belches.

"Gross," Amy mutters. "Anyway, my grandparents live in Las Vegas, and so does Mom's sister, my aunt Tam. She's a famous showgirl, isn't she, Mom?"

"That's right," Beth confirms listlessly.

Amy notices a road sign. "Oh, look! Gas, food, and lodging. It says it right there on the sign we just passed."

Cecil shifts in his seat and takes the last swallow of his beer. He crumples the can, then tosses it onto the passenger side floor. Amy moves her feet as if he's just thrown a live rattlesnake at her.

"Heeyyyy!" she protests.

Cecil chuckles. "Deepest apologies, your majesty."

Suddenly, the car judders and emits what sounds like a death rattle, the engine coughing and sputtering like an asthmatic giant.

Cecil pulls the car to the shoulder of the highway, the moment of crisis announced by the steam hissing from the edges of the hood in angry white plumes. The engine gives a final shake before he cuts it, plunging them into sudden silence broken only by the soft ticking of cooling metal and the occasional passing whoosh of a distant semi on the northbound side. No buildings are visible in any direction, just the empty highway stretching toward the horizon like a black ribbon and the vast, indifferent darkness surrounding them, punctuated only by the indifferent glitter of stars overhead.

"Oh, shit," Cecil mutters, his face illuminated by the green glow of the dashboard lights as he pops the hood release. He drums his nicotine-stained fingers against the steering wheel, jaw clenched in frustration.

He steps out into the cool night air, leaving Beth and Amy alone inside the car. Beth's worry is clear; she fidgets with the strap of her purse, glancing repeatedly at the rearview mirror as though expecting police lights to appear at any moment. Amy sits perfectly still, her face unreadable.

Outside, Cecil lifts the hood, which releases a cloud of steam into his face. He waves it away, coughing, and bends to examine the engine. His posture tells the story before he even returns to the car. Shoulders slumped, head shaking in disappointment.

When he slides back into the driver's seat, both Beth and Amy look at him expectantly, though with vastly different expressions. Beth's eyes hold desperate hope; Amy's contain only cold calculation.

"Just as I suspected," Cecil announces with the weary satisfaction of someone whose pessimism has been proven right. "She's held together with baling wire, bubblegum, a lick, and a promise. Surprised we made it this far."

"What are we gonna do now?" Amy asks plaintively.

Beth's anxiety grows. Somewhere behind them, a convenience store clerk lies dead on a bathroom floor, his blood drying on linoleum. By now, someone has surely found the body. Perhaps at this very moment, law enforcement is putting together the pieces, connecting this latest murder to the others, tracing the path of "Bonnie Rotten and Kid Vicious" down the California coast. What if there were CCTV cameras? She'd noticed more and more places were installing them these days. "Can we make it a few more miles?" she asks, the strain clear in her voice.

Cecil shakes his head, crushing her small bit of hope. "Not for another half hour or so. Engine's hotter'n two rabbits screwin' in a wool sack." He illustrates his crude metaphor with an obscene gesture that Amy pretends not to see. "Needs to cool down, and... Got any water?"

"Beer," Beth replies, the single word offering the only solution available.

"Gimme one," Cecil demands, already reaching toward her.

Beth hands him another can from the six-pack, and Cecil opens it with a satisfying crack. He takes a long drink, foam gathering at the corners of his mouth. His priorities stay clear, even in crisis—personal comfort comes first.

"I have to tinkle," Amy announces.

Cecil gestures broadly at the darkness beyond the car windows. "Nobody's stopping you."

Beth, ever practical despite her anxiety, hands Amy the tabloid. "Here, take this. Toilet paper."

Amy takes it and opens the car door, pausing to cast a baleful glare at both adults. "Don't look!"

"Nobody's going to be looking, Amy," Beth assures her with tired patience. "There's some bushes a few yards away. See?"

Amy exits the car, slamming the door behind her with force. The sound echoes briefly before being swallowed by the vast emptiness surrounding them. Insects hum, somewhere off in the distance. She moves away from the road, toward a cluster of scrubby bushes barely visible in the pre-dawn gloaming.

Behind the meager cover, Amy finishes her business quickly, then uses a page from the tabloid to wipe herself. With careful precision, she tears the entire newspaper into fragments, scattering the pieces in multiple directions, making sure that no one will be able to piece together the publication that ties them to their crimes.

A tarantula walks past her feet, its chelicerae raised and ready. Its movement is slow and deliberate, mirroring Amy's own careful actions as she removes her forest green hoodie. The furry arachnid pauses briefly, seeming to consider her presence before continuing on its nightly hunt. Amy watches it disappear into the darkness, a small predator in a vast, harsh landscape not unlike herself—dangerous when cornered, invisible when still.

With casual ease, she stuffs the hoodie as far as possible under a nearby bush, hiding it with fallen leaves and twigs. The evidence vanishes into the landscape, impossible to find unless someone knows exactly where to look. And no one will know to look here, she is certain; no one will connect this anonymous stretch of highway with the convenience store murder miles behind them.

Her task finished, Amy starts back toward the car, her silhouette trivial against the vastness of the night. As she nears the vehicle, a sound cuts through the silence. It's the unmistakable wail of a police siren, growing louder by the second. Amy freezes, her body instantly alert. The siren's pitch rises and falls, drawing closer with each oscillation. Red-and-blue lights will be visible soon, painting the landscape with their accusing colors, showing her guilt for all to see.

Inside the car, Beth and Cecil have also heard the approaching siren. Beth's face drains of color, her worst fears coming true. Cecil sits straighter, suddenly alert despite the beer he's been drinking. They both look out the windows, trying to spot where the sound is coming from.

Amy begins to run, not toward the car but away from it, into the deeper darkness beyond the reach of headlights. Self-preservation drives her into the shadows, away from adults who might slow her escape or, worse, use her as a bargaining chip to save themselves.

The siren grows louder still, seeming to come from all directions at once. Amy's heart thumps within her, not from running but from the mix of fear and forethought flooding her system. She's too young for prison. She's too young to die.

Then, as suddenly as it appeared, the siren passes. A police cruiser speeds by on the highway, lights flashing, continuing south without slowing.

Not for them. Not this time.

Amy watches from her hiding spot as the squad car shrinks in the distance, until it's nothing more than a fading pulse of light on the horizon. She stays motionless for several more beats, making sure that the danger has truly passed.

Only when she's sure does she come out of hiding, walking back to the car with the unhurried confidence of someone who has faced death and watched it pass by. Her face shows nothing of her fear, nothing of the backup plans that formed in her mind during those tense moments.

Beth flings open the car door the moment Amy appears, her relief obvious. "Amy! Where were you? Why did you run?"

Amy slides into the backseat with Beth, her expression carefully neutral. "I thought it might be better if they didn't find us all together."

Beth stares at her daughter, momentarily speechless. The thought behind Amy's words—the suggestion that she was ready to abandon them—hangs in the air between them.

Cecil breaks the silence with a low whistle. "Jesus H. Christ on a popsicle stick. Kid's got ice in her veins. Tougher'n a two-dollar steak, that one." He sounds impressed rather than disturbed, which only highlights the wrongness of the moment.

"Where's your hoodie?" Beth asks suddenly, noticing the missing garment.

"I hid it," Amy replies without elaboration. "It's too dangerous to keep now."

Beth nods slowly, accepting her daughter's decision even as she wonders when exactly their roles reversed, when the child became the strategist, the mother merely a follower. The thought rumbles uncomfortably in her mind, but she pushes it aside.

Cecil turns the key in the ignition, and the engine sputters reluctantly to life. The temperature gauge stays dangerously high, but the brief rest has bought them a few more miles at least.

"We should find somewhere to lay low for a while," Beth suggests, her voice steadier now that immediate danger has passed. "Maybe change our appearance. They're looking for a girl with blond hair and a green hoodie..."

"And a hot number with dark hair," Cecil adds, glancing

meaningfully at Beth's brunette waves. "Maybe y'all should both go blond. Be twins."

Amy smiles at this, the expression crafty rather than amused. "I've always wanted a twin," she says, echoing her earlier comment about the conjoined circus freaks.

"You know what," Cecil drawls, getting his bearings. "I know just the place we can lay lower than a pregnant possum. It ain't too far from here. Little spot outside Barstow where the sheriff's got cataracts and the locals mind their own business."

The car pulls back onto the empty highway, headlights cutting through the darkness that comes before dawn.

CHAPTER 11

Dawn breaks over a motel that time and neglect have worn down. Unlike the Budget Motor Inn, which at least tried to look respectable, this place has given up completely. Garbage spills from overflowing trash cans outside the check-in office, creating a stinking barrier that greets guests with the smell of acrid abandonment.

The motel's once-white paint has yellowed to the color of nicotine varnish, peeling away in sheets to show rotting wood beneath. The neon sign flickers on and off, several letters permanently dark, changing "SUNSET VISTA MOTEL" into "SUN ET V ST MOT L."

Cecil waits in the car, engine running to keep it from dying completely while Beth and Amy approach the office. Through the grimy plate glass window, they talk with the clerk inside.

Unknown to them, someone watches. A figure follows their movements with intense focus, studying every gesture, every interaction. The gaze goes to Cecil first, then lingers on Amy's small frame, on the way she stands beside her mother, poised like a miniature adult.

Inside the office, Beth empties her purse on the counter, scrounging for every coin and bill. She counts the money twice, her face falling as the math fails to change. Even Amy helps, fishing a few nickels and dimes from her pants pocket.

The receptionist, oddly cheerful given his surroundings, seems out of place among the motel's misery. His ample frame and smiling face don't match the decay around him. He watches Beth's desperate counting with kind eyes, eventually waving his hand and shaking his head as if to say, "That's okay." A small kindness in a cruel world.

Minutes later, Beth and Amy stand beside their car in the parking lot, talking with Cecil through his rolled-down window. The Chevy stays running, its labored idle sounding like an animal on its last breath.

"We were a dollar twenty short, but we can pay it tomorrow," Beth explains, relief in her voice. "The guy said there's a pretty good mechanic a couple of miles away." Then she pauses and adds, "Gonna have to come up with some way to pay him too..."

Cecil nods, accepting this small victory without comment.

Amy, however, shows an odd excitement, her eyes bright with childlike enthusiasm that seems strange given their situation, and her actions just hours earlier. "We're in Room 7. Lucky seven!"

Cecil raises an eyebrow, his expression saying volumes. "Real lucky, all right." He wrinkles his nose as the stench of garbage and neglect reaches him. "This place stinks so bad it could knock a buzzard off a gut wagon."

"Beggars can't be choosers," Beth replies practically. "Besides, you chose it. Come on, bring the car around, Cecil. We'll meet you there."

The room sits at the end of a row of identical doors, on the ground floor—an easy escape route, if they need one. Their car is parked directly in front, its dented frame and steaming engine perfectly matched to their lodgings. Both vehicle and motel share the same look of coming apart.

Inside, the room offers exactly what they've paid for, the bare minimum of shelter. A TV set with bent rabbit-ear antennas sits heavily on a particleboard chest of drawers, its thick screen coated in dust. An ancient mini-fridge hums valiantly in the corner, struggling to stay cold. A tiny desk area with one chair offers no real workspace. An ugly painting, a generic landscape in faded colors, is bolted to the dirty white wall, probably to prevent theft, though who would want it is a mystery. The bathroom door stands slightly open, showing chipped tiles and suspicious stains within.

Two full beds complete the space, their mattresses visibly sagging in the middle, edges soft with wear. The curtains are drawn against the morning light, keeping the room dark and hiding its many flaws.

Amy lies under the covers in one bed, her back turned toward the others, curled into herself like a wounded animal. Cecil moves on top of Beth in the second bed, his heavy breathing ragged and uneven, the only sound in the otherwise quiet space. His weight shifts the already wearied mattress with each mindless thrust. Beth makes no noise, her face turned toward the wall, her expression blank and eyes unfocused, as if her mind has gone somewhere far away, somewhere safer. Their coupling feels like a chore rather than passion, another transaction in lives built on what can be traded, as empty as the room itself. The smell of crack cocaine tarries, floating on dust specks that dance in the thin strip of sunlight between the worn curtains, a chemical fog that both causes and numbs their shared misery.

Amy turns on her side, facing away from the couple. She puts the pillow over her head, not only to block the sounds, which are few, but to create a wall between herself and the adults—a symbolic separation from things she can't control but deeply resents.

Hours later, with afternoon sun leaking through gaps in the shabby curtains, the room takes on a different feel. The trio has dressed in yesterday's clothes, minus Amy's hoodie. They move around the small space, unpacking the few things they've managed to keep in their life on the move.

Beth arranges toiletries on the bathroom counter with careful attention, bringing order to the only space she can control. Cecil sprawls on one bed, flipping through channels on the television, looking satisfied as though these dirty quarters represent some kind of victory. Amy organizes her few clothes in a drawer, her movements exact and efficient.

None of them notice the eyes observing them through the window—the watcher who studies their routine with disturbing interest, noting their habits, seeing their weaknesses. The observer stays just out of sight, barely breathing.

For now, though, they exist in the strange limbo of fugitives at rest. Tired, watchful, and utterly unaware that they themselves are being hunted by someone other than the law.

Outside, a diurnal owl lands on the roof of their car, its yellow eyes fixed on the motel room window. The bird seems drawn by the violence Amy carries within. It hoots once, the sound like mocking laughter, before spreading its wings and taking flight. The shadow it casts briefly darkens the dusty windshield, a passing eclipse that goes unnoticed by those inside. As it rises into the late afternoon sky, it joins two others circling overhead, their dark talons cutting against the amber light, nature's ancient witnesses to human folly, patient and uncaring about the desperation festering behind the motel's thin walls.

The stage is set. New players wait in the wings.

Cecil and Beth sit huddled on one of the beds, their postures matching the defeated dip of the mattress under them. The light filtering through the thin curtains casts everything in a sickly yellow glow, highlighting the worry etched into their faces. Across from them, Amy plays cat's cradle with a loop of yarn, her nimble fingers working the string with precision. The intricate patterns she creates—Jacob's ladder, witch's broom, cat's eye—seem to hypnotize her, giving her a brief escape from their dire situation.

"Well, there's nothing left to sell," Cecil announces, breaking the heavy silence. His voice carries the flat resignation of a man counting his last resources. "I need more supply, darlin'. What about you? You could... you know."

The hint is clear, unspoken but obvious. Beth's eyes drop to her lap, unable to meet his gaze or Amy's. The suggestion hangs over her like an eviction notice, familiar and suffocating.

"There must be another way," she replies softly, the words sounding hollow even to her own ears. "We'll think of something."

Cecil opens his palms upward in a helpless gesture, showing them as empty as their prospects. "Rent's due tomorrow. Car's still busted."

His bluntness cuts through Beth's fragile hope like a lumberjack's ax. These are facts, not opinions. Hard realities that demand answers rather than wishful thinking. The math doesn't care about their feelings; it sits before them like a judge, methodical and final, waiting for their response.

Amy stops playing, the yarn still looped around her fingers in a complex pattern. Her small hands have frozen mid-motion, holding the intricate cat's cradle in the space between them. Her gaze shifts from the string pattern to the adults with unsettling directness, too knowing for her years. "I'm hungry," she announces, her voice neither whining nor plaintive, but matter-of-fact.

"There's a whole bunch of bananas in the icebox," Beth offers, grabbing at this simple problem she can actually solve.

Amy makes no comment but crosses to the mini-fridge, ignoring the suggested fruit entirely to retrieve a chocolate bar, one of the ones she grabbed from the convenience store. She unwraps it carefully, the foil crinkling beneath her short, skilled fingers.

Beth rises suddenly, as though the room has become too small, too stifling with its unspoken expectations and limited options. "I need to take a walk," she declares, then adds after a moment: "Amy?"

Amy moves to her mother's side without hesitation, the chocolate bar clutched in one hand. Beth glances at Cecil, an unreadable message passing between them. "We'll be back in a bit."

Cecil doesn't respond, doesn't wish them well or ask when they'll return. He simply watches them go, his expression blank as the door closes behind them.

Outside, the desert heat hits them like a physical force after the motel room's tepid air conditioning. The October sun beats down mercilessly, turning the cracked pavement into a shimmering griddle below their feet. They walk side by side down a street that shows urban decline: a sad collection of liquor stores with faded signage, nail salons advertising discount services in hand-painted window displays, a pawn shop with thick bars on its windows and a "Cash for Gold" banner drooping in the still air, a strip mall with half its storefronts empty and papered over, a bus stop covered in layers of graffiti tags and foul language, and a few dive bars already doing business despite the early hour, their neon beer signs glowing weakly in the harsh daylight.

Amy reaches up and takes Beth's hand, a gesture so innocently guileless it creates a jolting contrast with the knowledge of what those small fingers have done. The chocolate bar, now softening in the heat, stays clutched in her other hand. "It'll be okay, Mom. Don't worry," she says, her voice showing more genuine emotion than usual, a rare softness breaking through her typically matter-of-fact manner.

Beth smiles down at her, squeezing the small hand in her own. A bead of sweat trickles down her temple as she studies her daughter's upturned face, searching for something. Reassurance, or forgiveness. For a moment, she lets herself believe in the comfort her daughter offers, to accept the strange role reversal where the child comforts the parent. "I know, baby. Somehow, we always manage, don't we?" The question hangs in the humid air, both casual and deeply sincere.

Amy's toothy, answering smile transforms her face, briefly erasing the coldness that usually lives there. "The two musketeers!" she declares with enthusiasm.

"What about Uncle Cecil?" Beth asks, unable to stop herself from testing the boundaries of this tender moment.

The effect is immediate. Amy pulls her hand away as though burned, her smile vanishing into the afternoon heat. The façade of childhood drops away, revealing the canny creature under her skin

—the one who stabbed a bookstore clerk, who killed a convenience store employee, who is still deciding Cecil's fate, and who sees the world as a collection of obstacles to be removed.

Beth sees her mistake instantly but can't find the words to fix it. Before she can try, Amy trots ahead, putting distance between them.

"Look, Mom," she calls back, stopping to allow Beth to catch up.

They've reached an intersection where a homeless woman sits on a milk crate, her weathered skin showing a life of immeasurable hardship. She looks to be in her sixties, though street living might have aged her prematurely. A small, skinny dog sits patiently beside her, tied with a makeshift leash made from rope. The animal's ribs show through its matted fur, but its eyes stay alert and true.

As Beth and Amy watch from a distance, two passersby stop before the woman. Wallets open, dollars and coins change hands. Not much, but enough to show how effective the sad tableau is. The dog, it seems, turns the woman from something to avoid into a fellow human being needing help.

Amy's gaze fixes on this exchange, absorbing its meaning with frightening intensity. Her eyes track the money changing hands, the grateful nod of the homeless woman, the continued loyalty of the dog despite its evident hunger. She's studying economics at its most basic level. The currency of sympathy, the value of looking vulnerable. Her fingers twitch slightly at her sides, as if mentally counting the coins that fall into the woman's weathered palm.

Beth recognizes the scheming happening behind her daughter's eyes and feels a familiar chill clambering up her spine. She knows that look. It appears just before violence erupts, just before Amy changes from child to predator. It's the same steely, merciless stare that came before the incident with the classroom hamster, the boy on the playground, the elderly neighbor.

"Let's keep walking," Beth suggests, trying to divert Amy's

attention from the helpless woman. "There might be a park nearby."

But Amy stays transfixed, her mind already several steps ahead, plotting a course that Beth can sense but can't see clearly yet.

As twilight falls and the street lamps flicker to life, casting long, sinister shadows across the decaying urban landscape, the homeless woman's day ends with a transaction far removed from the coins and bills that had clinked in her paper cup throughout the day.

In a filthy alley, tucked away beside a dumpster reeking of putrefaction, she slumps against the tag-scarred brick wall, her throat cut open with one neat slash. Her lifeless eyes are rolled back, showing only the whites, while her tongue lolls obscenely from her mouth. A red pool spreads from her, turning the unyielding concrete into a grotesque pillow that cradles her final rest. Nearby, the broken neck of a bottle lies on the ground, its jagged edge crusted with drying blood, a silent witness to the violence that has played out in this forgotten corner of the city.

Back in Room 7, behind locked doors, Amy sits cross-legged on the bed she claimed as her own. The dull light from the bedside lamp casts reaching shadows across the curling wallpaper. Beside her, the homeless woman's small dog trembles nervously, its matted fur still damp from the rain, its eyes darting around the unfamiliar surroundings. The terrier mix occasionally whimpers, as if sensing the lingering desperation that clings to these walls like hamburger grease and hoary cigarette smoke.

Cecil watches from his position by the window, his expression a mixture of disbelief and reluctant acceptance. "You expect us to feed another mouth?" he asks, gesturing toward the animal, then looks pointedly at Beth. "What were you thinking, woman?"

Beth crosses her arms, looking down. "I told you, the lady paid us to take him. We need money. What else could I do?" she lies, trying not to look at Amy.

Cecil purses his lips. He looks over at Amy and the dog. "That dog is going to the pound. First thing tomorrow!" he declares.

Amy puts her hands over the dog's ears. "Don't you listen to the mean man."

Cecil turns his attention back to Beth. He snaps his fingers. "Let's see," he demands.

Beth walks over to her purse, which is sitting on the desk by the window. She takes out her wallet, the worn, pitted black leather folded at the corners from years of use, returns to Cecil, and hands it to him with reluctance clear in her outstretched arm.

He looks inside, thumbing through the contents with a scowl, and takes out a few bills. He leaves some in the wallet, barely enough to notice. "That's not enough to fix the car. Not near enough," he grumbles, crumpling the money in his fist before shoving it into his pocket.

"But we can pay for another two nights here, get some food, do our laundry..." Beth replies, her words trailing off uselessly. Her shoulders slump slightly as she watches what little security they had disappear into his pocket, knowing her argument wouldn't change anything. But as long as Cecil believes the story, that's what matters.

Cecil takes a deep breath, then belches. "You do what you need. I'ma go get drunk as Cooter Brown," he declares.

With that, he turns and leaves the room, slamming the door shut behind him.

Beth sighs, then goes to Amy and pets the dog. "What are you going to call him?" she asks.

Amy makes a show of thinking. But of course, she already has a name picked out. "Jo-Jo!" she announces.

The dog looks up, as if approving.

"Jo-Jo the Dog-Faced Dog. I like it," Beth says.

They laugh.

"Well, we'd better get him some food. And us. Then we need to do the laundry..." Beth continues.

Amy frowns. "Awww, do we have to?" she complains.

"Yes, ma'am. Get your clothes together," Beth instructs.

Amy plucks her socks from the floor, then heads into the bathroom for her nightgown.

A scorpion skitters across Amy's pillow, its stinger raised and ready, gleaming under the harsh fluorescent light. No one inside notices its presence, just as they fail to see the greater danger gathering around them like storm clouds on the horizon, silent and patient, waiting for the perfect moment to strike. They exist in the space between crimes past and crimes yet to come, suspended in a fragile bubble of temporary safety that will, like all things, eventually burst.

The scorpion abandons its perch on Amy's pillow when Beth's shadow falls across the bed. It darts sideways, multiple legs moving in perfect cadence, and disappears beneath the mattress. Its retreat is silent, tactical, a predator's instinct to remain undetected until the perfect moment presents itself.

Amy emerges from the bathroom, nightgown draped over her arm. She tosses it onto the growing pile of laundry with casual disregard. "Can Jo-Jo come with us to the laundromat?"

Beth glances at the trembling dog. "I don't think they allow pets."

"I'll make him be quiet," Amy promises, her voice dropping to a register that makes Beth's skin prickle.

Crouched under the bed, the scorpion settles into stillness, its patience absolute. Like Amy, it understands the value of waiting—the power in appearing harmless until the moment to strike arrives. Both predators know their strength lies not in size but in venom, in the capacity to deliver pain disproportionate to their physical presence.

The scorpion's carapace gleams dully in the shadows, its pincers held ready. Amy's small hands gather her clothes with similar precision, each movement economical and purposeful. Nothing wasted, nothing revealed. The girl and the arachnid share this quality. An unnerving efficiency, a coldness that registers the world as a series of obstacles or opportunities rather than connections.

"We should hurry before the laundromat gets busy," Beth says, glancing nervously at the door as if expecting Cecil's return at any moment.

Amy nods, her face blank as she considers this new plan. The scorpion similarly assesses changes in its environment—vibrations through the floor, shifts in light and shadow—constantly recalculating risk and reward. Both creatures exist in a perpetual state of tactical awareness, their survival dependent on reading situations correctly, on knowing when to remain hidden and when to act. The scorpion's stinger curves upward, poised and ready.

"I'll get the socks," Amy offers suddenly, her voice sweet, her eyes watchful.

Jasper, an impossibly waifish preschooler, his face pressed against the grimy laundromat window, watches Beth and Amy with solemn interest. His eyes hold the unsettling intensity unique to children who have seen too much too young, who have learned to watch rather than take part.

A woman's hand lands on his shoulder, both protective and controlling. "Jasper! What have I told you about spying?" Her voice mixes weariness and affection.

Jasper looks up at his mother with big, blue Keane-worthy eyes, his face crumpling instantly at her scolding. The wail that follows seems too much for such a gentle rebuke, suggesting a child whose emotions have been damaged by things beyond his control.

Carla kneels beside him, her wasted figure easily folding into a crouch. Despite her rough appearance, her hug is tender as she pulls him against her chest. "Now, now, kiddo. Don't cry."

The sobs stop as quickly as they started. Jasper wipes his eyes with hands so dirty they leave smudged trails across his already grimy face. His clothes hang loosely on his frail frame, suggesting hand-me-downs or cheap store purchases worn far beyond their intended life.

His mother stands, straightening to her full height, which isn't much. Her thirties have not been kind so far... or maybe they've been exactly as cruel as she expected. Her stringy hair falls limply around a face that might once have been pretty before life carved its disappointments into her skin. Her outfit screams desperation: faded short-shorts showing too much loose, stretch-marked thigh, a deeply scooped tank top with no bra, and battered cork wedge heels that add scant height while making every step harder. It's the uniform of a woman whose only marketable asset is her body, and even that value is quickly dropping.

She takes Jasper's tiny hand in hers and leads him into the laundromat where Beth and Amy are sorting clothes.

Inside, Beth examines Amy's face with focused care, like someone who understands the danger of missed details. Her thumb, wet with saliva, reaches out to wipe away a small spot of dried blood near Amy's ear, a ghastly reminder of the homeless woman's execution. The gesture is intimate, practical, and terribly normal, considering what it erases.

Beth turns at the sound of approaching footsteps, her body automatically tensing before she sees Carla and Jasper. Her gaze moves past the woman to fix on the child, a soft gasp escaping her lips. Something about the boy strikes a chord deep within her, a motherly reflex that even years of enabling Amy's violent disposition hasn't completely erased.

"Well, who are you?" Beth crouches to Jasper's eye level, her smile changing her entire face. "Aren't you a handsome young man! Those eyes of yours are just like little stars."

Jasper responds with a shy smile of his own before ducking behind his mother's legs, using her as a shield between himself and this unfamiliar attention. Something about his retreat hints it's not merely shyness but a learned caution, a survival skill. His small fingers grip at the worn fabric of Carla's cutoffs, knuckles whitening slightly with the strength of his hold.

Beth straightens as the other woman moves, closing the distance between them. Carla's smile reveals stained teeth, several of which are missing or chipped, creating a jagged landscape that somehow makes her appear both vulnerable and dangerous. The smell of cheap perfume clings to her like a second skin.

"Hi. I saw you two in here and thought I'd introduce myself. I'm Carla." She speaks with the forced brightness of someone unused to friendly conversations, her voice carrying a slight tremor that betrays its artificial cheer. "I'm staying at the motel too. Well, sometimes." A meaningful pause, her eyes quickly checking Beth's reaction. "I'm an old friend of Cecil Hickman's."

The news lands like a stone in still water, creating ripples of meaning. Beth extends her hand automatically, social training overriding her surprise. "Oh, really? Why didn't you come over? Say hi to Cecil?"

Carla's shrug broadcasts volumes. "Oh, I dunno if he'd be happy to see me." Another pause, heavy with unspoken history. "It's been a good few years. At first, I wasn't even sure if it was him. I, uh, saw y'all check in."

"Hm." Beth's response gives nothing away, a placeholder while she processes this unexpected connection.

Amy watches the interaction from several steps away, her expression hardening into clear disapproval. Her territorial impulse flares at this outsider with past claims on Cecil—a man Amy loathes but considers, in her own twisted way, part of her limited resources.

"I'm Beth," her mother continues, not noticing Amy's darkening mood. "And this is my daughter, Amy."

Beth quickly turns her attention back to Jasper, winking at him with exaggerated friendliness. "And who's this little ragamuffin?"

Carla's grin widens with pride. "That's my son, Jasper."

The boy peeks out from behind his mother's legs, curiosity briefly winning over caution, before retreating again into his self-made fortress.

"He's shy," Carla explains, ruffling his reddish hair affectionately.

"That's the age." Beth nods with knowing sympathy. "Amy was always hiding too. Now she's a little ham!"

Amy's face twists with disdain at this description. "Am not!" she protests, indignant at being described in such terms.

Beth's smile turns indulgent. "Whatever you say, Porky."

The impromptu nickname provokes a glare from Amy, who stalks away to sit on a nearby bench, physically removing herself from a conversation she finds beneath her.

"Will you be staying long?" Carla asks, her casual tone masking the calculation.

"No," Beth replies. "We're just going to get my car fixed and move on." She hesitates, then adds with forced casualness, "You ought to say hi to Cecil before we leave. Come over later? We're in Room 7."

Carla fidgets with her hair, twisting the frayed ends between her fingers, a nervous habit revealing more uncertainty than her words. "Okay. I guess." Her voice wavers slightly, but she nods.

Jasper watches Amy from his protected position behind his mother, his little hand still clutching the faded fabric of Carla's jean shorts. His China-blue eyes are wide and wary, unblinking in their assessment.

Amy stares back at Jasper with laser focus, like a predator honing in on a small, tasty creature in its territory. Her jaw tightens almost imperceptibly as she studies every detail of this silent child who has managed to commanded everyone's attention without saying a single word.

And somewhere beyond their awareness, other forces gather. Police bulletins circulate with updated descriptions of "Bonnie

Rotten and Kid Vicious." The convenience store clerk's body has been bagged and tagged, added to the growing list of their victims. The beggar woman's absence has been noticed by regular passersby, though her death remains undiscovered for now.

The wheels of consequence turn slowly but surely. For this moment in the laundromat, however, they exist in a strange bubble of normalcy. Just two mothers with their children, making small talk while clothes tumble in industrial dryers. The blandness of the scene only highlights its underlying menace, like poisonous mushrooms growing in a well-kept garden.

Outside, the newly acquired dog waits tied to a bicycle rack, panting in the afternoon scorch. His tongue hangs from his mouth, dripping saliva onto the hot concrete as occasional passersby give him a wide berth. His presence marks another change, another adaptation in the evolving pattern of Amy's criminal development. From solo killer to accomplice, from impulse to plan, she changes her methods with frightening skill, adding tools and shedding limitations with the efficiency of a natural hunter.

CHAPTER 14

Carla knocks on the door with a confidence that is at odds with her circumstances. Her knuckles rap three times, precise and deliberate, as Jasper presses himself against her leg, his arms hugging the worn fabric of her jeans, eyes wide with uncertainty.

"Who is it?" Beth's voice calls from within, wariness evident through the thin door, the words tinged with the caution of someone who has learned to expect trouble.

"It's the cops! Come out with your hands up!" Carla responds with unexpected playfulness, her voice carrying a hint of the woman she might have been in another life—a college student with friends and inside jokes, not a street-walking single mom fighting to survive on society's edges. The flash of humor illuminates her face briefly, softening the hard lines that years of addiction and struggle have carved there, while her hand drops to Jasper's head, ruffling his hair with gentle reassurance.

The door swings open to reveal Beth's broad, toothsome smile.

Something about meeting Carla has awakened a long-buried desire for female friendship, for conversation that doesn't revolve around survival or cleaning up after Amy's evil deeds. Their connection, fragile as it might be, feels like finding water in a drought.

Inside, the room has changed slightly. Beth has put a scarf over the lamp, casting soft amber shadows across the walls, and placed some scraggly daisies in a glass of water, a humble attempt at making this temporary space feel homey. The room smells faintly of drugstore air freshener, masking but not quite covering the underlying scent of cigarettes and crack pipes.

She lets the pair inside the room and hands Carla a generic beer, condensation already beading on its aluminum surface. She sits on one of the full beds beside Carla, and they chat companionably as tinny a.m. pop music crackles through the clock radio's weak speaker.

Jasper settles quietly on the floor, his narrow digits tracing patterns on the stubbled carpet, his silence a presence rather than an absence. Amy joins him, engaged in what appears to be play. Jo-Jo lies between them, his energy drained by trauma and change. Amy strokes his wiry fur with fake gentleness, her actions a perfect copy of normal childhood affection, though she looks at him with cool detachment.

"I'm whipped," Carla announces after a long swallow of beer. She tosses the comment casually, as though exhaustion is simply part of the daily weather of her life. "Got any benz?"

Beth shakes her head. "Maybe when Cecil gets back."

Carla responds with a sigh that speaks of long-practiced patience with delayed gratification. "You working?" she asks, the euphemism hanging between them like familiar shorthand.

"Not these days," Beth replies, nodding toward Amy. "Trying to be good."

The irony of this statement seems lost on her. Beth's idea of "good" extends only to certain kinds of wrongdoing; murder, it seems, falls outside these boundaries in her moral math.

"I hear ya." Carla nods with tired understanding. "Someday..."

"It's not easy. I know," Beth says, the words showing genuine empathy born of experience.

In the background, the children create a picture of innocence that hides the darkness surrounding them. Amy dominates the interaction, speaking almost exclusively to the dog while Jasper giggles occasionally but stays silent. His muteness seems less a physical limitation than a psychological adaptation, a retreat from a world that has given him little reason to speak.

"He loves animals," Carla observes with tenderness, watching her son's gentle interactions with the mongrel. "When we get our own place, I promised him a puppy and a kitten." She pauses, reality intruding on the fantasy. "*If* we get our own place."

Beth places a reassuring hand on Carla's arm, the gesture carrying the weight of shared struggle. "You will," she affirms, then switches topics. "How old is Jasper?"

"He's five."

Beth's gaze softens as she watches the boy. "He's so cute," she says, then lowers her voice to a confession. "I wanted a little boy."

The admission hovers like a hummingbird for a moment before Beth returns to normal volume. "I love my little girl, though." She deliberately raises her voice, making sure Amy will hear what follows. "Though she did damn near kill me in labor."

Amy rolls her eyes but says nothing.

"No epidural?" Carla asks, wincing in sympathy.

Beth responds with a dismissive sound. "Huh! Hardly. Did it all on my own."

"Ouch," Carla acknowledges, knowing the grit required for such a thing.

"All's well that ends well," Beth reflects, then adds, "No birth certificate, though, no record. No baby pictures." A sigh escapes her. "I like keepsakes."

"Me too," Carla agrees. "But of course, it's hard to keep the sakes when you're always moving."

Beth raises her beer can in salute. Carla mirrors the gesture, and they drink together in a toast to nomadic survival. "Ain't it the truth? I really want to put her back in school though. She's been running wild too long."

Amy, now brushing Jo-Jo's fur with her pink hairbrush, overhears this assessment.

"She needs some discipline," Beth concludes.

"Do not!" Amy protests, sticking her tongue out.

Beth responds in kind, matching her daughter's gesture. "Do so!"

Amy returns to grooming the terrier while Jasper sits nearby, absently picking his nose. The women laugh at this typical mother-child exchange, finding brief lightness in ordinary conflict.

The mood shatters as the door flies open without warning.

Cecil stumbles in, his movements uncoordinated, swaying unsteadily on his feet. He blinks several times, his eyes struggling to adjust to the room's light and process the scene before him. His shirt is half-untucked, stained with what might be motor oil or something worse, and the sour smell of cheap whiskey follows him like a shadow.

Recognition dawns slowly across his features as his gaze settles on Beth, then shifts to Carla. His expression changes from confusion to disbelief, then hardens into something ugly. His fingers flex and curl at his sides, knuckles whitening, then reddening.

"What're you doing with my ex-wife?" he demands, the words slurring slightly but the accusation crystal clear. Spit flies from his lips as he speaks, and he takes another unsteady step into the room, causing Jasper to shrink back, his fingers freezing mid-pick.

The revelation hits like a thunderclap in the small room. Beth's eyes widen as she processes this new information. Cecil and Carla, once married. The connection Carla hinted at in the laundromat suddenly becomes clear, taking on dimensions Beth hadn't expected. A thousand puzzle pieces rearrange themselves in her mind.

Beth stands, smoothing down her sweater with suddenly trembling hands. "Hey, why don't we go out for a drink? Clear our heads a little?" Her voice aims for casual but lands somewhere closer to desperate.

Cecil grumbles, swaying slightly where he stands, but can't resist the offer of more alcohol. His bloodshot eyes narrow with suspicion, but his addiction makes the decision for him. "Yeah, I could bend an elbow."

Beth just wants to defuse any possible situation before it explodes. The tension in the cramped room is suffocating, and Jasper's wide, frightened eyes keep darting between the adults like he's watching a dangerous tennis match.

"Amy can watch Jasper," Beth says, nodding toward her daughter. "She's great with little kids."

"Okay," Carla agrees dubiously, her bony fingers worrying at the frayed cuff of her sleeve. She glances at Jasper with the anxious look of a mother who rarely trusts her child to anyone else's care.

Jasper waves "bye-bye" with his small, grubby hand, his face lighting up with a rare grin as if to say he understands and will be fine without his mother for a little while. Amy gives a snakelike smile in return, her eyes assessing as she looks at the little boy who's suddenly become the center of everyone's attention. Her lips curl upward, but the warmth doesn't quite reach her gaze.

The tavern matches the motel in squalor, a rundown establishment serving those needing oblivion rather than pleasure. It's the kind of place where dreams come to die quietly in the bottom of a glass. A few barflies perch on stools like carrion birds, nursing drinks and regrets in equal measure. A fluorescent light flickers overhead, casting sickly shadows across faces weathered by hard living and harder choices.

Beth, Cecil, and Carla play a halfhearted game of pool, each holding a plastic cup of cheap whiskey in one hand and a lit cigarette in the other. The jukebox plays a mournful country song, its twanging lament for lost love providing a fitting soundtrack. Smoke drifts like suspended judgment, lit by the pool table's overhead lamp.

They abandon the pool table and find a corner booth, sliding into the cracked vinyl seats. The table wobbles when Cecil sets his drink down too hard, whiskey sloshing over the rim of his glass. Carla scooches in next to him, leaving Beth no choice but to take the opposite side.

"This place hasn't changed," Carla observes, running her fingertip around the rim of her glass. "Same sticky tables, same sad jukebox."

Cecil grunts in agreement. "Same watered-down drinks." He downs his whiskey anyway, signaling the bartender for another round.

Beth lights a fresh cigarette, the flame briefly illuminating the hollows of her face and the hint of green in her hazel eyes. "You two know this place?"

"Used to come here when we first got together," Carla explains, her voice softening with the memory. "Before everything went to shit."

Cecil snorts. "Before *you* went to shit, you mean."

"Let's not do this, Cecil." Carla's voice carries a weariness that implies this is well-worn ground.

Beth jumps in, steering toward safer territory. "How'd you two meet, anyway?"

"Bus station," they answer in unison, then exchange surprised glances at their synchronicity.

"I was seventeen," Carla continues. "Running away from home."

"I was twenty-three," Cecil adds. "Running toward something better."

The waitress arrives with fresh drinks, her wan face a roadmap of wrong turns. She drops them off without a word and moves on to the next table.

"What about you, Beth?" Carla asks. "Where's Amy's father?"

Beth shrugs. "Long gone. Didn't stick around to see what he created."

"Men rarely do," Carla murmurs out one side of her mouth.

Cecil raises his glass in mock salute. "Present company excluded. I tried to make it work."

"You tried to make *me* work," Carla corrects him. "Big difference."

Beth taps her cigarette against the ashtray. "So how long were you two married?"

"Three years, two months, seventeen days," Cecil recites with surprising precision.

"You counted?" Carla looks genuinely surprised.

"Longest I ever stayed with anything," he admits, a flash of vulnerability crossing his face before he drowns it with another belt of booze.

"We really should get back to the kids," Beth suggests.

Cecil dismisses her worry with casual callousness. "Relax. Amy's old enough to babysit. Hell, I never had anyone to watch me at all, and I turned out fine."

The statement contains multiple layers of satire that Cecil himself fails to recognize. He takes a long swallow, then gives Carla an appraising once-over, his bloodshot eyes lingering with possessive familiarity. A burp punctuates his assessment.

"Goddamn, woman. You still look the same," he declares, the compliment backhanded at best.

She responds with a harsh laugh that contains no real humor. "You don't!"

Cecil grins, his silver tooth catching the dim light. "I know it. I look even better." He puffs out his chest with pride. "Come on, now. Admit it."

Carla gives him a gentle shove, the playful gesture carrying echoes of physical interactions that once defined their relationship. "I plead the fifth," she replies, neither confirming nor denying his ridiculous claim.

Cecil shakes his head and turns to Beth, seeking a different audience for his complaints. "Elizabeth here appreciates me. You never did."

The statement carries a threatening undertone, a reminder to Beth of expected loyalties. He leans forward, conspiratorial. "You wanna know what this one here did to me when we was husband and wife, huh?"

Meanwhile, the children have been left to their own devices—a dicey proposition when one of those children is Amy Elder. Jasper remains fully clothed and shoeless, while Amy has changed into her frilly nightgown and pastel green socks with lace trim, her hair pulled back in a short ponytail. The contrast between her innocent appearance and her true nature creates a mental clash that only heightens the menace of the scene.

They lie on the bed watching television, the bedside lamp casting anemic light across their faces. Jo-Jo snores softly on the floor nearby, still reeling from the sudden change in his circumstances. He whines occasionally, as if wondering where his mistress is. On the screen, an old black-and-white horror film plays, showing a man raising a knife, poised to stab a female victim, a mirror image of Amy's own preferred method of killing.

Amy picks up the remote and abruptly turns off the TV. She seems uncomfortable. "This is boring. Let's do something else."

The boy looks at her expectantly but stays silent. His vulnerability radiates from him in waves, seen by Amy not as something to protect but as something to potentially exploit.

"I know! Do you like Hide-N-Seek?" she suggests, her voice containing fake brightness.

Jasper nods, accepting her suggestion without suspicion.

"Okay. I'm going to hide. You close your eyes and count to ten..." She pauses, considering his abilities. "Can you count?"

Jasper blinks, thinking about the question, then nods again.

"Okay," Amy continues, then adds with stern emphasis, "No peeking. I mean it."

Jasper shakes his head solemnly and covers his eyes with small, dirty hands, a gesture of compliance that puts him further at her mercy.

Amy turns off the lamp, plunging the room into darkness relieved only by the faint glow of the powered-down television screen. She slides from the bed and wriggles under it with snakelike ease, positioning herself where she can watch without being seen.

Her hard gaze fixes on Jo-Jo as she waits, perhaps deciding whether the dog might reveal her position. His sorrowful brown eyes open briefly, registering her movement, but the animal stays still, primally sensing the danger of drawing her attention.

After a few moments, Jasper finishes his quiet counting and begins to move. He crawls from the bed with slow, careful movements, allowing his eyes to adjust to the darkness. Shapes gradually emerge from the gloom as his vision adapts.

Beneath the bed, Amy lies surrounded by her hidden treasures: a Barbie doll with hacked-off hair, a wadded-up T-shirt, her pink hairbrush, and most importantly, her switchblade. Jasper's bare feet move within reach of her position, his vulnerable flesh exposed and tempting.

The television, though turned off, keeps a faint ghostly glow, a spectral blue-white haze that barely lights the surrounding darkness. Across its curved surface, a fly crawls with careful precision, each of its six legs moving in perfect sequence as it navigates the static-charged landscape. It pauses now and then to clean its gossamer wings in a gesture of whimsical self-absorption, antennae twitching as if sensing approaching danger. From the ceiling, a spider descends on a nearly invisible silken thread, lowering itself with patient, deliberate momentum into the scene of predation unfolding below, its octet of spindly limbs delicately balanced against gravity.

These creatures watch, witness, but do not interfere as Jasper unknowingly places himself in striking distance of Amy's hidden position, his innocent movements mirroring the fly's oblivious wandering while Amy waits, coiled and watchful as the descending spider, her fingers already inching toward the switchblade among her treasured possessions.

CHAPTER 15

In the tavern, the three adults continue their dance of mutual damage. They've switched to cheaper beer on tap but haven't slowed their swilling. The amber liquid disappears down their throats with practiced efficiency, each empty glass a small victory in their undeclared competition. Their eyes grow increasingly unfocused as the night wears on, yet they persist with the grim determination of people committed to their chosen form of self-destruction.

Cecil leans forward, his voice rising several octaves as he recounts perceived injustices with the righteous indignation of the eternally wronged. "No lie: my brother. My own goddamn brother!" he declares, shaking his head with overwrought disgust. "And everyone blamed me. *Me!* He could fall into a barrel of shit and come out smelling like roses. Myself, on the other hand, I could fall into a barrel of titties and come out suckin' my thumb."

Carla lifts her beer bottle, finds it empty, and without hesitation reaches for Cecil's, taking a long swallow. The casual theft speaks to a closeness that outlives their separation, a familiarity that allows for certain liberties despite their dissent.

"But it was your fault," Carla counters, her voice steady despite the brew clouding her system. "Cole was there to pick up the pieces. What else was I supposed to do? I couldn't live with your parents in that god-forsaken double wide forever while you was out gallivanting…"

"Huh. Gallivanting!" Cecil seizes on the word with ersatz amazement. He turns to Beth, drawing her in as an audience for his mockery. "You hear that? Gallivanting. Them's at least *three* syllables." His attention swings back to Carla, condescension dripping from every word. "Where'd you learn yer vocabulary? Slut school?"

Carla rolls her eyes, her mouth twisting with angst. "Why did I think things might be different? Same old Cecil, always ready with the put-downs." She glances toward Beth, then back at him, hurt flashing across her face. "I can't believe you brought her here." Her voice catches slightly, tinged with something like betrayal. "This was *our* place. The one good thing we had together, and you had to ruin that too."

A verbal grenade, carelessly tossed into Beth's lap. She shifts uncomfortably in her seat, the tension between the former spouses creating a suffocating pressure. "Can we talk about something else?"

Cecil waves his hand dismissively, unwilling to give up his control of the story. "Yeah, yeah. Sure. Long story short, Cole dumped her ass six months later."

The casual cruelty of his summary proves too much. Carla begins to rise, dignity temporarily winning over her desire for continued oblivion. Cecil's hand shoots out, grabbing hers with uncomfortable force. His fingers press into her flesh, applying just enough pressure to threaten worse.

Carla winces, the expression so brief it might be missed by anyone not looking for it. Beth notices, however, and in that moment recognizes a pattern she knows intimately—the calculated use of force followed by manufactured sweetness.

On cue, Cecil's face transforms, anger melting into honeyed charm. "Come on, darlin'. Don't get yer knickers in a knot. I's just reminiscing. Bygones."

Carla settles back into her seat, following the path of least resistance. "Bygones," she echoes, the word hollow.

Cecil reaches into the front pocket of his shirt, the gesture infused with the drama of a magician preparing his finale. "I've got something I know you like..." he announces, producing a small white pill between his thumb and forefinger. He displays it briefly before returning it to his pocket. A promise and a lure, bait dangled before a fish he knows will bite.

Amy's game of hide-and-seek continues with increasing peril. Jasper methodically searches the room, moving from closet to bathroom with the focused attention of a child who takes his games seriously. Inside the bathroom, he stretches his small body upward, trying to reach the light switch that is poised stubbornly beyond his grasp. Undeterred, he peers into the bathtub, then looks up at the ventilation grid mounted high on the wall above the toilet, possible hiding places checked and dismissed.

Returning to the main room, his search is interrupted by Jo-Jo, who struggles to his feet and approaches with friendly intent. The dog's tail wags hesitantly, an offering of friendship that Jasper accepts without question. The boy kneels, wrapping his arms around the mutt's scruffy neck in a genuine hug that the animal returns by nuzzling closer.

The force of canine affection knocks Jasper over, sending both tumbling to the floor in a tangle of limbs and giggles. "Doggy!" he cries. The sound of Jasper's laughter fills the room, innocent and pure against the backdrop of sordid circumstances. It's a precious moment. This child who seldom speaks, finding joy in the simple company of the old dog. Jo-Jo licks Jasper's face enthusiastically, bringing more delighted squeals from the child, whose small hands pat the mutt's shaggy coat with unrestrained affection.

From her hiding place, Amy watches this love-fest with growing fury. Her eyes narrow, jealousy and possessiveness sharpening to dangerous points. The dog—*her* dog—has betrayed her, choosing this intruder over herself. Being forgotten, even momentarily, registers as an unforgivable offense.

The moment of potential violence is interrupted by the sound of a key in the lock.

The door swings open and light floods the room, revealing Cecil in the doorway, one hand holding Beth's and the other holding Carla's. All three stumble forward, their movements loose and uncoordinated as they collapse onto the nearest bed in a tangle of limbs and merry laughter.

Jasper stays on the floor, arms tightening around Jo-Jo as he senses the shift in atmosphere. He's seen his mother in this state before, understands what follows, and seeks comfort in the mutt's warm, solid presence. His small fingers curl deeper into Jo-Jo's fur, his body tensing almost imperceptibly. The joy that had lit up his face moments before is gone.

Amy stays hidden, watching the scene unfold from her concealing cave, thinking about her next move. Her breath comes slow and measured, her earlier rage temporarily suspended as she weighs this new development. The adults' arrival has changed the game, requiring a new plan.

Carla's gaze eventually finds her son, her eyes struggling to focus through the alcohol and whatever pill Cecil has given her. "How are you, baby boy? Did you miss Mama?" she asks, her words running together. There's soft affection in her voice, a tenderness that comes through her drunken haze. She reaches out a trembling hand toward Jasper, her red nail polish catching the light.

Jasper clutches Jo-Jo tighter, his body language saying what his voice cannot: wariness, resignation, the caution of a child who has learned to weather his mother's storms.

Carla sits up unsteadily, and Cecil follows, his hands immediately finding her breasts with drunken entitlement. "*I missed Mama,*" he declares, the juvenile humor baring yet another layer of his stunted emotional development.

Beth stays on the bed, no longer laughing, her expression shifting toward discomfort as she watches Cecil's hands on his ex-wife.

Carla removes his grasp with practiced deflection, maintaining a smile to avoid confrontation. "Oh, you. Stop it now," she says, the words playful but the intention firm.

She rises and makes her way unsteadily toward Jasper, prompting Jo-Jo to bolt for the bathroom, animal senses recognizing the unpredictability of intoxicated humans. "Where's Amy?" Carla asks, suddenly noticing the girl's absence.

Jasper shrugs, unable or unwilling to reveal Amy's hiding place.

Seizing the moment of maximum dramatic effect, Amy explodes from underneath the bed, launching herself at Jasper with a feral battle cry. "Rrrrrrow! I'm a monster...!" she shrieks, her sudden appearance and aggressive movement meant to terrify.

The tactic succeeds. Jasper grabs his mother's legs, instantly dissolving into tears. His crying is silent at first, then builds to hitching sobs.

Beth sits up, maternal authority asserting itself through her inebriety. "Amy Andrea Elder. What do you think you're doing?"

Amy transitions seamlessly from predator to performer, climbing onto the empty bed and arranging herself in a posture of innocent play. She flops down on her back, spreads her arms wide, and makes a pretend snow-angel on the bedspread, the picture of girlish exuberance. "Nothing. We were just playing Hide-N-Seek," she explains.

Cecil looks from Amy to Jasper, who has already stopped

crying and is wiping snot from his nose with the back of his hand. Something about the boy's quick recovery suggests practice, a learned ability to swallow fear and pain to avoid further attention.

Cecil approaches Amy with unexpected swiftness, turns her over, and delivers a single swat to her behind. "That is not how you play, missy!" he scolds, his voice sharp but controlled.

He then moves to Jasper, patting the boy's head with awkward gentleness. "You okay, little man?" His tone shifts completely, softening around the edges, revealing the uncertain tenderness of a man who never learned how to comfort a child.

The sudden attention from this volatile adult triggers fresh tears from Jasper, his small body visibly tensing. His shoulders hunch toward his ears as if trying to make himself smaller, disappear entirely. The boy's eyes dart toward the door, a reflexive measure of escape routes that no five-year-old should need to make.

Amy sits up on the bed, her glare burning holes in Cecil's back. The casual punishment hasn't cowed her; instead, it fuels the simmering rage that grows within her by the day. Cecil's tender nape, exposed to her as he comforts Jasper, becomes a target she mentally notes for future reference.

Cecil turns, catching her expression. "See what you did?" he demands, shifting blame with well-practiced ease.

Amy offers no response, her silence more menacing than any verbal reply.

Carla lifts Jasper onto her hip, shushing him. The boy stops crying immediately, his emotional display shutting off as though controlled by a switch. Jo-Jo peeks cautiously from the bathroom doorway, checking whether it's safe to come out.

Beth watches the entire scene with passive detachment, neither stepping in nor commenting.

Cecil's attention shifts to Carla, curiosity overriding tact. "Whose kid is he, anyway? Ain't mine. Ain't Cole's."

The question hangs, invasive and heedless. Carla doesn't

dignify it with a response, moving instead toward the door. "It's late. We've got to go."

"Where you staying?" Cecil persists, unwilling to give up his perceived right to information.

"Here. I picked up a few extra bucks," Carla replies, the meaning clear to everyone present. After a brief hesitation, she adds, "Room 2."

Cecil pats his chest pocket where more pills remain tucked away, the gesture a reminder of leverage kept. "Well, you and those few extra bucks know where to find us."

He punctuates the invitation with a smirk, the implication clear. The transaction remains open—drugs for sex, companionship for chemical escape. The oldest exchange in their shared past continues unchanged by time or circumstance.

Carla leaves the room without further comment, taking Jasper with her into the night.

Amy crawls under the covers, her expression unreadable as she processes the evening's events and considers adjustments to whatever plans are forming in her young but deadly mind. Jo-Jo ventures cautiously from the other room, settling onto the floor with a weary sigh that seems to convey the weight of the world.

Cecil joins Beth on the bed, shaking his head in wonderment. "Of all the dumb luck. Carla!"

Beth crosses her arms, intuition and observation coming together into insight. "Looks to me like you still have feelings for her."

Cecil's response is immediate and defensive, his frown hiding deeper reactions. "Huh. Worst mistake I ever made, marrying that floozy. She's smoked more meat'n Hickory Farms."

Beth glances toward Amy's bed, where the girl has turned her back to them, seemingly asleep but likely absorbing every word. "That's not a very nice thing to say."

"She's not a very nice woman," Cecil counters. "Not once you get to know her. She's a hustler and a speed freak. You saw how she is... I'm telling you, that one's dropped more pills than a three-fingered pharmacist." His voice rises with righteous indignation. "She's got no business bein' a mama, that's for damn sure."

Beth swallows hard, looking down at her hands as Cecil's judgment hits too close to her own vulnerabilities. "It's not easy being a mother. I'm sure she's doing her best."

Cecil snorts derisively. "Oh, like you? Yeah. Mother of the fucking year awards, all 'round." He raises his hand, index finger circling in the air to indicate universal failure.

Beth turns away, tears welling in her eyes. Not from the sting of his words, but from their alignment with her own secret fears. What kind of mother allows, enables, and covers up her daughter's murders? What kind of mother uses her child as the blade that carves their path through the world, no matter how willing that child may be?

Cecil realizes he's gone too far, his survival instincts alerting him to the danger of alienating his current meal ticket. He sighs, placing a peace-making hand on Beth's shoulder. "Come on now, darlin'. I'm sorry. I didn't mean it." He pauses, then changes tactics. "How 'bout a little kiss? Come on."

Beth is unresponsive, her body stiff at his touch.

Undeterred, Cecil begins kissing her ear and cheek with exaggerated enthusiasm, making loud smacking sounds that mimic cartoon affection. The performance is so ridiculous that Beth can't maintain her hurt; a reluctant laugh escapes her.

"There's my girl," Cecil crows. "You should be smiling. You know why?"

Beth's eyebrows rise in cautious curiosity. "No. Why?"

Cecil reaches into his other shirt pocket and produces a small wad of folded bills, presenting them like a magician revealing the card you selected. "Doubled our money. There's a new kid in town, and he's already numero uno."

Beth's smile returns, financial security temporarily

outweighing emotional concerns. "Can you take the car to the mechanic tomorrow?"

Cecil nods, adding a wink for emphasis. "First thing in the morning. Then it's you, me, and Amy makes three to Miami, F-L-A."

From the other bed, Amy turns over, revealing that she's been listening all along. "What about Jo-Jo?" she asks, concern for the dog seemingly genuine.

Cecil shrugs, adopting a magnanimous air. "Why the hell not? Jo-Jo the Dog-Faced Dog too. The more the merrier!"

He reaches over and gives Amy's ponytail a harsh tug. The small cruelty doesn't go unnoticed by Amy, whose mental list of Cecil's offenses gains another entry.

Jo-Jo closes his eyes, seemingly resigned to his fate with this strange, dangerous family.

Dawn's light filters through the thin motel curtains, casting weak golden beams across the rumpled beds where Amy and Beth lie sleeping, sharing one mattress while Jo-Jo has claimed the other as his territory. The dog's presence on Cecil's abandoned bed seems both rebellious and fitting—the lowest-ranking member rising in the hierarchy during the wannabe alpha's absence.

Amy wakes first, consciousness returning to her with immediate clarity. There's no groggy transition, no slow emergence from dreams, just the snap from sleep to alertness that has served her well. Her small body, still clothed in the frilly nightgown and lacy socks, shifts as she sits up and surveys the room. The digital clock radio displays 5:48 a.m. in harsh red numbers, marking another day in their fugitive existence.

She yawns with convincing normalcy, then reaches up to free her tangled blond hair from yesterday's ponytail. The rubber band joins other small possessions on the nightstand, tokens of a childhood that exists only in its most superficial trappings. Without a backward glance at her sleeping mother, Amy slips into the bathroom and shuts the door behind her.

Beth stirs at the sound, waking with considerably more reluctance than her daughter. Her eyes open to reveal mascara smudges, raccoon rings that, combined with her rumpled clothing from the night before, paint a familiar landscape.

Her attention shifts to Jo-Jo, whose tail begins thumping rhythmically against the bedspread at the first sign of human awareness. The dog's expression contains unmistakable guilt despite his continued defiance of spatial boundaries.

"No dogs allowed on the bed," Beth mutters, her voice raspy from hungover sleep.

The mongrel maintains eye contact but makes no move to obey, having already figured out the hierarchy of rule enforcement in this makeshift household.

"Whatever." Beth reaches into the nightstand drawer and takes out a pack of cigarettes and a lighter, the morning ritual that comes before all others. She lights up, drawing the smoke deep into her lungs before exhaling with a sigh that turns into a small cough. The nicotine hits her bloodstream, providing chemical stability like blood to a vampire.

Rising from the bed, she moves to the window and pulls the curtains aside. Sunlight momentarily blinds her, but as her vision adjusts, a significant absence becomes apparent. The parking space where their car should be sits empty, the stained concrete offering no explanation for what's missing.

The toilet flushes behind the bathroom door, followed by the sound of running water. Moments later, Amy emerges, her expression immediately questioning.

"Where is he?" she asks, cutting straight to the issue that Beth has just discovered.

Beth turns from the window, keeping a carefully neutral

expression. "Uncle Cecil went to have the car fixed. Just like he said."

The words sound hollow even to her own ears, but she stuffs down her doubt. Amy accepts the explanation with a noncommittal shrug, moving to the mini-fridge and opening it with casual entitlement.

"There's only one banana left," she announces, distaste evident in her tone. "Can I go get some mini donuts from the vending machine? Please-please-please?"

"There's change in my purse," Beth replies, settling back onto the bed, cigarette poised between her trembling fingers.

Amy turns her attention to her mother's purse, rummaging through it with methodical thoroughness. "No, there's not," she reports after a moment.

Beth glances over, mild concern beginning to penetrate her nicotine haze. "Then use a dollar. Get change up front."

Amy continues searching, agile fingers exploring every compartment and crevice. "There's no money in here."

Now Beth rises, alarm finally registering. "Are you sure? I had eight bucks last night, after we left the tavern."

As the implications solidify, Amy returns the purse to the dresser with careful deliberation. "Maybe he needed it to fix the car," she suggests, her tone neutral but her eyes watchful, noting her mother's reactions.

"Maybe," Beth echoes, the word hanging between them, a flimsy excuse they both recognize as false.

"When's he going to be back?" Amy probes, twisting the verbal knife.

Beth stretches, affecting casualness, and takes another drag from her cigarette. "I don't know. It's early. He probably just got to the garage, anyway." She pauses, adding with forced optimism, "I hope the car made it that far."

"I'm hungry," Amy declares.

Beth's patience thins. "Well, eat the banana."

Amy shakes her head as she mimes vomiting. "It's all squishy and gross."

"Well, then," Beth replies, lips pursing with annoyance. "I guess you'll just have to wait."

Amy's attention shifts strategically to Jo-Jo, using the dog's needs as a stand-in for her own. "What about Jo-Jo? He can't eat rotten old bananas. He already ate the one can of food you got him. Yesterday."

Beth stands, signaling the end of the negotiation. "Let him catch a rat."

"Gross!" Amy exclaims.

Beth moves toward the bathroom, hoping for refuge in routine. "I'm going to hop in the shower. Take the dog for a walk. Be good."

Amy responds with a mocking gesture, hands pressed together in prayer-like innocence, her smirk undermining the angelic pose.

As the bathroom door closes behind Beth, Amy retrieves the stopgap leash—a length of rope that once belonged to the homeless woman. She loops it around Jo-Jo's neck, and the dog's energy visibly increases, his body language showing excitement at the prospect of going outside.

"Come on, boy," Amy says, making kissy sounds.

She leads Jo-Jo to the door and opens it, the harsh, rising sunlight flooding into the dim room. Amy squints against the brightness, then her gaze dips downward.

Something on the ground before her causes her to freeze, her body suddenly motionless except for her eyes, which widen almost imperceptibly. She keeps staring downward, taking in the unexpected sight on their threshold.

With deliberate slowness, Amy pulls the door shut, staying inside the room. She lets go of Jo-Jo's leash, allowing it to drop to the floor as she walks with unusual hesitation toward the bathroom door. The dog whines softly, confused by the canceled walk.

Amy knocks on the bathroom door, the sound tentative rather than demanding. "Mom?"

The shower runs steadily, Beth unhearing or ignoring her daughter's call. Amy's next attempt carries more force, her voice rising sharply. "Mo-om!!"

The water continues its steady rhythm, but Beth finally responds. "Wha-at?" Her voice carries the usual exasperation of a parent interrupted during a rare moment of privacy.

Amy leans against the door, her small body suddenly appearing younger, more vulnerable. "Come out. You need to see something."

Beth's sigh of irritation carries clearly through the door. "I'm in the shower! Geez!"

"It's important," Amy insists, adding after a beat of silence, "Mo-om!!"

The sounds of interruption follow—water diverted from showerhead to faucet, shower curtain rings scraping along the metal rod, wet feet on linoleum. Then suddenly, the bathroom door flies open with enough force that Amy stumbles backward.

Beth stands in the doorway wrapped in a tiny white towel, water dripping from her hair and down her shoulders. Her face, partly cleansed of yesterday's makeup, now bears smeared remnants of mascara and eyeliner, creating a haunted quality that matches the situation's growing tension.

"This had better be good, young lady," she warns, voice tight with authority that seems increasingly hollow given their circumstances.

Amy says nothing, simply turns and leads the way to the motel room door. Beth follows, clutching the towel with one hand, water still dripping down her legs and forming small puddles on the carpet.

Amy opens the door again, more slowly this time, and both females stare down at the threshold.

There, curled into a small, motionless ball, lies Jasper, his eyes closed, body unnaturally still in the morning light.

CHAPTER 17

Beth gasps and her hand flies to her mouth, the everyday morning concerns of hunger and missing men instantly overshadowed by this new development. She turns to Amy, seeking confirmation that what she's seeing is real.

"Is he okay?" she asks, voice hushed with concern.

Amy offers only a noncommittal shrug, her expression unreadable as she surveys Jasper's motionless form. The detachment in her gaze suggests she's already thinking about how this unexpected turn of events might affect their precarious situation.

Beth steps forward, and as she bends down, the towel comes loose, momentarily forgotten in her concern. Her hand reaches out tentatively, touching the boy's shoulder with gentle fingers.

"Jasper?" she calls softly.

The boy stirs at her touch, consciousness returning gradually. He sits up, blinking groggily. His small body seems smaller still, as though the night spent alone has physically reduced him.

"Poor baby," Beth croons, genuine concern warming her voice.

"How long have you been sleeping there? Where's your mommy? Is everything okay?"

She takes his cold hand in hers, and he stands on unsteady legs. With one hand securing her slipping towel and the other guiding the boy, Beth gently pulls Jasper into the motel room.

Jo-Jo, sensing the disruption to the room's dynamics, dashes to the far side, watching the boy with rapt attention. The dog sits, head tilted, assessing this latest development with canine wariness.

"Amy, shut the door," Beth instructs, leading Jasper further into the room.

Amy complies, stepping forward to close the door with deliberate slowness, her movements suggesting reluctance rather than obedience. The soft click of the latch sounds unnaturally final in the quiet room.

Outside, the world is waking up. Birds tweet their morning songs, men hack, cough, and spit in the parking lot, radios play scratchy tunes through thin walls, and cars rumble to life with sputtering engines.

Beth kneels before Jasper, her hands moving over his compact form, checking for injuries or signs of mistreatment. "Where's your mommy, huh? Are you okay?"

Amy crosses her arms, tilting her chin upward in a posture of superiority that seems both childish and unnervingly adult. "He's mute," she announces with clinical detachment. "That means he can't talk."

Beth shoots her daughter a stern glance over Jasper's head, then pulls the boy into a protective embrace. "Don't you say that, Amy. He's just shy."

Jasper responds to the hug by clutching at Beth, a whimpering sound escaping him. The sound breaks something open in the atmosphere, a hairline fracture in his carefully maintained silence.

"I think he's slow," Amy declares, doubling down on her assessment with casual disregard.

Beth kisses the top of Jasper's head. "Shh. Don't you listen to her," she whispers against his curly, strawberry-blond hair.

Stepping back, Beth takes Jasper by the shoulders and turns him to face Amy, using the boy as a physical barrier between herself and her daughter's steely gaze. "You apologize, Amy Andrea," she commands, then adds with firm decision, "I'm going to finish my shower, then go pay Carla a visit."

Jasper looks at Amy, his expression wary. He wipes his raw, runny nose with the back of his hand.

Amy rolls her eyes dramatically. "Gross," she pronounces, the single word connoting multitudes of disdain.

Amy hears Beth finish her shower with rushed, impatient movements, then the hurried rustling of clothes being yanked on. Within minutes, the front door slams as her mother storms out, undoubtedly to track down Carla, or possibly even Cecil himself. Amy suspects the two have run off in her mom's car, but she wants to be sure before she rubs it in. She's witnessed plenty of Beth's blunders when it comes to men, and she's sure Cecil won't be the last sorry mistake.

After Beth leaves, Amy moves around the motel room with purposeful efficiency, now dressed in blue jeans and a blouse patterned with dark green leaves. Her hair is pulled back in a neat ponytail, flip-flops slapping against her heels as she paces. She's the picture of practical preparedness, a child going through mature motions with unsettling ease.

Jasper is sitting cross-legged on the floor beside Jo-Jo, who endures the boy's persistent petting with resigned tolerance. The dog occasionally scratches at fleas, whining softly as though protesting his general situation rather than the boy's attention.

Amy retrieves one of the empty paper bags from the floor, methodically unfolding it and standing it upright. As she moves around the room gathering possessions, she delivers a monologue that Jasper neither acknowledges nor responds to.

"This has happened before," she informs him with the world-weary tone of a much older person. "We've got to leave soon. I bet he took the car, and he ain't coming back. Bet your mom went with him."

Jasper continues his rhythmic petting, seemingly oblivious to Amy's words, though the tension in his narrow shoulders suggests otherwise.

Amy continues collecting items—clothing, toiletries, her switchblade carefully wrapped in a pilfered washcloth—and placing them in the paper sack. An open suitcase sits nearby, already partially filled with Beth's stuff.

"We'll have to ride the bus. Or maybe even hitchhike," she continues, not looking at Jasper as she speaks. "We can't take you with us. You'll only slow us down."

The airy cruelty of her assessment floats like a ghost, unacknowledged by its recipient but nonetheless delivered with finality. Jasper's warm fingers continue their steady thrum through the wiry fur, his downcast eyes revealing nothing of what might be churning beneath his silence. Amy knows her words have landed—they always do—even if Carla's boy lacks the capacity or courage to respond. It's almost disappointing, how easy it is to wound someone who won't fight back.

Beth stands before the front desk, her appearance transformed from the hungover, harried woman of earlier. She wears a second-hand sundress and espadrilles, her face scrubbed clean of yesterday's sins, her hair still damp from the shower. The transformation is superficial. Behind the presentable exterior, anxiety tightens her features as she grips the edge of the counter with tensed knuckles.

The same clerk who checked them in sits behind the desk, his perpetual smile creating a contrast with the words he delivers. "That's terrible. But yes: she definitely checked out." His cheerfulness seems wrong in the face of Beth's obvious distress.

He consults his ledger with performative thoroughness,

running a plump, fleshy finger down the column of room numbers and times. "Says here, at four this morning. Paid cash for the outstanding balance."

Beth shakes her head, processing this new abandonment, another in a long string of disappointments she should have anticipated. "Did she say anything about her son? Jasper?" Her voice catches slightly on the child's name. "Is someone coming to get him?"

The clerk's smile stays fixed, agreeable but not engaged. "We're not family services here, ma'am. I don't know anything about her son. She didn't leave no notes for nobody, neither." He shrugs, the gesture showing his indifference.

"Damn it," Beth mutters.

He glances at the clock behind him, which reads 7 a.m., before delivering his next blow. "By the way, ma'am, if you're going to stay here another night, that'll be eighteen dollars. Check-out time is now."

"What? I thought it was ten a.m."

The clerk lifts his shoulders dismissively, indicating that whenever he declares it's time to leave, that's what it is.

Beth's gaze drops to the floor, her posture showing defeat before she even speaks. "My gentleman friend went to get the car fixed, and he has all our money. Can't we have a grace period, just this once? I promise, he'll be back real soon and I'll pay you."

The clerk's grin shifts, warmth draining from it to reveal his true apathy. "No grace periods."

Beth wrings her hands, desperation creeping into her voice. "But I've got two kids in the room and nowhere to go. He'll be back in less than an hour. I swear."

The man shakes his head with finality: no exceptions, no mercy, no accommodation for women with children and no resources. Rules are rules, and those without money have no rights to space or even dignity.

Beth sighs, the sound containing generations of female resignation. "What am I supposed to do?"

The clerk spreads his legs while remaining seated, looking pointedly at his crotch before raising his gaze to Beth's face. His toothy smile returns, the proposition unspoken but unmistakable.

Her stance sags with recognition of the inevitable undertaking. Without a word, she begins to move around the desk, accepting the terms of her temporary reprieve.

"Lock the front door. Close the blinds," the current holder of Beth's fate instructs, his voice dropping to a conspiratorial register.

The scene fades to black in Beth's mind, but sounds penetrate the darkness—the metallic slide of a bolt being thrown, the eager whisper of a zipper being lowered.

Amy continues packing, her movements methodical and unhurried. She knows this drill. The abandonment, the improvisation, the carefully considered sacrifices necessary for survival. The boy keeps petting Jo-Jo with gentle persistence. In his touch lives the desperate hope of connection, of somehow anchoring himself to something living and warm in a world where adults disappear without warning and children are left sleeping on cold concrete thresholds.

Outside the motel, the day brightens, the sun indifferent to the banal human dramas unfolding below its rays. Somewhere on the highway, Cecil drives Beth's car toward whatever new scam or temporary paradise has captured his imagination. He's unwittingly escaped Amy's crosshairs—for now. Maybe Carla sits beside him in the passenger seat. Or, somewhere else, perhaps, she pursues her own escape, freed from responsibility.

Amy pauses in her task, her gaze settling on Jasper with new assessment. Her expression shifts slightly as she reconsiders his potential value. Maybe he isn't just an inconvenient burden.

Perhaps, like Jo-Jo, he might serve a purpose in her continuing survival.

"Hey, Jasper," she says, addressing him by name for the first time. "Maybe you could come with us after all. People feel sorry for kids with dogs. They might feel even sorrier for two kids."

He looks up, meeting her eyes with cautious hope, unaware that in Amy's world, usefulness is the only protection against elimination.

The room grows still as Amy, having finished her self-appointed task of packing up, finds herself with nothing to occupy her hands or mind. She casts about for something, anything, to relieve the boredom, the awareness of time passing without the promise of movement or change.

Her gaze lands on the worn paperback that has been a fixture in their wandering existence. With Beth absent, the book's appeal intensifies. Amy retrieves it from the paper sack. Her pad of her index finger traces the scuffed, embossed title before she thumbs through the pages, her eyes scanning for the most gruesome and compelling entries.

She settles cross-legged on the itchy sisal carpet, the book open in her lap. Jasper, intrigued by this new activity, crawls closer. He sits beside her, his small body a silent question.

"Listen to this," Amy announces, her voice dropping to a hushed, dramatic murmur, her green eyes gleaming with a mixture of mischief and malice. "This is the story of a man who was born with two faces. They called him 'the Two-Headed Nightmare.'"

She reads with fervor, detailing the man's life. His ridicule, his pain, his isolation from the world. As she speaks, her voice takes on the tempo of a practiced storyteller, each sentence designed to cause a shiver of horror.

"And look at this picture," she says, turning the book toward Jasper so he can see the grainy black-and-white photograph. The image shows a man with a second, smaller face protruding from his left cheek and jawline, a freak of nature captured for posterity.

Jasper's eyes widen, and he recoils slightly, his gaze flicking between the photograph and Amy's eager face. She watches him closely, searching for any sign of fear or disgust.

Undeterred by his lack of reaction, Amy turns the page. "And here's the story of a girl who had the body of a spider. They say she could climb walls and ceilings, her eight legs moving in perfect harm... harmony."

She continues to read, her words painting a vivid picture of spider-like deformities and the girl's lonely existence in a traveling sideshow. All the while, she studies Jasper, looking for the slightest indication that her words have hit their mark.

Jasper's lips part in a silent gasp, his small hands balling into fists at his sides. His stare stays fixed on the book, on the strange and terrible images it contains. Amy, satisfied with his response, leans in closer, a sadistic smile playing at the corners of her mouth.

"And this one," she says, her voice dropping to a near-whisper, "is about a boy who was born without any skin. They called him 'the Living Skeleton.' People would pay just to see his raw, red muscles and the bones poking through."

As she describes the boy's tragic life, the physical pain he endured, and the horrified stares he attracted, Amy's tone takes on an almost gleeful quality. She's no longer merely recounting the stories from the book; she is performing them, enjoying the shock value and the power it gives her over Jasper's silent attention.

Amy closes the book with a decisive snap, her presentation concluded, leaving Jasper to process the barrage of unsettling images and stories she has so vividly brought to life. She sets the book aside, her eyes still fixed on him, waiting for his reaction—and finally, his lower lip begins to quiver.

"I hope you don't have nightmares tonight," Amy says with a wink.

Amy tucks her switchblade into her back pocket with the rote efficiency of someone handling a familiar tool rather than a weapon of death. The metal presses against her through the denim, a welcome reminder of her power, her control, her ability to reshape her world through violence when necessary.

She steps over to the dresser, her attention caught by the banana peel curling brownly in the nearby trash can. Gnats fly in lazy circles above the rim, like vegetarian vultures. Her gaze shifts to Jasper, revulsion etching itself across her features as she makes the connection.

"I can't believe you ate that," she says, her voice dripping with disgust. "You're gonna be sick later."

The banana she had deemed too disgusting to eat has apparently met a less picky eater in Jasper—another mark against him in Amy's careful checklist of human weaknesses. The boy's willingness to eat food she rejected suggests both desperation and lower standards, qualities Amy notes with the aloof detachment of a scientist observing lab subjects.

Her attention shifts back to the book of freaks sitting by the TV set. She picks it up with unexpected tenderness, her fingers once again tracing the cover with something like affection. The stolen volume represents one of her few personal possessions, a treasure of abnormality that speaks to something basic in her nature.

She takes the book to the bed and climbs up, settling herself against the pillows like a teacher preparing for a lesson. "I'm going to read you another story," she announces, the offer containing neither kindness nor any real desire to entertain—merely a way to fill time while asserting control over their shared space.

Jasper lies down next to Jo-Jo on the floor, curling against the dog's warmth. The animal remains the only source of comfort in this uncertain situation, and Jasper gravitates toward it with the inborn need of a child seeking security in a chaotic world.

Amy flips through the book, finding her place with ease. When she begins to read, her voice transforms, becoming fluid and articulate, in contrast to her mother's halting, uncertain pronunciation. Amy reads with perfect diction and understanding, revealing an intelligence that makes her deadly nature all the more worrying.

"Grady Stiles was known as the Lobster Boy," she begins, the words flowing with precision. "His fingers were fused together on both hands, like the claws of a sea creature. He started performing in the sideshows when he was just a child..."

Meanwhile, in the motel office, a different performance unfolds. The clerk's moist, doughy hands tangle in Beth's hair, controlling her movements with casual brutality as he pushes her head downward. His expression holds neither passion nor particular cruelty, merely the satisfaction of a deal going according to plan, services rendered for accommodation extended. Beth's eyes flutter closed for a moment, a silent prayer for strength floating up to the cosmos. She endures the indignity, her mind a thousand miles away, dreaming of a future where such compromises are a distant memory.

Beth's humiliation buys temporary shelter for her daughter and their unexpected ward. Just another sacrifice in a lifetime of them, another piece of herself traded for survival. The clerk's face shows nothing but the most basic pleasure, unaware or unconcerned that the woman kneeling before him has mothered a killer who would not hesitate to open his throat given motive and opportunity. Unknown to him, Beth's thoughts are not of the present but of the safety of her child and Jasper, the mute boy who, despite his silence, has suddenly become an essential part of their makeshift family.

Back in the room, Amy continues her reading, unaware or unconcerned with her mother's degradation. "As an adult, he was an abusive husband and father," she recites, perhaps finding echoes in this description. "He forced his family to work in the sideshow, and... confined to a wheelchair, he developed incredible upper body strength that, when combined with his temper and alcoholism, made him quite dangerous."

The fascination in her voice is clear as she continues, obviously identifying with this historical figure who transformed physical abnormality into a source of power and fear. "On the eve of his daughter's wedding in 1978, he shot and killed her husband-to-be and was convicted of third-degree murder. But because no institution was equipped for his handicap..."

She interrupts herself with a giggle, delighted by the macabre wordplay. "Get it? HAND'y cap?"

Jasper's eyes remain closed, his body language suggesting he has mentally withdrawn from the room, from Amy's voice, from the disturbing content she shares with such glee.

Amy notices his apparent disengagement and responds by increasing her volume, unwilling to be ignored. "—he received fifteen years' probation instead," she practically shouts. "He's still out there... *somewhere.*" The ominous conclusion is a phantom threat that mirrors Amy's own deceptive existence.

Outside the motel office, Beth emerges into the harsh daylight, squinting against the sudden brightness that seems to spotlight her shame. She spits forcefully into the bushes, the gesture conveying all her disgust and self-loathing. She wipes her mouth with the back of her hand, as though the physical evidence of her degradation might be so easily erased, and walks on, shoulders squared with determined dignity.

Her path takes her back toward Room 7, where Amy continues reading and Jasper seems not to hear. Beth moves with the mechanical efficiency of someone compartmentalizing trauma, tucking the recent past into a mental box alongside countless similar experiences. Her mind already shifts to practical concerns —how long their reprieve will last, whether Cecil might return, what to do about Jasper, how to feed two children and a dog with no money and no transportation.

Inside her, something hardens further. Another layer of protective callus forming over a core that was once tender and hopeful. The pattern repeats with such regularity that she barely notices anymore. Crisis, sacrifice, temporary stability, then inevitable collapse, leading only to the next inevitable crisis. The cycle spirals downward, each revolution taking her further from any possibility of escape or redemption.

The sun climbs higher in the bald sky, illuminating the decrepit motel with unforgiving clarity. Paint peels, concrete cracks, and rusty stains broadcast neglect and decay. Yet within this physical manifestation of societal indifference, lives continue— damaged, desperate, and dangerous.

Beth reaches for the doorknob, steeling herself to face whatever new challenge waits inside. The door swings open to reveal Amy, book still in hand, miming normality with precision, while Jasper pretends to sleep and Jo-Jo watches with wary animal wisdom.

Another day begins for them, their fates bound together by circumstance and survival. Behind them lies a trail of bodies; ahead, the path is uncertain. But Amy's switchblade rests securely in her back pocket, ready for whatever comes next.

CHAPTER 19

Beth stands before the bathroom mirror, applying makeup with rushed efficiency. Not for vanity, but for business. Foundation covers fatigue, mascara widens eyes dulled by experience, lipstick creates the illusion of life where none remains. Her fingers work methodically, changing her face into something marketable, a weapon in the arsenal of survival. Each stroke of concealer hides not just physical flaws but the mounting psychic scarring. She reaches for her disposable razor, dulled by the weeks, and runs it down each armpit.

In the main room, Amy and Jasper share the bed with Jo-Jo, a Rockwellian picture of domesticity. The television casts dancing shadows across their faces, briefly uniting them in the passive communion of watching. For this space in time, they look almost like ordinary children.

Amy rises suddenly, drawn to the window by restless energy. She pulls the curtain aside, her small face hardening as she confirms what she already knows: the parking space remains empty, another broken promise written in absence.

"He's not back yet!" she calls out, the words pitched between indictment and observation. Her voice carries the pitch of disappointment she's too young to name but old enough to expect, a familiar tension settling across her narrow shoulders.

Beth appears in the bathroom doorway, her face partially transformed by makeup that fails to hide her exhaustion. "He'll be back," she lies, the fantasy maintained for reasons even she doesn't fully understand. "You behave. Watch TV."

Amy returns to the bed, her movements slow and exaggerated to show her displeasure. "I'm hungry," she announces, the simple biological need weaponized as accusation.

Beth retreats to the bathroom mirror, continuing her paintjob. "I know, baby," she calls from beyond the doorway. "We're all hungry. I'll be out for just a little while, and I'll bring back some food."

"A lot of food," Amy counters, her voice brightening with sudden enthusiasm. "McDonald's!"

Beth reenters the room, attaching cheap hoop earrings that complete her carefully constructed exterior. The costume is complete—generic attractiveness assembled from dollar-store components, designed to extract maximum value from minimum investment.

"French fries?" she offers, the question a negotiation rather than a query.

"And a shake!" Amy adds, sensing an opening. After a pause, she adds, "And a hamburger for Jo-Jo!"

The dog recognizes his name, tail wagging with Pavlovian response to potential food. His simple, hopeful reaction appears almost comical against the complex human manipulations surrounding him.

"Promise," Beth agrees. In her world, promises are currency, devalued through constant inflation but still traded nonetheless.

Beth retrieves her purse, the meager container of her worldly possessions. Her hand pauses momentarily on the doorknob, hesitation betraying her awareness of what comes next. Another transaction, another piece of herself exchanged for necessities. "Be good," she says.

The door closes behind Beth with a finality that seems to release agitation from the room. Amy's posture immediately shifts, the performance of childhood petulance abandoned now that its primary audience has departed. She sprawls on the bed, manipulating her Barbie doll with distant interest, not playing so much as mimicking the expected behaviors of girlhood, a ritual followed without joy.

Jasper sits on the floor again, his attention focused entirely on working through the dog's patchy fur with gentle persistence, the repetitive motion seemingly as comforting to him as to the animal. In this contact lives Jasper's only certainty—the tangible warmth of another living creature who accepts touch without judgment or threat.

Amy observes this ongoing connection with mounting irritation. "You're going to pet the fur right off that dog," she declares, the criticism smoke-screening deeper possessiveness. Her words zing through the air, sharp-edged and unacknowledged, another failed attempt to assert control.

She pats the bedspread beside her, attempting to redirect the animal's loyalty. "Come here, boy. Jo-Jo!" Her voice rises with artificial sweetness, a tactic she's learned from adults. Honey-coating commands to disguise their true nature.

The dog acknowledges her call with a quick tail wag but stays where he is. This small rebellion further sours Amy's expression, another tally mark in her mental ledger of perceived injustices.

"Come on," Amy insists, her voice hardening with command.

Jo-Jo stays put, his animal intuition recognizing genuine safety with Jasper despite Amy's assumed position of nominal ownership.

The betrayal, minor though it might seem, registers on Amy's face as a darkening storm cloud. She frowns, looking at Jasper with unmistakable menace. The boy doesn't meet her gaze, either from self-preservation or habitual avoidance.

Amy sighs theatrically, shifting tactics. "I'm bored. Aren't you?" The question requires no answer; Jasper's silence is a given. After a deliberate pause, inspiration strikes—or appears to. "I know! Let's give Jo-Jo a bath."

The suggestion stands suspended, innocent on its surface but harboring veiled threat in its execution. Amy's flat, calculating eyes reveal the true nature of her proposal. Not hygiene but control, not care but dominance, another move in the psychological chess game she plays with everyone around her.

Outside the motel, Beth walks toward the streets where transactions occur without paperwork or receipts. Her gait suggests determination rather than desperation, another performance in a life composed of them. She moves with practiced efficiency, navigating the cracked sidewalks and avoiding eye contact with passing strangers. The neon signs from nearby establishments cast sickly colors across her face, highlighting the hard lines around her mouth that betray years of similar errands.

Behind her, sequestered in Room 7, two damaged children and one wary dog await her return, a fragile ecosystem of need and manipulation temporarily balanced like a plate spinning on a stick, but inevitably unstable. The air inside that room grows heavier by the minute, charged with unspoken threats and jeopardy, the kind of atmosphere where small cruelties can bloom into something far worse.

Beth crosses the street and steps into the blur of the tavern, dark as a coal mine. Her entrance goes unnoticed amid the cacophony of clinking glasses, raucous laughter, and hacking coughs. The dim lighting cloaks the room in a deceptive warmth, a stark contrast to the cooled stares she receives upon crossing the threshold. She walks with an air of casual indifference and scans the room, her eyes briefly meeting and then sliding past those of the patrons.

Her gaze lands on a man seated alone at the bar, his slouch suggesting a weariness that matches her own. She approaches, the stool next to him an invitation she accepts with a silent nod.

The bartender, a middle-aged woman with sharp eyes and a sharper tongue, gives Beth a once-over. "What'll it be?" she asks, her tone implying that she already knows the answer.

Beth orders the cheapest swill. She ignores the bartender, her focus trained on the man beside her. His eyes stay fixed on his glass, swirling the remnants of his vodka as if the answers to life's questions might be found at the bottom.

She leans closer, her voice barely above a whisper as she speaks to him. "Looking for some company tonight?" Her question is direct, devoid of pretense. There's no room for games in her world, only tit for tat.

The man turns to her, his eyes lingering on her painted face. For a moment, there's a flicker of something—pity, perhaps, or regret—before it hardens into resolve. "Not interested," he grumbles, turning away and signaling for the check.

Beth's expression doesn't waver, but inside, there's a subtle shift. She's familiar with rejection, yet each time it chips away at a resilience already worn thin. She finishes her drink in a single gulp, the burn of cheap alcohol a temporary anesthetic.

Rising from the stool, she moves on to the next prospect, a group of men huddled around the pool table where she had laughed with Cecil and Carla. She approaches with a sway in her step, a mimed seduction designed to appeal to their basest needs.

"Care for a game?" she offers, her smile bright against the dingy backdrop of the tavern.

One of the men, younger than the rest with a cocky grin, eyes her up and down. "Depends on what you're playing for," he retorts, his friends snickering at the innuendo.

Beth holds his gaze, her resolve momentarily strengthened. "Winner takes all," she replies, the double meaning clear.

The young man's smirk fades, replaced by a look of discomfort. He shakes his head, stepping back from the pool table. "Nah, I'm good. We're just here to play some pool."

The laughter from his friends feels sharper this time, a stab at her lowly status. Her age. Her brokenness. Beth nods, her pride stinging from the public dismissal. She slinks away quickly, the walls of the tavern seeming to close in around her with each step, the floorboards creaking under her worn shoes like a mocking chorus.

She leaves the bar, the cool night air a harsh slap against her flushed face. Her reflection in a nearby storefront window is an unwelcome reminder of her defeat—hair disheveled, eyes hollow, shoulders slumped under the blow of another rebuff. She pauses for a moment, gathering herself before moving on to the next place, the next possibility.

Amy tests the bathwater's temperature with an almost scientific precision, her steady hand hovering just above the rising surface. The hot water flows from the tap in a rush, filling the stained tub with clarity that will soon be muddied by Jo-Jo's unwashed coat. Steam rises in tentative wisps, creating a humid atmosphere in the already cramped bathroom. The mirror above the sink has begun to fog at its edges, reflecting Amy's concentrated expression in increasingly blurred detail.

In the doorway, Jasper and Jo-Jo stand frozen in a diorama—the boy's eyes wide with apprehension, the dog's body tensed with wariness. The preschooler's fingers twist anxiously in the hem of his T-shirt, his tiny body seeming even smaller as he shrinks against the doorframe. The terrier's ears have flattened slightly, his normally lively tail now hanging motionless between trembling hind legs.

"It's almost full," Amy announces, her voice carrying the false brightness of a grand spectacle. "Bring him over here."

Jasper takes a hesitant step forward, his bare feet padding on the grimy linoleum, toes curling slightly as if trying to grip the floor for stability. Jo-Jo, possessed of more immediate, animal instinct, bolts back into the main room with a sudden burst of self-preservation, nails scrabbling frantically against the worn floor as he disappears around the corner.

Amy rises from her kneeling position beside the tub, her hands clenching into fists as rage darkens her features. The transformation happens in an instant. Childlike pretense dropping away to reveal the rapacious creature beneath, her jaw tightening and eyes narrowing to glittering points. "Jo-Jo!" she snaps, the name becoming command and threat simultaneously, her voice pitched low and menacing.

Outside on the street, Beth pauses in her purposeful walk toward potential paying customers. Her gaze is drawn upward by the garish flash of neon against the afternoon sky, a billboard advertising "LIVE NUDE GIRLS!" in pulsing pink lettering.

Her reflection wavers in a storefront window below the sign—cosmetics carefully applied, clothes selected for maximum appeal with minimum protection, a woman transforming herself into marketable segments while maintaining the illusion of wholeness. Beth stares at herself for a moment, recognition and alienation mingling behind her eyes before she continues her journey toward whatever temporary salvation she can secure.

Back in the motel bathroom, Amy returns triumphant, carrying the squirming dog in arms that belie their childish appearance with surprising strength. The animal twists and writhes in her grip, whining softly, paws paddling air, already sensing the impending bath.

Amy brushes past Jasper without acknowledgment, treating

him as an unimportant obstacle rather than a participant. The boy's presence registers as little more than furniture in her single-minded focus. With glacial efficiency, she drops Jo-Jo into the water, the action containing neither cruelty nor kindness. Merely purpose, the mechanical execution of a task she's chosen to complete.

Jo-Jo yelps as he hits the scalding water, the sound sharp with panic and betrayal. He scrambles desperately, claws scrabbling against the slick porcelain as water flies in all directions, soaking Amy's clothing and splashing Jasper where he stands, frozen in mute observation. The bathroom fills with the frantic sounds of splashing and canine distress echoing off the cracked tile walls.

"No! Be still," Amy commands, pressing down on the dog with both hands, forcing his trembling body deeper into the water. "You're a dirty, dirty dog!" Her expression is concentrated, lips pressed into a thin line of determination.

The little boy backs away from the scene, his thumb finding his mouth in stupefied self-soothing. His eyes widen with concern for the animal that showed him kindness, but he remains silent, unable or unwilling to intervene. He retreats into the main room, carrying the weight of his helplessness like an anvil.

Jo-Jo fights against Amy's unyielding hands, his efforts growing weaker as he focuses on keeping his head above water. His eyes roll wildly, reflecting the bathroom ceiling and the grimacing alpha's face in desperate rotation.

On the high windowsill above the tub, a glossy black widow spider crawls with deliberate patience, its venomous body gleaming in the harsh fluorescent light. The spider watches the proceedings with eight unblinking eyes, a noiseless witness to the small cruelties that prefigure larger ones. Its front legs raised in mock supplication, it grooms itself with the self-absorbed focus of a perfect killing machine, indifferent to the human drama played out around it.

Beth shuffles into the room, her physical demeanor suggesting both exhaustion and relief. Her purse dangles from one shoulder, and in her opposite hand she carries a fast food sack, its bottom darkened with grease that promises satisfaction of a primal need. The smell of salt, fat, and processed meat infiltrates the stale motel air, an appetizing announcement of temporary abundance.

Jasper stays where he has been for hours, slumped against the pillows of one bed, thumb still anchored in his mouth. He barely glances up as Beth enters, his body language communicating a retreat so profound it borders on disconnection.

Amy has transformed herself during her mother's absence, changing into her nightgown and green socks—her costume of innocence. She sits cross-legged on the other bed, the *Sideshow Freaks* book open on her lap, its unsightly illustrations matching the interior landscape of its reader. At Beth's entrance, her face arranges itself into an expression of childlike delight.

"Mom! I thought you'd never come back," she exclaims, the performance flawless in its simulation of normal little-girl dependence.

Beth responds with a tired smile, moving toward her daughter with the offering of food. "I'm not only back, but I have burgers, fries, and hot apple turnovers," she announces, the statement carrying pride disproportionate to the meager feast, as though she's returned from a heroic quest bearing precious gifts rather than fast food bought with her body's currency.

Amy jumps up in seemingly genuine excitement, her book tumbling to the floor where it lands beside her Barbie doll.

Beth's tired chuckle carries affection mixed with bone-deep weariness. "Don't be a barbarian. Sit back down, and we'll have a little picnic on the bed. Doesn't that sound like fun?" The invitation attempts normalcy in a context that defies it. After a beat, she adds, "Jasper?"

The boy's gaze drops downward, avoiding connection, his

silence a wall between himself and these strangers who now control his destiny.

Beth's attention shifts to Amy, maternal intuition sensing the aftermath of something amiss. "What's wrong with him?" she asks, suspicion threading through concern.

Amy offers a noncommittal shrug, her expression masterfully blank. "He seems fine to me," she replies with indifference, then adds after a strategic pause, "I told you he was slow."

Beth approaches Jasper, concern overriding her exhaustion. She touches his forehead with the back of her hand, checking for fever with the automatic gesture of experienced parenthood. She gently removes his thumb from his mouth, searching his face for clues. "Are you okay, sweetheart?"

He responds by immediately reinserting his thumb, the coping gesture his only defense against the chaotic world that has swallowed him. The message is clear: he cannot or will not communicate beyond this physical statement of withdrawal.

Beth rests her hand on his small shoulder, offering comfort through touch where words have failed. "How about some french fries? Bet you're hungry," she suggests, using food as both enticement and potential bridge across his silence.

Meanwhile, Amy attacks the paper bag with zeal, spreading its contents across the bedspread. The unwrapping of a burger becomes a tactical operation, hunger and impatience driving her movements. "Come on, Mom!" she urges, demanding the attention Beth has directed elsewhere.

"In a second," she replies without looking at her daughter. "You go ahead."

Amy freezes, her eyes narrowing as she observes the interaction between her mother and Jasper. Jealousy flares, sharp and possessive, at this diversion of maternal resources to the interloper. With deliberate provocation, she sets down her unwrapped burger. "I'm not hungry," she announces, the sulking both childish and calculated.

Beth's attention remains on Jasper, her fingers detecting dampness in the fabric of his shirt. Suspicion crystallizes into certainty as she makes the connection. "Your shirt is damp," she observes, then glances over her shoulder at Amy. "What did you do to him?"

Amy crosses her arms, the defensive posture betraying guilt despite her nonchalance. "I didn't do anything. We were just giving Jo-Jo a bath earlier, that's all."

It's then that Beth notices the dog's absence, her eyes sweeping the room with sudden concern. "Where is he?" she asks, then calls out, "Jo-Jo! Here, boy."

Amy's hand rises, finger pointing toward Jasper in accusation. "He did it. Jasper did it."

Beth stands, suspicion straightening her spine. "Jasper did what?"

Amy's gaze drops to the floor in fake contrition. "Nothing," she says, the word contradicted by her quick glance toward the bathroom.

Beth follows the visual cue, moving toward the doorway with growing dread. She flicks on the light, illuminating the scene. She stands motionless before the tub, looking down at what's inside. Her head moves slowly from side to side in a gesture of profound disappointment.

When she turns around, her face reflects the unwanted wisdom of repeated disillusionment, yet another confirmation that her daughter's nature is warped and... sinister. The bathroom light casts harsh shadows across her features, highlighting the lines of worry that have deepened over years of similar incidents. She approaches Amy, her steps heavy with the knowledge that no discipline, no consequence, no maternal guidance can alter the fundamental darkness that flowers within her child.

"Oh, Amy," she says, the words containing volumes of dashed hope and resigned acceptance. Her voice barely rises above a whisper, but the quiet desperation behind it fills the room more effectively than any shout could.

Amy responds by picking up her burger and taking a defiant bite, chewing with exaggerated enthusiasm while maintaining eye contact. A challenge rather than an apology. Ketchup smears at the corner of her mouth, but she makes no move to wipe it away, instead savoring her mother's discomfort as much as the food between her teeth.

The McDonald's bag sits on the bed between mother and daughter, its golden arches promising happiness while delivering only temporary satiation. Like everything else in their lives, it represents the counterfeit version of what others take for granted —family, security, normal childhood, all simulated but never truly experienced.

As night falls completely, Room 7 cradles three damaged souls. One woman who sells herself in fragments to protect a daughter beyond salvation, one girl whose capacity for violence is matched only by her talent for deception, one silent boy adrift in a world that has repeatedly failed him. One soul, that of the beleaguered dog, lingers, tethered to this unspeakable evil.

Nearby, the packet of half-eaten french fries lies on its side, its contents writhing with maggots. The squirming white larvae transform the treat into something nightmarish, an apt metaphor for the deceptive appearances that masks the rot beneath. Like Jasper's silence, the infestation exists without commentary, without explanation—nature simply reclaiming what was discarded. The grease-stained container, once bright with color, now hosts life of the most primitive kind, converting abandoned pleasure into the stuff of revulsion.

In the half-light of Room 7, the undulating mass seems almost hypnotic, a miniature universe of hunger and consumption playing out in the lonely shadows.

CHAPTER 21

Beth moves through the ritual of bedtime, her robe belted tightly around her waist as though the terrycloth might shield her against the accumulated traumas of the day. She tucks Amy into bed with tenderness, pressing a kiss to her daughter's cheek, the gesture containing all the contradictions of their relationship, her affection flowing toward a vessel incapable of truly receiving it.

Jasper occupies Beth's bed, his small body curled into a defensive position even in sleep, knees drawn to chest as though warding off invisible threats. When she joins him, her arm settling around his shoulders with protective response, he doesn't stir—exhaustion having finally claimed him after hours of vigilant anxiety, his five-year-old frame surrendering to slumber only after fighting it for fear of nightmares. The nightstand lamp clicks off under Beth's hand, plunging the room into darkness broken only by ambient light seeping through thin curtains, casting elongated shadows across the walls like silent sentinels guarding their troubled rest.

Silence settles briefly, the momentary peace as fragile as blown glass.

"Mom...?" Amy's voice emerges from the darkness, shattering the peace.

"What?" Beth responds, flat, fatigued.

"Why does Jasper get to sleep with you?" The question implies layers of possessiveness and jealousy, emotions that might seem childishly normal if not for the switchblade that enforces them.

Beth lowers her voice to a whisper, ostensibly to protect Jasper's rest but perhaps also to diminish the confrontation. "Shh. You'll wake him up."

Amy modulates her volume accordingly, but her persistence is undiminished. "But why?"

"You know why," Beth replies, the cryptic response acknowledging unspoken truths between them. "Now go to sleep."

The command resonates, temporarily obeyed but not accepted. Moments pass, measured by the hum of the ancient air conditioner and the distant sound of cars passing on the highway.

"He's not coming back, is he?" Amy finally asks, her question pivoting to Cecil's absence with characteristic abruptness. The question carries no emotional weight, merely a calculation seeking confirmation. "And she's not, either."

"I don't know, honey," Beth admits, raw honesty emerging in the gloom. "But we've got to stay here for a while longer, in case they do. We can't just leave Jasper."

The boy sleeps through this discussion of his fate, his consciousness mercifully absent from deliberations that treat him as object rather than subject. His steady breathing provides rhythmic counterpoint to the tense conversation.

"Yes, we can," Amy counters with icy practicality. "Or what about the hospital, maybe leave him at the fire station?"

The suggestion reveals her awareness of society's systems for abandoned children, knowledge she has perhaps gleaned from overheard conversations or TV, storing it away as potentially useful information for future contingencies. Her mind works constantly, assessing and categorizing, even in this moment of apparent childhood petulance.

Beth's arm tightens around Jasper's sleeping form, her body language betraying what her words will soon confirm. "He needs a mother," she says simply.

Amy turns away, facing the wall in a physical rejection of this new reality. "When we leave, is Jasper coming with us?" she asks, the question pointed and direct, a demand for clarity in their shifting family configuration.

"Good night, Amy," Beth responds, using finality rather than concession to end the conversation.

Morning brings transformation, both external and strategic.

Beth and Amy stand on the doorstep of a house in an affluent neighborhood, their appearances carefully curated for their current con. Amy's hair is pulled back in a short ponytail, secured with a green ribbon that complements her eyes and her clean shirt, jeans, and tennis shoes—the costume of an ordinary, middle-class child. Beth wears her standard sundress and sandals, the uniform of approachable motherhood.

Props complete their disguise: Amy holds a small open-faced box containing five off-brand chocolate bars, while Beth carries a clipboard that lends official credibility to their scheme. Around her wrist, partially hidden, is a roll of duct tape.

The house before them represents opportunity rather than shelter, set back from the road, isolated from neighbors, with a luxury car in the driveway signaling wealth within. The neighborhood is quiet, emptied by the rhythms of weekday work and school schedules. The timing, like everything else, has been carefully designed. Even the shadows stretch long across manicured lawns, providing additional cover for what's to come. This particular residence, with its ornate stonework and tall windows, stands apart from others they've targeted. More secluded, more affluent, more promising. The decorative water feature burbling in the front garden obscures sound, while the dense hedgerows offer natural screening from any passing vehicles. Beth had selected it after two days of reconnaissance, noting the predictable departure of adults each morning and the absence of security cameras that might capture their approach. Perfect hunting grounds for their particular brand of predation.

Beth rings the doorbell, the musical chime echoing inside the house with deceptive cheer. The homeowner who answers—a man in his sixties, well-dressed despite the casual loafer-style slippers that suggest retirement—peers out with the wariness of the privileged confronted by unexpected visitors. His gaze takes in the candy bars and clipboard, categorizing them within familiar and dismissible parameters. His posture relaxes slightly, the tightness in his shoulders easing as he seemingly mentally files them under "harmless interruption" rather than "potential threat." The gold watch on his wrist catches the afternoon light, another indicator of prosperity that Beth notes with assessment.

"Sorry. No solicitors," he says, the easy refusal of someone accustomed to turning away those who come begging for money or his precious time.

Amy steps forward, as if stepping onto a stage. "Oh, we're not sol... soli..." She stumbles over the word with deliberate imperfection, making herself seem callow and innocent. "Um. Well, this is for charity. I'm selling candy bars so my class can take a field trip to see the Grand Canyon next week."

Beth rests her hand on Amy's shoulder, completing the tableau of mother-daughter wholesomeness. "I'm her mom. Hi," she adds, the simple introduction designed to neutralize their presence, to render them unthreatening.

The man remains unmoved, his caution reasonably intact. "Well, my wife isn't home right now. She's the one who makes these decisions, and..."

"Oh, please?" Amy interrupts, her voice climbing into the register of childish pleading. "Please-please-please? It's only fifty cents a bar."

Beth chuckles indulgently, playing her role. "Honey, the man said no."

"But I really want to see the Grand Canyon," Amy persists, her eyes widening with manufactured enthusiasm. "Mister, have you ever seen it? I've never been anywhere, ever. This is my only chance, and I just have these five bars left."

The performance is masterful—vulnerability and innocence precisely calibrated to overcome any barriers. The homeowner considers, his resistance weakening as Amy activates deeply ingrained social programming about helping children and supporting education.

He opens the door wider, a fatal lowering of boundaries. "Five? That's all?" he asks, seeking confirmation that his investment will be minimal, contained.

Amy nods with enthusiasm, sensing victory. "Yes. You're our last stop. Please?"

A flicker of suspicion crosses the man's face, rational caution attempting one last stand. "Why aren't you in school on a Thursday?"

But the question comes too late. He has already stepped back from the doorway, the physical invitation superseding verbal hesitation.

Beth and Amy quickly cross the threshold, entering the space that will soon transform from home sweet home to grisly crime scene.

Inside, domestic order awaits destruction—furnishings carefully selected over decades, photographs documenting a life's journey, possessions accumulated through years of work and saving. All of it vulnerable to the marauders who've just been invited inside. The living room breathes with comfort—a worn leather sofa bearing the impressions of countless evenings, bookshelves lined with leatherbound hardcovers meant to be simply decorative, a collection of ceramic figurines arranged with meticulous care. On the mantel, family snapshots track the passage of time through changing hairstyles and widening smiles—treasured memories soon to be reduced to evidence markers in police photographs.

As the door closes behind them, Amy's expression shifts subtly, patience replacing enthusiasm now that the role has served its purpose. Beth's hand remains on her daughter's shoulder, but the gesture has transformed from maternal affection to something closer to restraint, a futile attempt to control forces she has enabled but cannot contain.

The homeowner gestures toward the living room, unaware that his routine courtesy has brought on the beginning of his end. "Come in, please. Would you like some water? Or maybe lemonade? I think we have some in the fridge."

"That would be lovely," Beth replies with false warmth, her eyes already cataloging valuables, exits, potential weapons. "The lemonade, I mean. It's so hot today. Already!"

"Yes, please," Amy echoes, her gaze fixed on the man with a particular intensity. "I'm really thirsty."

He droops a bit, as if he'd been hoping they'd decline his hospitality and be on their way. "I'll just be a moment. Make yourselves comfortable."

As he disappears into the kitchen, Beth and Amy exchange a glance that contains volumes of unspoken communication—timing, methods, division of labor all confirmed in a single look between accomplices.

The roll of duct tape slides from Beth's wrist into her palm, prepared but not yet deployed. Amy sets the candy box on a side table, her hand already reaching toward her back pocket where the switchblade waits, patient and purpose-built, like its owner.

The trap is set, the parts assigned, the outcome predetermined by patterns established long before this particular door opened to this particular con. Like actors in a macabre play they've performed countless times, Beth and Amy await their cue: the homeowner's return marking the transition from deception to violence, from performance to bloody reality. In the kitchen, ice clinks against glass as the target pours lemonade, unaware that these will be the last mundane actions of his life. The old man's footsteps signal the imminent drop of an invisible curtain that separates the prologue of their scheme from its inevitable coda.

CHAPTER 22

S unshine winks through closing blinds in horizontal bands, gradually diminishing until the final slat clicks into place and plunges the kitchen into forced twilight. Amy stands by the window, her small hand releasing the cord like a hangman with his noose, her face expressionless in the artificial dusk she's created.

The homeowner sits rigidly in a wooden kitchen chair, his hands secured behind his back with multiple wraps of silver duct tape that bite into his wrists. Beth kneels before him, applying the final strips around his ankles, binding them firmly to the chair legs with methodical precision. Her movements are efficient, practiced even, but her hands tremble, broadcasting her unmistakable remorse and regret like a silent confession. She tears the last piece with her teeth, the sharp sound cutting through the tense silence, before smoothing it with deft fingers against the cool wood of the chair leg, never meeting the man's wide, disbelieving eyes that silently plead for an explanation she cannot give.

On the kitchen table, a glass jar overflows with coins. Quarters, nickels, and dimes accumulated over months or years, perhaps for some specific purpose now rendered irrelevant. Beside it lie the props that facilitated their entry: the chocolate bars arranged in their open-faced box, the clipboard with its fabricated charity forms, edges worn from repeated handling. A half-full coffee cup grows cool, steam no longer rising from its surface, and a newspaper lies in sections, evidence of the homeowner's interrupted morning routine. The crossword puzzle remains half-completed, blue ink trailing off mid-word where his pen had dropped.

Anger rather than fear dominates the man's expression, the indignation of the privileged confronting the unthinkable violation of his sanctuary. His voice carries the certainty of someone accustomed to authority, to being heard and heeded.

"You will not get away with this, I assure you!" he declares, the words bolstered by a commanding, stentorian tone.

Beth ignores his pronouncement, focused on ensuring the tape's security around his ankles. Her face reveals nothing— neither pleasure nor regret, merely concentration on the task at hand.

"My wife will be home any minute," the man goes on, invoking absent rescue with desperate confidence. "And she will call the police!"

He directs his attention toward Amy, perhaps sensing her youth as a potential weakness in this criminal enterprise. "Do you want to go to Juvenile Hall? Do you, young lady? It's a bad place, I'm telling you."

The attempted manipulation reveals his fundamental misunderstanding of the situation, his assumption that Amy is a normal child who might be swayed by threats of institutional punishment, that Beth is merely a desperate mother driven to criminality by circumstance. He doesn't yet recognize the predators who have entered his home, doesn't understand that his threats carry no weight in the inverted moral universe they inhabit.

Beth tears another strip of tape from the roll with a sharp, ripping sound. She places it firmly over the man's mouth, silencing his protests and completing his helplessness. The silvery rectangle transforms his face into something less human, less individual—a canvas for fear rather than a vehicle for expression.

He glares at the pair, his eyes communicating what his voice no longer can. Rage, indignation, the dawning horror of complete vulnerability. His breathing quickens through his nose, each exhale a muffled testament to his rising panic. The tape pulls at his skin with every tiny movement, a constant reminder of the control that has been taken from him. In his gaze flickers the terrible realization that the social contract he has relied upon his entire life, the basic assumption of safety within his own home, has been irreparably shattered.

Amy surveys the kitchen with the assessment of a child contemplating a candy store's offerings. "Mom, I'm hungry," she announces, the mundane request jarring in its normalcy against the context of captivity and imminent violence.

Beth's gaze sweeps the well-stocked kitchen. Cupboards, refrigerator, a loaf of bread resting beside a toaster. The domestic abundance presents itself for their consumption, another resource to be plundered. "Let's see what we have here," she responds, moving from the breakfast nook into the main kitchen area.

She opens cabinets with casual entitlement, exploring another family's provisions as though browsing in a store. "I see some peanut butter..." she observes, the ordinary comment rendering the extraordinary circumstance all the more disturbing.

While Beth catalogs available food, Amy regards their captive with unsettling intensity. Her appraisal contains neither childish curiosity nor sadistic anticipation—simply the assessment of a predator determining the most efficient approach to dispatching prey. The homeowner squirms under her gaze, perhaps finally beginning to comprehend the true nature of his situation.

"Want a PB and J?" Beth calls, the innocent question creating a moment of surreal domesticity amid impending horror.

Amy turns reluctantly from her study of the bound man, stepping away as though momentarily distracted from a fascinating exhibit. "Is there grape jelly? I don't like raspberry," she specifies, the preference for grape over raspberry incongruously normal given what will soon transpire.

Beth sorts through jars in the cupboard, examining labels in the dim light. "I think so…" she replies, focused on this mundane task while catastrophe gathers around them.

The homeowner's eyes dart frantically around the room, seeking escape or weapon. His gaze catalogues potential salvation. The wall-mounted phone beyond reach, the butcher's block of knives across the room, the coffee cup nearest to him but offering little offensive capability. Hope rises briefly with each possibility, then collapses under the reality of his immobilization.

Then revelation arrives in the form of newsprint partially obscured by other sections of the paper lies a story about "Bonnie Rotten and Kid Vicious," the mother-daughter serial killers terrorizing Southern California. The headline, bold and black against the gray page, connects to fragmented memories of recent news reports he'd only half-attended to over morning coffee. Recognition dawns in terrible clarity as he understands precisely who has entered his home, what fate awaits him, and why the girl's preference for grape jelly now seems so absurdly, horrifically mundane.

He tenses, eyes closing momentarily as the full horror of his situation penetrates his consciousness. His muscles lock involuntarily, as though his body might be able to fortify itself against the inevitable. A single tear escapes, tracing a path down his cheek— not from fear but from the profound understanding that his life has reached its endpoint through random, meaningless chance. The arbitrary nature of his selection as their victim strikes him as almost cosmically cruel. He shakes his head slightly, perhaps in denial, perhaps in final acknowledgment, then opens his eyes to face what comes, his expression settling into a portrait of resigned dignity in these final moments.

Amy stands before him, switchblade drawn and gleaming in the filtered light. The transformation is complete. No trace remains of the sweet child selling candy bars. In her place stands something ancient and terrible wearing a child's form, a predator evolved to exploit society's most fundamental protective reflex toward children.

The man attempts to move, pushing against the floor with his feet to scoot the chair backward. Muffled protests emerge from behind the tape, unintelligible except for the universal language of terror.

"No... I won't tell..." he manages, the words barely comprehensible through the gag, offering silence in exchange for life—a bargain it seems the child has no intention of honoring.

Her face becomes set in stone, all performance abandoned now that it serves no purpose. She steps forward with terrible purpose, thrusting the knife upward under the man's chin with precision born of practice. The blade finds the vulnerable flesh with unerring accuracy, sliding through the soft tissue under the jaw into the vital structures above. A scarlet fountain erupts, painting the room in a grotesque parody of an abstract artist's studio.

The man's eyes fill with tears, the body's final, involuntary response to catastrophic injury. He attempts to scream, but the sound emerges only as a wet gurgle as blood fills his throat, drowning his final protest before it can fully form. His body convulses, a marionette dancing at the end of its strings, then goes limp, the life extinguished from those terrified eyes, leaving behind a silence more deafening than any scream.

In contrast to this violence, Beth stands at the counter, back deliberately turned to the scene unfolding behind her. She begins to hum, a tuneless, mindless sound meant not to soothe but to block, to create an auditory barrier between herself and her daughter's actions. Her hands move with deft strokes, spreading peanut butter across bread with a butter knife, the mockery of this innocent tool against Amy's lethal blade creating an unintentional metaphor for their divergent roles. The soft sound of knife against bread occurs in perfect synchronization with the wet, muffled sound of Amy's blade penetrating flesh, the mundane and the monstrous happening in parallel universes that somehow occupy the same kitchen.

Blood flows with dreadful efficiency, pooling on the tile floor in an expanding circle of finality. The homeowner's body twitches with diminishing vigor as neural systems shut down, as consciousness flees, as the biochemical processes of life surrender to the absolute certainty of death. His eyes stay open but become increasingly vacant, the light behind them fading fast.

Amy steps back from her handiwork, observing the results with neither satisfaction nor remorse—merely the assessment of a job completed according to established parameters. Blood stains her hands and speckles her clothing, the physical evidence of violence that must be addressed before they can leave.

Beth continues spreading jelly on bread, her humming growing louder as though to compensate for the diminishing sounds of struggle behind her. Her ritual of denial persists until the final sequence is complete. Sandwich assembled, cut diagonally, placed on a plate as though this were merely lunch at home rather than murder in a stranger's kitchen.

Only when the task is finished does she turn, facing the aftermath of what she has enabled but not executed. Her expression registers multiple layers of emotion. Resignation rather than shock, weariness rather than horror, the look of someone confronting a familiar scene rather than an aberration.

"We need to clean up," she says simply, the mundane phrase encompassing both the blood-spattered floor and the crumbs from her sandwich preparation—all messes requiring attention, all evidence needing removal before they can proceed to the next phase of their operation.

Amy nods, already moving toward the sink to wash her hands, the switchblade, her face. The routine is established, practiced, efficient. Beth begins searching drawers for trash bags, for cleaning supplies, for the tools needed to erase their presence from this space.

The body slumps in the chair, life completely departed, leaving only the shell that once contained consciousness, personality, history. His warning about his wife's imminent return takes on new urgency now, a possible deadline rather than a threat.

Between them, mother and daughter will transform this scene, removing valuables, eliminating evidence, and relocating the body to delay discovery. The mechanics of murder's aftermath have been performed so often they require little discussion, just the choreographed movements of long-established collaboration.

The sandwich waits on its plate, perfectly assembled, a monument to the banality that coexists with atrocity in Amy's world. She will eat it soon, consuming calories with the same mechanical efficiency with which she has consumed a life, fueling her body for the next performance, the next kill, the continuation of a pattern that stretches backward into her short past and forward into a future limited only by capture or death.

In the gradually warming kitchen, blood begins to congeal, bodily functions cease, and the transformation of living person to cooling corpse progresses according to biological inevitability. Outside, the neighborhood remains blissfully quiet, unaware that death has visited one of its homes, that predators walk among its manicured lawns and carefully maintained properties.

The glass jar of coins will soon be transferred into Beth's bulky purse. The wallet will be located and relieved of cash and cards. Jewelry and other portable valuables will be assessed and selectively taken. And then they will leave, money in hand for whatever comes next.

CHAPTER 23

Mother and daughter sit cross-legged on the drooping motel bed, their postures mirror images of seasoned casualness. Between them, the stolen moments of normalcy taste like peanut butter and jelly—cheap food bought with ill-gotten gains. Jasper perches in Beth's lap, his small body accepting nourishment and closeness with the unquestioning gratitude of the truly abandoned. An open can of soda fizzes quietly nearby, its contents gradually flattening in the stale room air.

The TV plays an old black-and-white noir, the sound muted, actors' mouths moving in silent pantomime of emotions that no one in that room has the luxury of feeling. On the dresser beside it sits their macabre collection of trophies. The glass jar of coins gleaming with obscene fullness, the victim's wallet emptied of identification but heavy with cash, Beth's purse hiding their meager belongings, Amy's green hair bow a splash of innocent color amid the evidence of atrocity.

Amy's switchblade rests beside these items, cleaned and

sheathed, its lethal purpose temporarily dormant. A centipede crawls across the knife's handle with deliberate purpose, its many legs moving in hypnotic undulation, a living metaphor for the corruption that flows through their small family unit. Its segmented body navigates the contours of the weapon with unsettling familiarity, as though the creature and the blade were kindred spirits in this dingy sanctuary of moral compromise. The insect pauses momentarily at the hilt, antennae twitching in what could almost be mistaken for contemplation, before continuing its relentless journey across the instrument that has altered their collective fate beyond redemption.

"I'm worried," Amy announces, her voice containing the fake vulnerability she employs when seeking information or reassurance.

Beth responds with maternal instinct, automatic and genuine despite everything. "About what, my baby?"

"Well, what if he was my dad?" Amy asks, the question revealing one of her few authentic anxieties—the mysterious gap of her paternity, a void she fills with increasingly elaborate fantasies.

Beth smiles sadly, the expression flowing with tenderness mixed with the exhaustion of repeating comforting lies. "Your father wouldn't be that old."

"My grandpa, then," Amy persists, unwilling to release the possibility. After a calculated pause, she adds, "What if?"

"Why would you think that?" Beth counters, steering the conversation back to familiar mythological territory. "I told you: your dad is a famous guitarist. We met backstage after one of his concerts at the L.A. Forum. I'll tell you who he is when you're eighteen. You'll have to take a blood test, and... it's very complicated." She pauses, then adds with forced lightness, "Anyway, did that guy look like a rock star?"

Amy giggles, momentarily restored to genuine childhood by this shared fiction. "No," she admits, then sobering slightly, adds, "But there was something about his nose. It looked like mine."

The observation contains unsettling perceptiveness. Amy's capacity to recognize herself in others, to identify potential biological connections through physical similarities. It suggests deeper questions about nature versus nurture, about whether her homicidal tendencies might be inherited rather than developed through environment.

Beth feeds Jasper a small bite of sandwich, the gesture buying time while she formulates a response. She reaches out to touch Amy's knee, offering physical connection as substitute for honest answers. "Don't trouble yourself. We did what we had to do. Now we have enough money to take the bus to Mexico."

Amy brightens visibly at this information, genuine excitement breaking through her affect. "Really?"

But her enthusiasm dims almost immediately as her gaze shifts to Jasper, computing his impact on their plans. "Him too?"

Beth hugs the boy closer, her body language already answering before her words confirm. "Just until his mother comes back."

The lie looms obvious and enormous between them. Carla isn't coming back, Cecil isn't returning with the car, and Jasper has silently, unintentionally become a permanent addition to their twisted family unit.

"I don't like him," Amy declares, petulance masking deeper territorial intent. "He smells."

Jasper looks up at this moment, perhaps recognizing his name or sensing he's being discussed. He smiles at Amy, the expression containing no guile, just the simple desire for connection that children naturally seek.

Beth returns the smile, interpreting the gesture with willful optimism. "He likes you," she observes, adding with naïve hope, "big sister."

Amy mimes vomiting, the exaggerated disgust communicating both childish rejection and something darker—her unwillingness to accept this reconfiguration of their family unit, her resistance to sharing her mother's love. "Gross."

Beth's expression turns serious. She tenses, as if contemplating something. "Amy," she says so gravely that Amy becomes alert with attention, tuned in. "I'm going to tell you the truth about your dad. The real truth. Okay?" She sighs. "Only my sister, Tam, knows this." Amy smiles, ready for another fable. "No, I'm not kidding," Beth says. "He works at the Last Chance Casino, off the Strip. Or at least, he did, when... when you were born. And there's one more thing... This isn't easy, but—"

The moment of forthcoming truth shatters as a pounding knock rattles the motel room door. The sound reverberates with authoritative intensity, instantly transforming the atmosphere from tense family discussion to survival crisis.

Everyone inside freezes, muscles tensing in unison, breath held. For several heartbeats, they remain motionless, the half-eaten sandwiches forgotten in their hands. Even Jasper senses the shift, his small body going rigid beside Beth, eyes wide with visceral fear. Amy watches the boy's fingers curl into tiny fists, clutching at the worn fabric of Beth's sleeve, the same instinctive gesture she herself fights against making.

A strident male voice booms, "Police! Open the door!"

Silent communication passes between Beth and Amy—practiced partners in crisis management, their responses honed through multiple similar encounters. Beth rises, pointing toward the bathroom doorway with urgent clarity. Amy nods, gathering Jasper with efficient movements and disappearing into the small room, the door clicking shut behind them.

"Wait a second, I'm not dressed," Beth calls toward the door, her voice pitched to communicate embarrassed compliance rather than resistance.

The knocking intensifies, patience eroding with each impact. "We just have a few questions, ma'am," the officer responds, the polite phrasing belied by authoritative tone. "Open the door, or we will open it for you."

Beth glances at the bathroom door, mentally gauging the thin barrier's inadequacy as protection for Amy and Jasper. The flimsy pressed wood would offer no resistance if they decided to search the room, hardly more substantial than cardboard in the face of determined law enforcement. She can almost visualize it splintering under a single forceful kick. With no viable alternatives, she approaches the front door, movements deliberately unhurried to suggest innocence rather than the panic fluttering in her chest. She forces her breathing to steady, adopting the mildly inconvenienced expression of someone interrupted during their morning routine rather than a woman harboring fugitives. Each step across the worn carpet feels like walking through quicksand, time stretching as the knocking continues its impatient rhythm.

She removes the security chain and turns the knob, creating the smallest possible opening while arranging her features into a disguise of sleepy confusion. The crack proves sufficient invitation, and three police officers burst through with coordinated force, two male and one female, hands hovering near holstered weapons in trained readiness. They fan out into the small room, eyes scanning every corner as if expecting danger to materialize from the shabby furniture.

Beth stumbles backward, her face a tableau of terrified confusion, her hands fluttering to her throat. The door remains open behind the officers, an escape route unwittingly provided, the morning light spilling across the threshold like a path that could be taken.

The officers scan the room with professional efficiency, cataloging details with rapid visual assessment: the unmade bed, the half-empty coffee cup on the nightstand, the closed bathroom door. "What's going on?" Beth asks, injecting appropriate alarm into her voice while her mind races through possible explanations and alibis.

"We ask the questions, ma'am," the lead officer responds, establishing control through verbal dominance. His weathered face betrays nothing as he shifts his weight forward, badge catching the light. His gaze fixes on the closed bathroom door with particular intensity, lingering there with predatory focus. "Are you here alone?" The question reverberates, deceptively simple yet loaded with consequence.

"Yes," Beth lies smoothly. "My husband just stepped out... What's this about?"

The officer's attention shifts to the bed where three half-eaten sandwiches lie in obvious contradiction to her claim. "This room is registered to a Cecil Hickman," he states, eyes returning to the bathroom door. "He's not here? Are you sure?"

Beth glances toward the open front door. "Yes. My husband just stepped out," she repeats, reinforcing the fiction of Cecil as legitimate partner rather than absconded thief.

"We're going to need to see some I.D., ma'am," the female officer interjects, her tone slightly gentler but equally authoritative.

The third officer, silent until now, studies the glass jar of coins with suspicion. He exchanges meaningful glances with his colleagues, silent communication passing between them. The recognition of potential evidence, of inconsistencies requiring explanation.

"Sure," Beth agrees with false compliance. "My purse is just over there..."

She moves toward the dresser where her purse sits alongside the other incriminating items, positioning herself between the officers and the bathroom door in a seemingly casual movement that creates a critical physical barrier. The distance calculated, the moment prepared, Beth suddenly pivots, turning toward the bathroom with desperate intensity.

"Amy, RUN!!!" she shouts, the command bursting from her with a boom.

In that crucial second of divided attention, Beth launches

herself at the nearest officer, a human projectile propelled by fierce desperation. Her body collides with his, creating momentary chaos that expands the window of opportunity for Amy's escape.

The room explodes into motion—officers reaching for weapons and sputtering commands, Beth grappling with surprising strength born of maternal desperation. She claws, kicks, and throws herself against their restraint with the feral intensity of a cornered animal protecting its young.

Threats are issued with escalating urgency, voices overlapping in harsh barks of "Stand down!" and "Stop resisting!" but the thread between mother and daughter holds firm across the chaos... Beth sacrificing herself to secure Amy's freedom, the ultimate expression of their twisted bond. In this moment of violent clarity, the years of shared secrets and survival crystallize into a single, desperate act of protection that transcends their criminal entanglements, revealing the raw, primal love rooted in their damaged relationship.

She fights blindly, clawing and thrashing against trained professionals, knowing she will lose but determined to provide those crucial seconds of distraction. Her nails rake across an officer's face, drawing blood as another wrestles her toward the floor. In this final act, she becomes the mother she has always claimed to be. Not through nurturing guidance or moral instruction, but through savage protection of her offspring at any cost, even as Cecil's absence underscores his ultimate unreliability when it mattered most.

The coins in the glass jar catch sunlight streaming through the open door, transforming blood money into something briefly beautiful and transcendent, glinting like false promises as the world of Room 7 collapses into chaos and consequence.

Beth's hand closes around the switchblade lying on the bed, her fingers fumbling at the button awkwardly. The blade flicks out with a metallic snap, sunlight catching its edge and throwing a momentary prism against the wall. She holds it before her, arm extended, the weapon trembling in her grip, not only from fear but from the adrenaline surging through her system, the chemical tide of fight-or-flight flooding her veins, making her heart pound against her ribcage like seismic events.

"Don't come any closer," she warns, her voice carrying the unmistakable edge of maternal ferocity, low and guttural. Her eyes dart between the officers, considering distances, assessing threats, her mind operating on autopilot.

The female police officer raises her hands in a placating gesture, her voice adopting the measured cadence used for hostage negotiations and suicide interventions. "Calm down, ma'am. We aren't here to hurt you. We want to help you." Her badge catches the same sunlight that glints off the knife, a different kind of authority than the one Beth now wields.

She takes a careful step forward, maintaining eye contact with Beth—a dangerous miscalculation based on the assumption that Beth is rational, that she can be reasoned with, that she operates within normal parameters of human motivation. The floorboard creaks beneath her weight. "It's okay," she continues, edging closer, her hand hovering near her holster unconsciously. "Who's Amy? Is that your daughter?"

Beth's response is to extend the knife further. "Get away from me," she commands, desperation sharpening each syllable. There is no negotiation in her tone, no room for compromise, only the absolute priority of buying Amy time to escape, whatever the cost to herself.

The officers exchange glances, a silent shorthand born of training and shared experience. With synchronized caution, they unholster their weapons, the leather creaking ever so lightly. The sound is unmistakable in the confined space, the acoustic signature of imminent violence.

Each officer takes another measured step toward Beth, creating a tightening perimeter around her. The choreography of confrontation proceeds according to procedure, but something in Beth's eyes tells them this will not end according to protocol.

With the explosive suddenness of a cornered animal, Beth lunges forward. Her scream contains no words, only raw emotion. Rage, terror, the desperate knowledge that she has reached the terminus of her journey through this minefield called life. The knife arcs through air, seeking flesh, driven by the final evolutionary imperative to ensure her offspring's survival through her own sacrifice.

Time fractures into crystalline moments of hyperclarity. The revolvers rise in unison. Fingers tighten on triggers. The concussive blast of multiple gunshots fills the small room, reverberating off thin walls and cheap furniture.

Bullets find Beth's body with devastating accuracy—chest, neck, head—the fatal arithmetic of modern weaponry versus human flesh. Behind her, the glass jar of coins explodes into deadly confetti, a grotesque celebration of mortality. Shards of glass and metal discs fly through the air, quarters and dimes becoming unintended projectiles as they scatter across the room with lethal randomness. Stray bullets find the television screen, shattering it into a spider web of cracks that distort the frozen black-and-white image still playing silently, a macabre counterpoint to the unfolding tragedy.

Beth stumbles backward, her forward momentum arrested by the impact of the bullets. She careens into the dresser that supports the broken television, the cheap veneer splintering under the force of her fall. Her body begins to collapse, the tension draining from her muscles as she succumbs to the gravitational pull of death. Blood, bone fragments, and tissue spray outward in a red mist, painting the wall behind her with the abstract expressionism of violent death, a different kind of motel art that tells the story of a life ended too brutally.

As the echoes of the gunfire fade, the room is left in a surreal silence, the air thick with the metallic tang of blood and the acrid smell of gunpowder. The adrenaline-charged mother who had stood defiantly only moments before is now a crumpled form, her final act etched into the memory of those who had witnessed her last desperate moments.

As she falls, her hand finds and clutches Amy's hair ribbon, the small token of normalcy in their abnormal lives, the pretense of ordinary childhood that she maintained despite everything. Her fingers close around it as though it might anchor her to the world she's leaving, as though she might somehow transfer her protective energy through this small fabric connection to the daughter now beyond her reach.

Beth slides down to the carpet, leaving a red smear on the dresser's shoddy veneer. Blood blooms outward from her still form, the final offering of a body that has endured so much yet still obeys the basic laws of hydraulics. In her hand, visible against pale skin rapidly losing color, rests the pretty green bow, the period at the end of Beth's unfinished sentence.

No sooner does the trio of shooters turn away from Beth's bullet-riddled body than bathroom door splinters with a deafening crack as the lead officer's boot connects just below the handle. Wood fragments spray inward, the hollow-core door offering minimal resistance. The hinges tear from the frame, and the door crashes against the toilet tank with a hollow thud. "Police! Don't move!" he barks.

Jasper sits frozen in silent terror, his wide eyes the only indication he comprehends the destruction of the closest thing to stability he's known since being taken from Carla's arms.

All three officers burst through the opening, guns raised, expressions grim with adrenaline and the aftermath of lethal force. Their eyes sweep the small space, seeking additional threats, finding only one traumatized child.

From their perspective, the tableau presents itself with stark clarity: Jasper sits huddled on the floor beside the toilet, knees drawn up to his chest, tears streaming down his face in silent rivulets.

One officer checks behind the door, then drops to his knees to peer under the sink cabinet. "Clear here too."

They exchange glances of confusion mingled with mounting dread. The bathroom window remains firmly shut, painted over with layers of institutional white that have sealed it permanently closed. No child could have escaped through there.

"Where the hell is she?" The male officer holsters his weapon, running a hand through his hair as he surveys the tiny space again. "Amy! Amy!"

Above him, the air vent gapes open, its grill cover resting on top of the toilet tank—mute evidence of an escape route. It's far too small for any adult to give pursuit.

The female officer holsters her weapon first, moving toward Jasper with professional compassion. "It's okay now," she tells him, the platitude hollow against the backdrop of gunfire and death. "You're safe."

But the boy's eyes tell a different story. And silence speaks volumes about what he has witnessed with Amy, what he knows about the girl who has disappeared into the walls.

Outside, sirens approach. Reinforcements, ambulances, the full theatrical production of law enforcement responding to an officer-involved shooting. Yellow tape will soon transform this anonymous motel room into a crime scene, technicians will document and collect, detectives will theorize and deduce.

But they will not find Amy. Not today. Not here.

The parking lot has transformed from neglected asphalt to impromptu command center, cruisers arranged in haphazard constellation around the focal point of the scene. Crime scene tape flutters in the evening breeze, marking boundaries between ordinary reality and extraordinary violence.

From a distance, the scene resembles a macabre three-ring circus. Uniformed figures moving with unhurried efficiency, bystanders gathered at perimeters, news vans arriving with satellite dishes extended like curious antennae. The ecosystem of aftermath unfolds according to established protocols, each participant playing their assigned role in the theater of tragedy.

Two paramedics wheel a gurney toward the waiting ambulance, their movements perfunctory rather than urgent. The body bag enveloping Beth's remains lies flat and anonymous on the stretcher, zipped completely closed—no longer a person but a package to be processed, documented, eventually disposed of according to whatever minimal standards apply to indigent bodies. The metal doors of the ambulance slam shut with terminal finality, sealing away evidence of maternal sacrifice with the indifference of routine.

The bystanders cluster in small groups, consuming the spectacle. Death as entertainment, tragedy as social currency. They murmur theories and judgments, filling information gaps with speculation and prejudice, the collective breath of their whispers creating currents of rumor that will solidify into accepted narrative long before official conclusions emerge.

News crews unload equipment with the practiced poise of vultures arranging themselves at a carcass. Reporters adjust clothing and hair, preparing to transform blood and death into digestible segments for commercial interruption, their expressions shifting from bored to appropriately somber as cameras activate.

Near the motel office, several officers interview the clerk, who gestures with animated importance, suddenly central to events beyond his usual tedium. His perpetual smile has transformed to match circumstances, gravity replacing vacuity as he provides innocuous details that will appear in reports, databases, eventually court documents if necessary. He leaves out the nature of the payment Beth made for the room.

An employee from Child Protective Services holds Jasper's tiny hand, her grip neither comforting nor controlling, merely functional. The boy stands motionless beside her, his face a blank canvas upon which trauma continues to paint invisible patterns. His silence remains unbroken, a fortress constructed not of strength but absolute necessity. Around his stillness, adults move with bureaucratic purpose, already categorizing him according to available programs, facilities, and outcomes deemed statistically acceptable.

Above this choreography of aftermath, the seedy room's door stands open, a bright yellow banner creating a symbolic barrier between ordinary space and extraordinary events. The threshold represents passage in multiple dimensions—from life to death for

Beth, from captivity to freedom for Amy, from one form of abandonment to another for Jasper.

Inside, the room has been transformed into a taxonomy of evidence. Numbered markers punctuate significant items, creating a jumble of potential meaning for investigators to decode. A crime scene investigator's voice can be heard: "Dead dog in the closet." Another officer mumbles something about trace evidence, his latex-gloved hands methodically collecting fibers from the doorframe.

Beth's blood has mushroomed across the carpet in a dark pool, still wet in the center, drying to rust at the edges, the final tangible remains of her existence soaking into synthetic fibers that have absorbed countless other human secretions. The pattern tells its own story of violence, a Rorschach that investigators will photograph and measure with clinical detachment. Like the nameless stains from past occupants—the spilled wine, the vomit, the sweat of nightmares—Beth's essence now joins this palimpsest of human suffering, another layer in the motel room's unwritten history.

At the edge of this shallow pool, a praying mantis perches with predacious stillness. Its triangular head rotates with robotic precision, compound eyes registering movement without comprehension. Front legs raised in mock supplication, it preens itself with the narcissistic focus of a perfect killing machine, impervious to the human suffering in its midst.

CHAPTER 25

Miles away and hours later, under cover of darkness, a nondescript sedan pulls to the curb along Las Vegas Boulevard. The passenger door swings open, releasing not light but shadow into the neon-painted night.

Amy emerges from the vehicle, her small form silhouetted against the gaudy electric landscape of America's playground. Her eyes, shrewd and tactical despite the façade of childish features, scan the boulevard.

She leans back into the car briefly, addressing the unseen driver with feigned childish gratitude. "Thanks, mister!" The words contain perfect mimicry of normal appreciation, the performance flawless in its simulation of innocence.

The car door slams with percussive finality, and the sedan pulls away, its driver unaware of the nature of his passenger, of the bullet he has dodged through circumstance rather than caution. Taillights recede into traffic, anonymous as blood cells flowing through urban arteries.

Amy stands motionless on the sidewalk, a deceptively small figure amid the towering casinos and hotels, their façades glittering with promises of fortune that would never come true for most who sought them. Her hands are placed defiantly on her hips as she surveys her new territory. The bright lights of Sin City spread before her like a banquet of opportunity. Millions of strangers, thousands of potential victims, a wilderness of concrete and desperation where predators pass unnoticed among the perpetually distracted.

Green neon from a nearby casino strobes across her face, illuminating her features in pulses of alien light. The unnatural color transforms her appearance into something otherworldly, something that merely approximates humanity without embodying it. In this revealing illumination, Amy smiles. It's not the imitation of childhood joy she employs as camouflage, but the genuine expression of a predator assessing a target-rich environment. The smile contains no warmth, no humor, no connection to ordinary human emotion. It is the expression of something recognizing ideal hunting conditions, of appetite acknowledging abundant food sources, of evolutionary success acknowledging optimal circumstances for continuation.

Las Vegas spreads before her, unaware and unprepared. The city that embraces vice and excess, that markets itself as consequence-free indulgence, will now host something truly sinister within its gaudy exterior. Among the gambling addicts, the weekend revelers, the desperate dreamers and shrewd hedonists, something moves that understands humans as merely prey—walking collections of exploitable weaknesses packaged in predictable behaviors.

Amy steps forward into her new territory, her movements containing the confidence of a creature perfectly adapted to its ecological niche. Her small stature, her feigned innocence, her calculated vulnerability are all evolutionary advantages in a society programmed to protect children, to trust their apparent helplessness, to lower defenses in their presence.

Still, she will need to find an adult. Perhaps... maybe, just maybe, she will find her father here. Maybe, for once, Beth was telling her the truth.

Amy disappears into the flowing river of tourists, gamblers, dreamers, and schemers—one small shadow among many, unremarkable except for the particular emptiness behind her eyes, the specific absence where normal childhood should reside. The crowd absorbs her, unknowingly providing concealment for the contagion now moving among them.

Somewhere in the city that never sleeps, a child who never truly existed begins her hunt anew.

CHAPTER 26

The Last Chance Casino bustles with the usual Thursday night crowd. Not packed shoulder to shoulder like weekends, but busy enough that the dealers can't catch their breath between hands. The air is thick with cigarette smoke and sweat-prickled desperation, trapped under a ceiling of dim lights and slowly rotating fans that do little more than push the staleness around.

James Edison Elder deals blackjack with seasoned precision, his fingers moving across the felt with the efficient memory of decades on the job. The gold name tag pinned to his faded maroon vest reads "JAMES," though no one uses it. Customers address him as "dealer" when they're winning and considerably less polite terms when they're not.

"Hit me," says a middle-aged tourist in a Hawaiian shirt, his forehead glistening with the sweat of a man down three hundred dollars and climbing.

James slides a card face up. Queen of Spades. He strokes his goatee reflexively before calling it. "Twenty-two. House wins." James's voice carries no pleasure, no regret, just the flat pronunciation of mathematical certainty. He sweeps the man's chips toward himself with rote efficiency.

"Goddamn it," mutters the tourist, reaching for his watered-down mai tai.

James doesn't bother responding. He's heard every variation of anger, bargaining, and despair across this table. His face remains impassive under thinning hair gone gray at the temples, his eyes blank mirrors reflecting the flashing lights of nearby slot machines rather than revealing anything of himself.

The pit boss nods toward James. "Elder. Your relief's here."

James checks his watch. Ten forty-five p.m. Mike is early for once. He nods, counting out his chips for the register count, each stack aligned with perfect precision. His gnarled fingers move with practiced efficiency, the ritual of closing his shift as ingrained as breathing.

"Tough luck tonight," Mike says as he slides into James's vacated seat, his voice carrying the cheerfulness of someone who still believes in the promise of Vegas. "You heading straight home?"

James offers a noncommittal grunt as he signs his timesheet. Home is a relative term. A two-bedroom apartment in a building that had seen its best days sometime during the Truman administration. Fifteen years in the same unit, and it still feels temporary, like a motel room he's stayed in too long. The walls are thin enough to hear his neighbor's television, the carpet worn to threadbare paths between door, kitchenette, and bed... a physical manifestation of the ruts in his daily existence.

"Elder." The pit boss again, his voice carrying unusual urgency. "Office wants to see you before you clock out."

James pauses, his pen hovering above the timesheet. In seventeen years, management has never wanted to see him about anything good. "Problem with my count?"

"Dunno. Just delivering the message."

The walk to the management office takes him through the heart of the casino floor. James passes the craps tables where players cheer every roll like it's New Year's Eve, past the ringing carousel of slot machines where blue-haired old women feed quarters with religious devotion. Their happiness, or its gaudy simulation, seems to exist in another universe from his own.

The office door bears the name "Richard Winton, Floor Manager" in gold-lettered importance. James knocks twice, short and perfunctory.

"Come in."

Inside, Richard sits behind a desk cluttered with paperwork, his tie loosened, sleeves rolled up to show hairy forearms. But it's not Richard who catches James's attention. It's the woman in the plain navy suit sitting opposite the desk, and beside her—

A child.

The girl can't be more than ten, her slight body nearly swallowed by the oversized office chair. Blond hair cut in a longish pageboy frames a face that strikes James like a physical blow.

He's seen that face before. In photographs. In memory. In nightmares.

"Mr. Elder," the woman begins, rising to extend her hand. "I'm Margaret Reynolds from Clark County Child Protective Services. Thank you for meeting with us at this unusual hour."

James ignores her outstretched hand, his gaze fixed on the child who stares back with unsettling directness. "What is this?"

Richard clears his throat. "James, these people have been trying to reach you at home. They say it's regarding your daughter."

"Ex-daughter," James corrects automatically, the words aspirin-bitter on his tongue. "Haven't seen her in a decade. Whatever this is about, you've got the wrong man."

Margaret lowers her hand, her professional smile dimming slightly. "Mr. Elder, I'm afraid we need to speak with you regarding Elizabeth Elder. There's been an incident."

"Beth," he mutters, the name foreign in his mouth after so

many years of refusing to speak it. The memory hit like a poison dart. A quick sting, then a slow weakening, then a crumple to the ground. "What kind of incident?"

She glances at the child, then back to James. "Perhaps we could speak privately for a moment?"

Richard stands, grateful for the exit opportunity. "You can use my office. I'll be on the floor if you need anything."

When the door closes, Margaret's professional demeanor shifts subtly, compassion replacing procedure. "Mr. Elder, I regret to inform you that your daughter Elizabeth has passed away."

The words should impact him like a physical blow, but after the initial surprise of hearing his daughter's name, James feels only a distant, hollow echo where grief might be expected. Beth has been dead to him for years. This merely makes it official. "How?"

"There was an altercation with police in California. Elizabeth was..." Margaret's eyes drift meaningfully toward the child, who continues to stare unblinking at James. "She didn't survive the confrontation."

James follows her gaze to the girl, understanding dawning with cold certainty. "And this is..."

"This is Amy. Amy Andrea Elder. Your granddaughter."

The word drops like a stone, rippling through the stagnant pool of James's existence. Granddaughter. The concept seems absurd, disconnected from any reality he recognizes.

"Beth never told me she had a kid."

"According to our records, Amy is ten years old. Haven't found her birth certificate yet, but we have enrollment records out of California. She has no other living relatives that we can locate."

James's laugh holds no humor. "So you tracked me down. The grandfather she's never met. The man her mother ran away from."

Margaret maintains her professional calm. "Mr. Elder, in situations like these, we always try to place children with blood relatives before considering foster care."

"And if I say no?"

"Then Amy enters the system. But I would strongly encourage you to consider—"

"Consider what? I'm a sixty-two-year-old blackjack dealer who lives in a shitty apartment with bars on the windows. I work nights, sleep days, and my refrigerator has more booze than food. I've never raised a child. Not properly, anyway. The first one's been arrested more times than I can count. Drugs, theft, you name it. The last one who was in my care ran away at sixteen without so much as a goodbye note. Hasn't spoken to me since." James rubbed his bloodshot eyes with gnarled fingers. "I'm not exactly father-of-the-year material. Hell, I'm barely functioning-adult material most days."

Margaret's expression doesn't change, but something in her eyes hardens. "Mr. Elder, we're not asking you to win parenting awards. We're asking you to step up for a child who has lost everything."

James looks at Amy again. She sits perfectly still, her posture unnaturally rigid for a child her age. Her eyes, much greener but still somehow like Beth's, study him with an intensity that makes his skin crawl. Not the innocent curiosity of childhood, but something planning, assessing.

"What about her father?" he asks.

A flicker of something crosses Amy's face—so brief James almost misses it. Interest, perhaps. Or recognition.

"We have no information about the father," Margaret replies. "Elizabeth never listed him on school records."

"Typical Beth," James mutters.

"The child—" she catches herself, "Amy, said that her mom told her Amy's dad worked here."

He shrugs. "Could have, but that would've been ten years ago."

"Mr. Elder," she continues, her voice lowering slightly, "you should know that Amy has experienced significant trauma. She witnessed her mother's death. The authorities believe she may have been exposed to... other concerning situations while in Elizabeth's care."

"What kind of situations?"

Her lips press into a thin line. "The full reports haven't been transferred yet. This all happened very suddenly. We know only that Elizabeth's lifestyle was... irregular."

James snorts. "That's one word for it." He studies Amy, looking for other signs of the Elder family in her features. The resemblance is there—the shape of the eyes, the stubborn set of the jaw—but there's something else too, something he can't quite place. "Does she talk?"

"When she chooses to," Margaret answers. "She's been mostly nonverbal since the incident. She was caught hitchhiking two days ago... she..." The woman's voice lowers to a whisper, her professional demeanor cracking slightly. "She had a boxcutter on her... threatened the people who gave her a ride when they tried to take her to the authorities. The couple was quite shaken. They said she was perfectly calm one minute, then suddenly had the blade out the next."

The girl's continued stare makes James uncomfortable. He turns away, running a hand through his thinning hair. "I need to think about this."

"I'm afraid there isn't much time for deliberation, Mr. Elder. We need to place Amy tonight."

"Tonight? You can't just—"

"We can and we must. Either you take temporary custody while we process the permanent paperwork, or Amy goes into emergency foster care. Those are the only options available."

James turns back to Margaret, anger rising. "This is ridiculous. You can't just show up and dump a kid on me."

"She's *family.*"

The words hit harder than she probably intends. James feels the old familiar guilt twist in his gut like a corkscrew. "I don't know what to do."

"People often rise to meet circumstances, Mr. Elder." Margaret reaches into her briefcase and pulls out a thick folder. "Here's the temporary guardianship paperwork. If you agree to take Amy, you'll need to sign these forms. We'll schedule a home inspection within the week, and there will be regular check-ins from our office."

"And if the home inspection finds my place unsuitable? What then?"

"We'll cross that bridge when we come to it." She softens slightly. "Mr. Elder, Amy has been through enough transitions. What she needs now is stability. Family."

James looks at the folder, then at Amy. The girl has not moved, has not spoken, has given no indication that they're discussing her fate. She simply watches, her delicate hands folded neatly in her lap, a posture of patience that seems altogether wrong.

"Do you want to stay with me?" he asks her directly.

Amy tilts her head slightly, considering the question. When she speaks, her voice is clear and unnervingly steady. "I don't have anywhere else to go."

Not "I want to stay with you." Not "Please help me." Just the resignation of limited options. James recognizes the appraisal behind it. He's seen it in the eyes of gamblers who know they're playing a losing hand but have already pushed all their chips to the center of the table.

"Fine," he says finally, taking the folder from the CPS agent. "But don't expect miracles."

Margaret's smile returns, professional satisfaction at a case temporarily resolved. "No one's expecting miracles, Mr. Elder. Just basic human decency."

The paperwork takes thirty minutes to complete. Forms signed in triplicate, promises made in bureaucratic language, responsibilities outlined dispassionately. Through it all, Amy watches, silent once more, her gaze moving between James and Margaret as they negotiate the terms of her future.

When it's done, Margaret shakes James' hand.

"Is that it?" he asks.

"For now." She kneels before the girl, meeting her eyes directly. "Amy, you'll be staying with your grandfather for a while. I'll come check on you in a few days to see how you're settling in. If you need anything before then, you can call me." She hands the girl a business card, which Amy takes and studies carefully before slipping it into her pocket. "And don't forget your suitcase." It's more of a duffel bag, really, filled with donated clothes, a toothbrush and paste, a few basic necessities.

Margaret gives James one final assessment. "My number is on the forms if you have any questions. Day or night."

"I'll manage," James says, the words sounding hollow even to himself.

"I'm sure you will." Her tone suggests she's anything but sure. "Good night, Mr. Elder. Good night, Amy."

She leaves the office, the door clicking shut with a finality that echoes through the room. James listens to her sensible heels tapping down the hallway until the sound fades completely, leaving him alone with a granddaughter he doesn't know and the weight of responsibilities he never wanted.

"Well," he says, "guess we'd better go home."

Amy nods once, decisive, and falls into step beside him as they take an employee exit and head toward the employee parking lot. She doesn't reach for his hand. Doesn't ask questions. Doesn't show any of the fear or uncertainty that would seem natural in a child suddenly placed with a stranger. James notes her composure with a mixture of relief and discomfort. It's unnerving, this self-sufficiency in someone so small, as if she's already learned not to expect comfort from adults. He catches himself almost offering his hand, then shoves it into his pocket instead. The fluorescent lights of the parking structure cast harsh shadows across their faces as they walk in silence, two strangers connected only by blood and vivid green eyes.

Amy walks with purpose, as though this is merely the next scene in a play she's been rehearsing all along, her small footsteps keeping perfect time with his larger ones in the near-empty parking lot.

James's 1972 Chevy Impala sits alone under a flickering streetlight, its once-bright blue paint now dull and pocked with rust spots. He unlocks the passenger door first, holding it open with awkward formality.

Amy slides into the seat, her hands immediately finding the seatbelt, clicking it into place with practiced efficiency. James walks around to the driver's side, using those few seconds to compose himself, to try to grasp this sudden collision of past and present.

The engine coughs to life on the third try. As they pull away from the Last Chance Casino, James glances in the rearview mirror, half-expecting to see Margaret's car following them, ready to announce this has all been some elaborate mistake.

But there's nothing behind them except oil-stained parking spaces and the distant glow of the Strip, its glittery promises fading as they drive toward the shabby neighborhood James has called home for nearly two decades. The colorful fantasy recedes in the rearview mirror, replaced by the reality of sun-bleached stucco apartments and chain-link fences. James grips the steering wheel tighter, his sinewy fingers finding their familiar grooves as they enter the part of Vegas tourists never see, where the desert's harsh indifference creeps back in and the city's glamour can't disguise the quiet desperation of those who service the dream machine but never partake of its rewards.

A wasp, a type known as a tarantula hawk, lurks in the shadows behind James and Amy, pressed against the cool of the back window, its bottle blue body and reddish orange wings catching the headlights of passing cars as it balances on the dusty rear deck. The massive insect, notorious in these parts for its excruciating sting, twitches its antennae in the artificial glow, a silent passenger in James's battered sedan.

Like everything else in this forgotten corner of Nevada, it's beautiful and savage in equal measure, surviving on instinct in a landscape that offers little mercy. Its iridescent body, a hypnotic fusion of deadly purpose and evolutionary perfection, embodies the harsh dichotomy of the desert, where beauty and brutality coexist without contradiction. The creature waits with the patient indifference of something that has outlasted civilizations, empires, and the countless desperate souls who've come to this parched land seeking fortune only to find themselves hollowed out by its relentless sun and broken promises.

James's bloodshot eyes flick occasionally to the rearview mirror, not just for Margaret's phantom car, but as if sensing the predatory presence lurking behind him, another survivor making do in a place where forgiveness is as scarce as rainfall and second chances evaporate before they can be grasped.

CHAPTER 27

Amy stands motionless in the doorway of what James calls the spare room. The space barely deserves the name—more storage closet than bedroom, its dimensions so narrow that the twin bed nearly touches both walls. A bare light-bulb dangles from the ceiling, casting harsh light over random, mismatched cardboard boxes stacked in the corner.

"It's not much," James says, hovering awkwardly behind her. "Haven't had a reason to fix it up."

Amy steps into the room, the ancient beige carpet crunching slightly. It feels brittle, as if it might disintegrate. The bed is slop-pily made with a faded blue comforter, the fabric thin from the years of use. A small dresser with three drawers stands against the wall opposite the bed, its surface dusty except for a recently cleared rectangle where a cheap digital alarm clock now sits, its red numbers the only modern touch in the time capsule of a room. A milkcrate serves as a nightstand of sorts.

"Bathroom's down the hall," James continues, filling the

silence with unnecessary information, his words tumbling out faster as Amy's silence stretches on. "Towels in the cabinet under the sink. Kitchen's always open; help yourself to whatever you find. I'm not much of a cook, but there's cereal, maybe some mac and cheese. Cheese, bread. You know how to make a sandwich, right?"

Amy nods once, not turning to face him.

"Right." James shifts his weight, uncomfortable with her continued silence. "Well, I guess I'll let you get settled. It's late. I work nights, so I usually sleep till noon or so."

Still, Amy doesn't respond. She sits on the bed, examining her fingernails.

"Okay then," James says, retreating. "If you need anything, I'm just down the hall. Good night."

The door closes with a soft click. Amy waits, counting silently to thirty before turning to survey the room more carefully. The walls are painted a dingy off-white, bare except for a water stain in the corner near the ceiling. The window is small and covered with metal security bars, the glass grimy from years of desert dust.

Her fingers move deftly through her bag, removing the three T-shirts, two pairs of pants, a long nightgown, underwear, socks. Toiletries. When her clothing is arranged in the dresser drawers, Amy decides to check out the rest of the apartment.

She eases the bedroom door open, wincing at the slight creak of hinges. She pauses, head tilted, listening for any sign that James might still be awake. The apartment is silent except for the low hum of the refrigerator and the occasional tick from the wall heater.

She steps into the hallway, her bare feet silent against the carpet. The living room spreads before her, a small space dominated by a sagging couch and mismatched coffee table. A TV sits on a stand in the corner, its screen dark and reflective in the dim light filtering through vertical blinds.

Amy moves methodically through the room, fingers trailing

over surfaces. The bookshelf contains no family photos, just a row of dog-eared paperbacks with titles like *Casino Mathematics*, *Dealer's Edge*, and *The Art of Blackjack*. A notebook sits beside them, its cover marred with bottle and glass rings.

The kitchen counters are mostly bare. A coffee maker, a stack of mail, takeout menus magnetized to the refrigerator door. She opens each cabinet quietly, revealing mismatched dishes, a few glasses, and several boxes of cereal. The refrigerator contains little beyond condiments, jack cheese, a half-empty carton of spoiled milk, and a six-pack of beer.

Amy circles back to the living room, examining the entertainment center. No family photos here either, just casino promotional items, including a commemorative poker chip, a branded deck of cards still in its plastic wrapper, a small plastic trophy plated with gold paint, engraved with "Employee of the Month." She slides open a drawer under the television set to find several dealer uniforms neatly folded, pressed white shirts and black vests with the same Last Chance Casino logo embroidered on the pocket.

The walls are equally impersonal. No photos, no family portraits, not even generic decorative prints. Just blank spaces interrupted occasionally by a nail hole or faded rectangle where something once hung, like memories deliberately removed. The off-white paint has a institutional quality, as if the apartment itself is merely a place to exist rather than live.

Amy pauses at a small desk in the corner, running her fingers over a stack of papers. Work schedules, utility bills, a manual titled "Advanced Card Handling Techniques," and a notification for an upcoming dealer certification exam. Nothing to suggest James has two daughters, or any personal life beyond his job dealing cards. She rifles through a drawer filled with pens, paperclips, and casino-branded notepads, searching for any trace of the family man he once was.

Amy drifts toward the window, drawn by distant sirens cutting through the night. She slides open the glass, slowly, silently. Her fingers curl around the security bars, rust-pocked metal pressing against her skin as she peers through the tattered screen.

The neighborhood sprawls before her, a patchwork of neglect illuminated by flickering streetlights surrounded by moths and mosquitoes. The apartment complex sits in a forgotten pocket of Las Vegas, just a few miles from the neon-drenched Strip where tourists throw away money and inhibitions. Here, dreams don't glitter; they corrode. Identical two-story buildings with peeling paint form a horseshoe around a cracked, potholed parking lot. A shopping cart lies abandoned on its side. Three cars occupy spaces —one missing its front bumper, another balanced on concrete blocks instead of tires, and other belonging to her grandfather.

Beyond the complex, small houses crouch low to the ground, their yards more dirt than grass. Chain-link fences separate properties, some sections collapsed or missing entirely. A dog barks aggressively from somewhere nearby, triggering a chain reaction of howls and yaps that ripple through the darkness. The animal sounds desperate, angry at confinement.

Two blocks away, red-and-blue lights pulse against the night sky. The sirens that drew her attention have stopped, but new ones wail in the distance, a constant soundtrack to this part of town. Amy watches as a helicopter sweeps overhead, its searchlight painting harsh white circles on the streets below.

A man stumbles along the sidewalk across from the complex, his gait unsteady. He stops to argue with someone who isn't there, gesturing wildly at empty air before continuing his journey into the unknown. At the corner, three teenagers huddle around the faint orange glow of a shared cigarette, their laughter carrying unnaturally in the night air.

The wind picks up, sending a plastic bag tumbling across the parking lot like urban tumbleweed. It catches on a chain-link fence, flapping like a holey flag. The sound of breaking glass echoes from somewhere nearby, followed by muffled shouting.

This neighborhood exists in stark contrast to the Las Vegas of postcards and commercials. No fountains dancing to music here, no luxury hotels with marble lobbies. Just people struggling to survive in the shadow of excess, the glow of casino lights visible on the horizon like a cruel reminder of wealth just out of reach.

Amy returns to her room, closing the door softly behind her. She removes her clothes and slips into the nightgown, then slides between the sheets of the twin bed, springs creaking as she shifts to find a comfortable position.

The ceiling above has a hairline crack running diagonally from corner to corner. Amy traces it with her eyes in the dim light filtering through the thin curtains. Outside, car doors slam, voices argue, and music thumps from somewhere nearby.

She sees a small notebook and a stubby pencil lying on the milk crate that doubles as a nightstand. Amy flips past pages filled with addresses, phone numbers, and cryptic notations. Finding a blank page, she writes "James" at the top, followed by "Last Chance Casino" and today's date.

Morning arrives with harsh sunlight cutting through gaps in the curtains. Amy wakes instantly, eyes open and alert. The clock reads 8:37. She dresses quickly in jeans and a faded T-shirt, then makes the bed, smoothing every wrinkle from the frayed comforter.

Amy pauses in the hallway, head tilted toward James's bedroom door. His snoring rumbles through the thin wood, a rhythmic, congested sound that rises and falls with unsettling regularity. She stands perfectly still, counting the seconds between each labored breath.

The door isn't completely closed. A sliver of darkness shows between frame and edge, tempting her. Amy glances at the front door, calculating how long it would take to reach it if James suddenly woke. Her fingers brush against the cool metal of the doorknob, hesitating.

The snoring stutters, then resumes with a phlegmy catch. Amy pushes the door open another inch, wincing at the barely audible creak of hinges. The bedroom beyond is dark, blinds drawn against the morning sun. James lies sprawled across a queen-sized bed, one arm flung over his face, the other dangling toward the floor. The sheets tangle around his legs, exposing pale skin and dark hair.

Amy's eyes adjust to the dimness. The room smells of stale cigarette smoke and unwashed sheets. His uniform shirt hangs from the closet doorknob, black vest draped over the back of a chair. The nightstand holds an overflowing ashtray, empty beer bottles, and a prescription bottle with the label partially torn away.

She steps inside, moving with Ninja-like silence. On the dresser sits a wallet, keys, and loose change. Amy picks up the saddle-brown wallet, flipping it open to examine its contents. Driver's license, a credit card, casino employee ID. A few one dollar bills. No photos.

James snorts in his sleep, rolling onto his side. Amy freezes, billfold still open in her hands. His breathing settles back into its congested rhythm. She replaces the wallet exactly as she found it, then moves to the closet.

Sliding hangers quietly along the rod, she catalogs his possessions: a few button-down shirts, jeans, two pairs of dress pants. A shoebox on the shelf contains old receipts, a deck of cards, and a small notebook filled with numbers and shorthand notes. Nothing personal. Nothing to suggest connections to anyone outside these walls.

James mumbles something unintelligible in his sleep, his snoring momentarily interrupted. Amy slips back toward the door and slinks out.

In the kitchen, she finds a box of Raisin Bran and eats it dry from a chipped bowl. When done, she washes her bowl, dries it, and returns it exactly where she found it. She moves to the window, looking out at the apartment complex in daylight. A woman drags a screaming toddler toward a rusted sedan. An old man sits on a plastic chair outside his door, smoking and staring at nothing.

The scene is depressing but familiar. Amy's lived in worse places—motels with mystery stains on the carpet and cockroaches scurrying across pillows. Places where the smell of chemical smoke seeped into everything she owned, where her "uncle" Cecil belched out insults, where her mother cried in the dark.

Amy wipes away a rare tear and makes her way to the haphazard stack of boxes in the corner.

CHAPTER 28

The top one is sealed with yellowing packing tape coming up at the edges, but the box below it is open, its flaps folded over one another. She slides it out carefully, making no sound as she lifts it onto the bed.

Inside, the box contains the discarded artifacts of someone else's life. Women's clothing from a different era... a peasant blouse with embroidered flowers, faded jeans with bell bottoms, a suede vest with fringe along the bottom. Below the clothing lies a shoebox filled with costume jewelry, cheap rings with glass stones, beaded necklaces tangled together in a multicolored heap.

Amy lifts each item and examines it without expression, her fingers moving over the fabrics and beads without interest. The vest feels rough against her skin, the embroidery on the blouse faded and coming loose in places. Nothing here she can sell, no weapons. Just worthless relics, the kind of junk that accumulates in attics and basements across America.

Far above Amy's head, nestled in the corner of the crawlspace over the ceiling, is a lone brown bat, listening to her every move. It clings to the rough wood beam, its clawed thumbs hooked into a crevice where the joist meets the attic floor. Its wrinkled face twitches, ears rotating like tiny radar dishes catching every rustle from below. Eight years it has lived in this place, and it knows the sounds—the groan of settling wood, the skitter of mice, the drip of pipes that leak during heavy rain.

But this sound is new. The bat's nostrils flare, sensitive membranes detecting unfamiliar scents rising through the thin ceiling. Female. Young. Sweat with hints of uncertainty and determination.

The bat's heart beats rapidly, a thousand tiny pulses per minute. Its paper-thin wings fold tight against its furry body, leathery skin creased like an old umbrella. Beneath its chin, dried blood crusts from last night's feeding, a moth caught mid-flight and consumed in seconds.

It shifts position, crawling sideways along the beam without making a sound. Directly below, the human continues to move, unaware of being observed. The bat's vision, better than humans believe but not its primary sense, catches only vague movements through hairline cracks in the plaster. But its ears and nose build a complete picture—a stranger disturbing the dust of forgotten things.

The bat has survived in this house by knowing when to hide, when to hunt, when to flee. It recognizes the scent of blood in all living things. This new human's blood pulses strong and clean, unlike James's tainted fluid. Fresh blood. Healthy blood.

The bat's tongue darts across its teeth. Not to feed, it is too small for such ambitions, but in recognition of change. New humans mean new patterns to learn, new dangers to avoid. Or perhaps opportunity. It settles deeper into its hiding place, preparing to wait and listen. The bat has all the time in the world.

At last, Amy reaches the bottom of the box. There, nestled between layers of yellowed tissue paper that crackle at her touch, she finds three notebooks. They're bound in faded covers—one red, one blue, one green—their spines creased from use, corners dog-eared from countless turnings.

The first is covered in blue denim, decorated with sewn-on patches. A peace sign, a flower, the words "KEEP ON TRUCKIN'" in faded iron-on letters. Amy opens it to the first page, where girlish handwriting declares:

"Property of Beth Elder! Private! Keep Out!"

The date reads September 8, 1967.

Amy settles onto the bed, crossing her coltish legs under her. The diary's pages are filled with the looping script of adolescence, some entries covering multiple pages, others just a few harried lines. Many words are misspelled, scratched out, rewritten, under-lined for emphasis, the penmanship deteriorating when emotions seemingly ran high.

Her eyes move methodically over the first entry:

"Dear Diary, Mom got me this journal for my 13th birthday. She says I should write down my thoughts and feelings because keeping them inside is 'unhealthy.' Whatever. School started last week and it's SO BORING already. Dad's been in one of his moods since he lost his job at the garage. Mom says we have to be extra nice to him, but why should I? He's not nice to us when he drinks..."

Amy's expression doesn't change as she reads about the mundane complaints of a teenage girl—her mother—from years earlier. Boring teachers, itchy school uniforms, friends who talked behind her back. She traces the childish doodles in the margins. Flowers, hearts, the names of boys written and then aggressively scratched out. The looping handwriting gradually becomes more confident with each page, though the content remains trivial, focused on the petty dramas of adolescence.

The digital clock counts the minutes, then hours, going by. Her back stiffens from hunching over the journal, but she doesn't pause. Beth's early entries reveal nothing of note until

Amy reaches October, where the tone of the writing subtly shifts:

"I hate him! I HATE him! Mom's in the hospital again. She 'fell down the stairs.' That's what Dad told the neighbors. But I SAW him push her. I SAW it! And when I said I was going to tell, he grabbed my arm so hard it left bruises. He said if I told anyone, they'd take me away and put me in a home for bad girls. Like he did to Tam. (I miss Tam!!!) Mom will be home tomorrow. She made me promise not to say anything. Why does she always protect him? Why doesn't she just leave? I hate her too sometimes."

Amy's finger pauses on this entry, hovering over the angry words where the pen had torn through the paper in places. She turns the page, finding similar outbursts scattered among more typical teenage concerns. A failed test, a crush on a boy named David, complaints about chores and homework.

The pattern becomes clear as she reads—periods of normalcy punctuated by explosive violence, always followed by tense reconciliation. Beth's handwriting deteriorates during these cycles, becoming jagged and uneven, only to smooth out again as the household returned to its uneasy peace.

Amy turns to the second diary, this one a green composition book with "BETH'S THOUGHTS!!! KEEP OUT!!!" written across the front in silver marker. The date is two years later, 1969. The handwriting has matured slightly, the entries more measured, more resigned.

The first pages detail Beth's mother's declining health. Persistent headaches, unexplained bruising, frequent fatigue. By March, the diagnosis appears: "Mom has leukemia. Dad won't talk about it. He just drinks even more. The doctor says she needs special treatments, but Dad says we can't afford it because he's still looking for steady work. No insurance. I offered to quit school and get a job, but Mom says no. She says education is my only ticket out of here. Out of where? This house? This life? She won't say."

Amy reads on, her expressionless face betraying nothing as she reads about her grandmother's condition worsening through the spring and summer. The entries become shorter, more factual. Temperature readings, medication schedules, brief notes about good days and bad.

August 17, 1969: "Mom died today. 3:47 PM. I was holding her hand. Dad was at a bar somewhere. He didn't come home until after midnight. I didn't tell him right away. Let him sleep it off first. When I told him this morning, he broke all the plates in the kitchen. Then he cried. I've never seen him cry before. I didn't know what to do, so I just went to my room and locked the door. Someone came and took Mom's body... I don't know who. A funeral home, I guess. The house feels empty now, like all the air got sucked out. I keep expecting to hear her call my name. The neighbor lady brought over a casserole. She patted my shoulder and said something about God's plan. I wanted to scream. What kind of plan is this?"

The entries that follow chart a rapid deterioration. Beth stops going to school regularly, her attendance dropping to just two or three days a week. James's drinking gets worse, evolving from evening binges to round-the-clock stupors. Their isolation grows as neighbors and former friends drift away, uncomfortable with the palpable misery emanating from the Elder household. Christmas passes without mention; Beth's sixteenth birthday merits only a terse line about her father forgetting it entirely.

Amy closes the second diary and reaches for the third—a spiral-bound notebook with a cover so worn the original color is indiscernible. Red, probably. Opening to the first page, she finds the date: January, 1970. The neat handwriting of the early diaries is gone, replaced by a cramped, hurried scrawl.

"I'm pregnant. I can't believe I'm writing those words. I'm pregnant. Dad doesn't know yet. He'll kill me when he finds out. Not figuratively. Literally. I have to leave. But where can I go? No money, no job, no friends left. Maybe Aunt Tam would take me in? Dad always said she was a whore, but at least whores make their own money. Maybe she'd understand. I'll call her tomorrow from the pay phone at the gas station."

Amy's finger traces the words "I'm pregnant" with unusual intensity. The following entries detail failed attempts to contact Tamerlane, Beth's increasingly desperate search for solutions, and finally, the inevitable confrontation.

"He found the pregnancy test. I came home and he was sitting in the kitchen with it on the table in front of him. I thought he would hit me. Instead, he just asked who the father was. He looked scared. I couldn't tell him. I COULDN'T. So I lied. Said it was a boy from school. David (he moved away last year so Dad can't find him). He got quiet then, which was worse than yelling. He said I had two choices: get rid of it or get out. I said I'd leave. Been packing all night. Taking Mom's old jewelry to pawn. Don't know where I'm going yet. Anywhere but here."

The entries stop abruptly after that, resuming three months later with a different pen, different handwriting. More mature, more controlled:

"Still here. I'm showing now. Can't hide it anymore. Got a job at a diner, just washing dishes. It sucks. Baby moves all the time now. Strange to think there's a person growing inside me. A person that's half me and half..."

The entry trails off, the next words heavily scratched out, then continues:

"...half its father. Still don't know what I'll do when it comes. But I have to get out of here, for real. I finally found Tam. She's gonna help me."

Amy flips through more pages, scanning entries that detail Beth's growing isolation, her fear of the future, her ambivalence about the life growing inside her. Several pages have been torn out, leaving ragged edges in the spiral binding. The final entry reads:

"Tam figured it out somehow, said she'd suspected all along. Called me sick, disgusting. Threatened to call the police, to tell

HIM. I can't let that happen. We're leaving tonight. Heading west. I have almost three hundred dollars saved. Should be enough to get us far away from here. From him. From the truth. I'll burn this diary before we go. No evidence. No proof. Just me and my baby against the world. Forever."

But the diary hadn't been burned. It sits in Amy's hands now, the final piece of a puzzle she's been assembling her whole life.

Amy closes the notebook and returns all three diaries to their place at the bottom of the box. She rearranges the clothing exactly as she found it, then slides the box back into its position in the stack. No evidence that she's discovered anything at all.

She changes into her nightgown and climbs into the narrow bed. The sheets smell of dust and disuse, but she doesn't mind. She lies on her back, staring at the ceiling, connecting dots in her mind.

James Edison Elder is not just her grandfather.

He is also her father.

Over the weekend that follows, the knowledge settles into Amy's consciousness without shock, without disgust, without the emotional response that might be expected. It simply becomes another fact in the catalog of her existence—a piece of information to be stored and, perhaps, utilized.

Tomorrow, she'll be reborn where she was conceived. She'll begin school in this new place. She'll meet new people, establish new patterns, create a new version of Amy Elder for public consumption. The camouflage of ordinariness that has served her so well. A disguise worn so perfectly that even she sometimes forgets it isn't her real face.

Monday morning and brazen sunlight slants through dust-covered blinds, casting striped shadows across Amy's face. She's been awake for a few minutes now, lying motionless, listening to the sounds of James moving through his new, unwanted morning routine. His grumbling and cursing, shower running in short bursts, the coffee maker gurgling, the television murmuring weather reports and stock prices.

The knock on her door comes at precisely 7:30. "Amy? You up? We need to get going in fifteen minutes."

She doesn't answer but slides from the bed and dresses with efficient movements. The clothes she selects are the deliberately childish ones she picked out at Kmart yesterday—a pink T-shirt with a rainbow on the front, jeans with embroidered flowers on the pockets. The kind of outfit that disarms, that suggests innocence.

In the kitchen, James stands at the counter, pouring coffee into a travel mug. "There's cereal," he says without looking up. "Milk in the fridge. Grab whatever you want."

Amy pours herself a bowl of cornflakes, adding just enough milk to soften them. She eats standing at the counter, watching James from beneath lowered lashes. In daylight, his resemblance to her is more pronounced. The same shape of jaw, the same slight asymmetry to the eyes. She wonders if others will notice.

"School called yesterday after you were asleep," James says, still not making eye contact. "Said they need immunization records, birth certificate, that kind of thing. Said they'd take you anyway, get the paperwork sorted later. Social worker pulled some strings."

Amy nods, finishing her cereal and rinsing the bowl in the sink.

"Not much of a talker, are you?" James observes, finally looking at her. "Your mother was the same way after her mom died. Silent for months. Then one day wouldn't shut up."

Amy shrugs, wiping her hands on a dish towel. She had seen how well silence worked for Jasper—that little interloper—and finds she rather enjoys the power it holds.

"Right," James says, checking his watch. "Time to go. Got your stuff?"

She holds up a spiral notebook and pencil she found in the kitchen drawer, the only school supplies in the apartment.

"That'll have to do for now." James grabs his keys from a hook by the door. "We'll figure out the rest later."

The car ride to Watson Elementary passes in silence. James navigates morning traffic with one hand on the wheel, the other tapping nervously against his thigh. At red lights, he steals glances at Amy, as though trying to decipher an encrypted message.

James fiddles with the radio dial, country western twang filling the car's interior. Guitars and a man's voice lamenting lost love compete with the sound of tires and bad shocks on bumpy asphalt.

"You like music?" He glances at Amy. "This is the good stuff. None of that pop garbage they play these days."

Amy stares out the window, watching houses blur past, each one containing lives she'll never know. The music washes over her, meaningless.

"Listen." James turns the volume down slightly. "I know this is weird. For both of us. But there's something I want to clear up." He drums his fingers on the steering wheel in time with the beat. "You don't have to call me Grandpa. James is fine. If you ever decide to speak to me, that is."

Amy's eyes flick toward him, then back to the window.

"I'm not exactly thrilled about this situation either." He sighs, braking for a red light. "Wasn't expecting to become a guardian at my age. Had my life all figured out, you know? Work, fishing at Lake Mead on weekends, football on TV."

The light changes. James accelerates too quickly, making the tires chirp.

"But here we are. And we're family, whether we like it or not." His voice softens. "Only family either of us has left."

The next singer on the radio croons about highways and heartbreak as they turn onto a tree-lined street. School buses idle in front of a low brick building.

"Watson Elementary," James announces unnecessarily. "Your mom went here too. Tamerlane..." He trails off, then pulls into the drop-off lane. "Principal's expecting you. Said they'd have someone show you around."

Amy gathers her meager supplies, hand on the door handle.

"Hey." James's voice stops her. "We'll figure this out. Somehow."

Children stream through the main entrance, their voices a cacophony of excited shrieks and laughter. "Want me to walk you in?"

Amy shakes her head, opening the car door before he can insist.

"I'll pick you up at three fifteen," James calls after her. "Wait by the front office if I'm late."

Amy doesn't acknowledge him, simply joins the flow of children toward the entrance, blending seamlessly into the crowd. Another skill honed through years of practice—becoming invisible when necessary, unremarkable, just another face in a sea of indistinguishable youth.

Inside, the school smells of floor wax and cafeteria food, of chalk dust and the peculiar combination of pencil shavings and sweaty children. It's been a year since Amy has been to school, but she knows her way around. They're all the same to her. She follows the signs to the office, where a harried secretary looks up from a stack of attendance sheets.

"Can I help you?"

"I'm Amy Elder. I'm new."

The woman checks a list on her desk. "Ah, yes. Fifth grade, Mrs. Winters. Your grandfather called yesterday." She pulls a form from a drawer and slides it across the counter. "Have him fill this out tonight. For now, I'll take you to your classroom."

The classroom buzzes with the energy of twenty-eight children settling into their morning routine. Mrs. Winters, a woman in her fifties with silver-streaked brown hair pulled into a severe bun, stands at the front, writing the day's schedule on the chalkboard.

"Mrs. Winters? This is Amy Elder, your new student," the secretary announces.

The teacher turns, her expression shifting from annoyance at the interruption to professional warmth as she spots Amy. "Welcome, Amy. We're so glad to have you join us." She gestures to an empty desk in the third row. "You can sit there between Michael and Jenny."

Amy walks to the assigned desk, keeping her eyes down, aware of the stares from her new classmates. The feeling is familiar. The assessment, the categorization, the instant judgments formed on minimal information. She's experienced this ritual in a half-dozen schools across three counties.

"Class, this is Amy," Mrs. Winters says. "She's just moved here from California. I expect everyone to make her feel welcome." Her tone suggests dire consequences for those who fail to comply. "Now, let's continue with our geography lesson."

The morning passes in a blur of administrative tasks and rudimentary lessons. Amy answers when called upon, raises her hand occasionally to maintain the appearance of engagement, and observes her classmates with covert precision. By lunch, she's identified the social hierarchy. The popular girls clustered at one table, the boys showing off at another, the outcasts finding solitary corners or forming their own defensive alliances.

She chooses an empty table, opening the paper bag lunch James hastily assembled that morning. A peanut butter sandwich, an apple, and a small bag of potato chips. The food holds no interest for her; it's merely fuel, consumed while she continues her survey of potential allies and enemies.

"You're sitting at *our* table."

Amy looks up to find three girls standing across from her. The leader, a blonde with a butterfly clip in her hair, plants her hands on her hips with practiced authority.

"I didn't see any names," Amy replies, her voice neutral.

The blonde's eyes narrow. "We always sit here. Everyone knows that."

"I'm not everyone. I'm new."

The girl exchanges glances with her friends, perhaps surprised by Amy's failure to immediately capitulate. "What's wrong with you? Can't you talk right?"

Amy continues eating, apparently unperturbed by the challenge. "I talk fine."

"You talk weird. Like a robot or something." The girl leans forward, her next words pitched for maximum impact. "My mom says your mom got shot by the police. Is that true? Was she a criminal?"

Something flickers in Amy's eyes, a brief flash of something that makes the blond girl step back. But it's gone so quickly it might have been imagined.

"Yes," Amy answers simply. "She was."

The admission throws the trio off balance. They'd expected denial, tears, or angry rebuttal—not calm confirmation. Uncertain how to proceed, the blonde makes a dismissive noise.

"Whatever. You're weird. Just find somewhere else to sit tomorrow." She motions to her friends, and they move to the far end of the table, glancing back occasionally as though Amy might contaminate them from a distance.

Amy finishes her lunch methodically, neither hurrying nor lingering. When the bell rings, she follows her classmates back to the classroom, maintaining the careful distance she's established. Present but separate, visible but unseen.

The rest of the school day passes without incident. Amy answers questions correctly but not brilliantly, participates in group activities without drawing attention, and observes the complex social dynamics of fifth grade with the detachment of an anthropologist studying an unfamiliar tribe.

CHAPTER 30

When the final bell rings, Amy waits on the front steps as instructed. James's blue Impala pulls up seventeen minutes late, its engine coughing in protest as he parks in the fire lane.

"Sorry," he says as she slides into the passenger seat. "Got held up. How was school?"

Amy shrugs, buckling her seatbelt with a loud click.

"That good, huh?" James pulls away from the curb, merging into the line of cars exiting the school grounds. "Look, I know this isn't ideal. Neither of us asked for this situation. But we're stuck with each other for now, so we might as well make the best of it."

Amy stares straight ahead, watching the side streets of Las Vegas slide past the window. Pawn shops, liquor stores, wedding chapels, and billboards advertising shows on the Strip. Each gaudy sign, each neon promise seems to mock the gray reality of her current circumstances.

James sighs, giving up on conversation. They drive in silence until reaching a small grocery store several blocks from the apartment complex, its faded sign flickering in the late afternoon sun. "Need to pick up a few things," he explains, parking in a space near the entrance, the car's tires crunching over scattered pebbles in the worn lot. "Come on."

Inside, James grabs a plastic basket and moves through the narrow aisles at a brisk pace, navigating the fluorescent-lit space briskly. Amy trots to keep up. He adds white bread, a half-gallon of milk, more cereal, packaged lunch meat, a few TV dinners with overly saturated photos on their boxes, and a six-pack of cheap beer to the basket without consulting Amy about preferences or needs. Each item lands with a decisive thud against the plastic.

Amy watches as he adds to the basket, noticing how he calculates costs in his head. His lips move slightly, tracking the mounting expense with visible concern, his forehead creasing each time he checks a price tag. She recognizes the familiar dance of budget anxiety—the mental arithmetic of someone who counts every dollar.

At the checkout, he counts out bills from his worn leather wallet, the transaction depleting his already sorry cash supply. Amy notices but shows no reaction, simply takes one of the grocery bags when offered and follows him back to the car.

"Got to make a stop on the way home," James announces as they pull out of the parking lot. "Need to see a man about a moonlighting gig."

The "man" turns out to be a small, wiry individual with tattoos covering both arms, standing outside a pawnshop on a street just off the Strip. His ink-stained skin tells stories of prison time and hard living, the faded blue designs climbing up to disappear under the sleeves of his tattered T-shirt. The neon sign above the pawnshop flickers intermittently, casting a jaundiced glow across the cracked sidewalk where he waits. James parks the car at the curb, kills the engine, and rolls down the window with a mechanical whirr that seems too loud in the sudden quiet.

"Wait here," he instructs Amy. "Lock the doors. I'll be five minutes."

She watches through the windshield as her grandfather and the tattooed man exchange words, then disappear inside the shop. The street around her pulses with early evening energy. Tourists seeking the promise of the nearby casinos, locals going about their business with the resigned air of those who live in the shadow of others' pleasure.

A bus rumbles past, its side advertising "GIRLS! GIRLS! GIRLS!" at the Sapphire Gentlemen's Club. Amy's gaze follows it, fixing on a smaller ad beneath the garish main image: "The Velvet Slipper Lounge. Las Vegas's Most Elegant Ladies." The accompanying image shows a silhouette of a woman in profile, feather boa draped across bare shoulders.

When James returns fifteen minutes later, Amy hasn't moved, her posture exactly as he left it. If he notices the intensity of her study of the street, he gives no indication.

"Got some extra work," he explains, starting the car. "Filling in for a poker dealer at the Golden Nugget. Three nights this week." He glances at her. "That's gonna take me from before dinner till after you're asleep. I can see if Mrs. Babayan next door would check on you."

Amy shakes her head. She is ten years old and has seen more of life's brutality than most adults. She has killed. The concept of needing supervision is almost laughable. Of course, James doesn't know about any of that. Yet.

"Figured you'd say that," James mutters. "Uppity. Like your mother." He pulls into traffic, heading toward the apartment. "You can zap one of those TV dinners. You know how to use a microwave, right?"

Amy nods, gaze now fixed on a phone booth they pass. Her mind is already calculating distances, schedules, opportunities.

The next morning follows the same pattern. Cereal, silent car ride, school. But Amy has a plan now, a purpose beyond simple observation. During lunch, she approaches the pay phone near the cafeteria, a couple of dimes and a nickel hidden in her palm. She waits until the lunch monitors are distracted, then slips to the phone, drops in the coins, and dials a number she memorized from the side of the bus.

"Velvet Slipper Lounge," a woman's voice answers, sounds of glasses clinking and faint music in the background.

"I'm looking for Tamerlane," Amy says, her voice carefully modulated to sound older than her years.

A pause. "Tam doesn't come in till five. Who's asking?"

"Tell her Beth's daughter called." Amy hangs up before the woman can respond, turning to see a lunch monitor watching her with suspicion.

"Phone calls aren't allowed during school hours," the woman says, approaching with clipboard in hand. "What's your name?"

"Amy Elder. I was calling my grandfather. I forgot my medication this morning."

The lie flows effortlessly, accompanied by a facial expression carefully calibrated to suggest embarrassment rather than deception. The monitor's suspicion softens.

"Next time, use the office phone. You need a pass."

"Yes, ma'am. Sorry."

Amy returns to the cafeteria, satisfied with this first step. The pieces are in motion.

For the next three days, she cultivates normalcy. She participates in class, completes homework at the kitchen table while James watches television, and eats the frozen dinners he leaves for her before departing for his night shifts. She learns his routine. Up at noon, coffee while reading racing forms, shower at two thirty, dress for work at three, return around four a.m., collapse into bed after two beers.

On Thursday afternoon, when James drops her at the apartment before leaving for his shift at the Golden Nugget, Amy waits exactly twenty-five minutes before shouldering her school backpack and leaving. She has timed the bus routes, calculated transfers, created alibis for potential questions.

Amy climbs aboard, dropping her coins into the fare box. The driver—a heavyset woman with hair pulled tight under her uniform cap—barely glances at her.

"Transfer?" the driver asks, already reaching for the slip of paper.

Amy shakes her head and moves down the aisle. The bus interior smells of cigarettes, cheap perfume, hairspray, body odor, and the lingering phantom of fast food. She selects a seat halfway back, away from the few other passengers but not so far as to draw attention.

A man in a rumpled security guard uniform dozes across from her, chin bobbing against his chest with each pothole the bus encounters. His name tag reads "Earl," and his shoes are scuffed at the toes. Two seats ahead, an elderly woman clutches a plastic shopping bag from a 99-cent store, its contents clinking softly with the bus's movement.

Outside the windows, the suburban Las Vegas afternoon blurs by. Laundromats with faded signs. Check-cashing storefronts with bars on their windows. Liquor stores advertising hot dogs and cold beer.

The bus lurches forward, stopping every few blocks to exchange passengers. A teenager with a Walkman blasting tinny music loud enough for everyone to hear through the headphones. A woman in nurse's scrubs, dark circles under her eyes suggesting the end of a long shift. Two men speaking rapid Spanish, their conversation punctuated with occasional laughter.

Amy catalogs each face, each detail, filing away information with the methodical precision that comes naturally to her. The way the nurse's hands shake slightly as she counts out her fare. How the security guard's uniform is a size too large, suggesting recent weight loss. The way the elderly woman watches the passing storefronts with vacant eyes.

At Maryland Parkway, a woman boards with twin toddlers, their matching outfits stained from the day's adventures. She struggles to manage them and her oversized purse while paying the fare. The bus driver waits with resigned patience.

"Fremont Street next," the driver announces as they approach downtown, the Strip's smaller, seedier cousin coming into view with its canopy of lights just beginning to illuminate in the approaching dusk.

Amy pulls the cord, the bell chiming softly. She slides from her seat, moving toward the rear exit with unhurried confidence.

The Velvet Slipper is just around the corner, its neon sign visible even from here—a stiletto heel rendered in purple light. The lounge sits on the edge of downtown, its exterior a snapshot of faded elegance. Purple velvet curtains visible through tinted windows, a neon sign depicting a high-heeled shoe flickering irregularly above the entrance. A hand-written sign on the door reads "OPEN 4 PM - 4 AM."

Amy approaches with confidence beyond her years, pushing open the heavy door and stepping into the dim interior. A barstool, where the doorman would usually be sitting, is empty. Amy's eyes protest, having gone from the desert's brutal winter sun to pitch black. The abrupt transition leaves her momentarily vulnerable, something she detests.

She blinks a few times, allowing her vision to adjust to the murky atmosphere. A long bar stretches along one wall, mirrors behind it reflecting bottles and the tired faces of early afternoon drinkers nursing glasses with practiced indifference. Small tables cluster in the center of the worn carpet, while along the opposite wall, plush velvet booths, their fabric faded from years of use, provide shadowy alcoves for private conversations and discreet exchanges.

A dancefloor stretches across the back of the joint, elevated just enough to command attention. Colored lights, electric blues and muted pinks, strobe gently over the nude bodies of two listless strippers. They move mechanically through their routines, eyes vacant and movements perfunctory, performing for the scattered audience with the detached professionalism of shift workers counting down to quitting time. The bass-heavy music pulses at a volume just loud enough to provide rhythm without drowning out drink orders, creating a soundtrack of manufactured desire that fools no one.

A woman behind the bar looks up, cigarette dangling from her lips, a thin trail of smoke curling toward the stained ceiling. She's wearing a low-cut crop top that reveals a faded tattoo across her collarbone and a micro miniskirt that hasn't been fashionable in a decade. Her hair is Lucille Ball red, clearly from a bottle, that hasn't been refreshed in weeks. She narrows her eyes, instantly assessing the young intruder. "We don't serve minors, kid. Beat it," she says flatly, her voice rough from years of cigarettes and late nights.

"I'm looking for Tamerlane," Amy says, standing her ground. "I'm her niece."

The cigarette freezes midway to the ashtray. The woman studies Amy with new interest, eyes narrowing as she takes in the resemblance.

"Jesus Christ," she mutters. "Wait here." She disappears through a beaded curtain behind the bar.

Amy stands motionless, aware of the stares from the handful of patrons nursing drinks in the artificial twilight of the lounge. She catalogs exits, assesses potential threats, maintains the outward appearance of a normal child while her mind calculates a dozen contingencies.

The beaded curtain parts, and a woman emerges. Tall, slender, with shoulder-length dark hair streaked with premature gray. Her face shows the careful maintenance of someone fighting against time. Makeup applied in several layers, skin taut around the eyes suggesting a few cosmetic tweaks. She wears a black silk blouse and fitted pants, a far cry from the glamorous showgirl Beth had described in her stories.

"What kind of sick joke is this?" the woman demands, stopping several feet from Amy, arms crossed defensively across her chest.

CHAPTER 31

"No joke, Aunt Tam," Amy replies flatly. "I'm Amy Elder. Beth was my mother."

"Was?" Tamerlane's expression shifts from suspicion to something more complex—a flickering kaleidoscope of confusion, disbelief, and the first tendrils of dread. "What do you mean, 'was'?"

"She died. A week ago. Police shot her in California." Amy delivers this news with the flat affect of reading a grocery list, her emerald eyes never wavering.

The blunt delivery seems to physically impact Tam. Color drains from her face as she reaches for the edge of the bar to steady herself, knuckles blanching against the polished wood. She swallows hard, then motions to the bartender with two fingers raised. "Bourbon. Neat." Her voice sounds hollow, disconnected. Turning back to Amy, she gestures toward a booth in the corner, authority hardening her tone. "Sit. Now."

Amy slides into the booth, her small frame dwarfed by the high velvet back. She arranges herself with deliberate elegance, hands folded neatly on the table. Her aunt joins her moments later, placing her freshly delivered drink on the table with a hand that trembles slightly, ice clinking against glass in the sudden silence between them.

"Beth is dead." It's not a question now, but a statement she's testing for truth. "And you're her kid."

Amy nods once.

"How old are you?"

"Ten."

Tam does the math quickly, her expression darkening. "And who's taking care of you now? How did you even get here?"

"My... um, grandfather. Child services picked me up. Some narc reported me. I was trying to find you..." Amy swallows, then shrugs. "So, I'm living with James."

Tam's face hardens at the name, hatred flashing bright and unmistakable before she controls it. "That bastard." She takes a long swallow of her booze. "He hasn't changed, then? Still guzzling booze like it's the fountain of youth? Still dealing cards? Still miserable and alone?"

"Yes."

"And hitting? Is he hitting you?"

Amy shakes her head. "No. He mostly ignores me."

"Small mercies." Tam studies Amy more carefully now, looking for something specific in her features. Whatever she sees causes her to drain her glass and signal for another. "You look like her. But you've got *his* eyes."

"I know."

The simple acknowledgment thrums between them, heavy with implication. Tam's second bourbon arrives, and she takes a smaller sip this time.

"How much do you know?"

"Everything," Amy says. "I found Beth's diaries."

Tam closes her eyes briefly. "Christ. I told her to burn those."

She opens her eyes, fixing Amy with a penetrating stare. "What do you want from me? Money? A place to stay? Because I gotta tell you, this ain't exactly a place for a child."

"I want information," Amy replies. "About Beth. About him. About you."

"Why? What good does any of that do you now?"

"Knowledge is power." The adult phrasing sounds incongruous coming from a child, but Amy delivers it with such conviction that Tam doesn't laugh.

"You're not like other kids, are you?" Tam observes. "There's something... I can't put my finger on it." She leans forward slightly, studying the girl's face with growing unease.

"I'm just me," Amy says simply, as though this explains everything.

Tam sighs, relenting. "Fine. What do you want to know?"

"How did you find out? About my mom and... your dad."

The question is so direct, so unexpected, that Tam almost chokes on her drink. "Jesus. You don't start small, do you?" She dabs at her brick-red lips with a cocktail napkin, leaving a smear of gloss, her hand trembling slightly. "I found out because I came home unexpectedly. I wanted to get some of Mom's clothes. I wasn't there when she died." Tears fill her eyes but don't fall. "I walked in and... Well, let's just say it was obvious what was happening."

"What did you do?"

"What could I do? I was nineteen, working as a cocktail waitress, barely making rent. I confronted him, told him I'd go to the police. He beat me so bad I couldn't work for two weeks." She traces a thin scar along her jawline. "Souvenir. After that, I tried to get Beth to leave with me, but she wouldn't. Said he needed her. Stockholm syndrome or some shit." Tam's voice hardens with the memory.

"Her diaries say you yelled at her. Called her dirty, disgusting." Amy's voice was flat, but the words hit hard.

"I didn't mean it. I was trying to shake her up. Get her to do something." Tam's defense was a whisper, a feeble attempt to justify the unjustifiable. She cringed, the memory of her own cruelty still a festering wound.

"When did she finally leave?" Amy asked.

"When she got pregnant with you." Tam's gaze dropped to the floor, the weight of the past pressing down on her. "She called me from a pay phone, her voice so weak I could barely hear her. She was terrified. I wired her money for a bus ticket to anywhere but here.

"Didn't hear from her again until she called again when you were about two. She was strung out, paranoid. Said someone was after her. Said there was something wrong with you. Like..." Tam paused, her eyes lifting to meet the inquisitive gaze of her listener, "I don't know. Like I said, she was out of her damn mind." The words were a shield, an attempt to deflect the horror of what her sister had become, the fear that perhaps there had been a grain of truth in Beth's delusions.

Amy absorbs this information without visible reaction. "Did you ever tell anyone? About James and Beth?"

"Who would believe me? Dad had friends in the department. Cops go to his table all the time. Besides, by the time I had the guts to try, Beth was long gone." Tam swirls the amber liquid in her glass, watching the light catch in its depths. "Why are you asking all this? What's your angle?"

"I need to understand my history," Amy says. "To plan my future."

Tam barks a harsh laugh. "What future? You're ten. Living with that monster. What kind of future are you planning?"

Amy doesn't answer directly. "Did you ever want to kill him? For what he did to Beth? To you? He did it to you too, didn't he?"

The question lands like a slap. Tam stares at Amy, really seeing her for the first time. The bourbon glass freezes halfway to her lips, amber liquid catching the light in suspended animation. Something icy trickles down her spine. Not fear exactly, but a primal recognition of wrongness.

"What kind of kid asks something like that?" she whispers, her voice barely audible over the dull hum of the ancient refrigerator. The child across from her, with those unsettling green eyes, suddenly seems less like Beth's daughter and more like something else entirely.

"The kind who's seen people die," Amy replies, her voice unchanged, her stare steady. "The kind who knows there's more than one way to deal with obstacles."

"You have quite a large vocabulary for a little girl," Tam says with an uncomfortable chuckle.

"Do I?"

Tam sets her glass down carefully, the soft clink against the table like a tiny warning bell. "Listen to me very carefully, Amy. Whatever you're thinking, whatever you're planning—don't. You get caught, and you'll end up in juvie until you're eighteen, then straight to prison. That's no kind of fucking life." Her fingers remain curled around the base of the glass, her rings glinting in the gently strobing light on the dancefloor.

"And this is?" Amy gestures around the dim lounge with a sweep of her small hand, taking in the pitted ceiling, the flickering neon beer signs, the lingering stench of desperation that no amount of cleaning and scrubbing could ever remove.

"There are worse things," Tam says, her voice dropping to a rough whisper that barely carries over the thrum of the bass from the dancefloor. The scar along her jawline, a silvery line marring the otherwise smooth skin, seems to stand out more prominently in the bar's harsh shadows, as if accentuating her words with its own silent punishment. "You can take that to the fucking bank." Her eyes, dark pools that have seen too much, hold Amy's gaze, and for a moment, something haunted flickers behind them—a glimpse into darker places that even Amy hasn't managed to conjure.

"I don't trust anyone," Amy replies simply, her expression reflecting nothing but cold certainty. Her small face settles into an expression far too ancient for her years.

For a long moment, they regard each other across the table, the aging lounge hostess and the child with adult eyes, each recognizing something familiar in the other, some shared damage that creates a bridge across the gaps of age and experience.

"You should go home," Tam says finally. "Before that fucker gets back from his shift. Before someone calls the cops about an unaccompanied minor in a bar."

Amy slides out of the booth, adjusting her backpack straps with practiced efficiency. "Will you help me?"

"Help you what? Run away? Kill him? What exactly are you asking?"

"I haven't decided yet," Amy answers with a shrug.

Tam stares at her, drink forgotten. "You're serious."

"I'm always serious."

After a long pause, Tam reaches into her purse and pulls out a business card, its edges bent and softened. She scribbles something on the back before handing it to Amy. "My home number. Don't call the lounge again. Too many ears." She hesitates, then adds, "I can't promise anything. But... I've got no love for James Edison Elder. Never have, never will."

Amy studies the card before tucking it carefully into her pocket. "That's a start."

"Go on now."

Amy turns to leave, then pauses. "She talked about you sometimes. Said you were the only person who ever tried to help her."

"Fat lot of good it did her," Tam mutters.

"Still. She remembered." With that, Amy walks out of the Velvet Slipper Lounge into the harsh late afternoon sunlight, leaving Tam staring after her, hand already reaching for another glass of liquid oblivion.

Amy hears the heavy door swinging shut behind her with a dull thud that seems to mark the boundary between two worlds.

The card from Tam feels like a talisman in her pocket—not quite a promise, but a possibility. She touches it through the fabric of her jeans, reassuring herself of its presence as she navigates the cracked sidewalk toward the bus stop three blocks away.

A shortcut presents itself, a narrow path cutting through the outdoor seating area of the Desert Bloom Café, its perimeter lined with surprisingly lush flower beds. Defying the harsh, dry Nevada winter, riots of purple sage and yellow brittlebush create a momentary oasis in the urban landscape.

Amy slips between the tables, drawing curious glances from the patrons nursing their iced coffees. She ignores them, focusing instead on the quickest route through the garden. Her mind is elsewhere, calculating probabilities and planning next steps with the methodical precision that comes naturally to her.

Lost in thought, she nearly misses the slight movement at her feet. A tiny brown creature darts across her path. It's a desert shrew, no bigger than her thumb, its pointed snout twitching frantically as it freezes in momentary panic.

Amy's foot hovers inches above the creature. She stops abruptly, watching with detached curiosity as the shrew recovers from its shock and retreats toward a small hole between the flower bed stones.

Before disappearing completely, the insectivore turns, baring needle-like teeth. It emits a high-pitched shriek that slices through the ambient café chatter, a sound disproportionate to its tiny size, vibrating with territorial fury.

The shrew's tiny black eyes, like liquid obsidian beads, fix on Amy with unmistakable aggression. Its entire body trembles with the effort of its warning cry, whiskers quivering as it takes in her scent, her presence, categorizing her as an intruder in its domain.

Amy stares back, a flicker of recognition passing across her features. Something in the creature's disproportionate rage resonates with her—small but dangerous, overlooked but lethal.

CHAPTER 32

Amy leaves the café, the shrew's defiant shriek lingering in her mind as she catches the bus back to her neighborhood.

The ride passes in a blur of monotonous stops and strangers' conversations.

Amy settles into a seat near the back of the bus, her mind still churning over her meeting with Tam. As the vehicle lurches forward, fragments of conversations drift through the air like wayward myna birds, gradually pulling her attention away from her thoughts.

"—told him I wouldn't be caught dead at another one of his family reunions. Not after what his mother said about my potato salad—"

Two rows ahead, an elderly woman clutches her purse while speaking emphatically to her seatmate. Amy finds herself leaning slightly forward. "Eight dollars for a haircut! Highway robbery, I tell you. And she still couldn't get my bangs right."

Across the aisle, a teenager with vibrant blue hair chats loudly with a mousy girl hunched beside him: "Nah, dude, the sequel was garbage. Complete character assassination. Like they forgot everything that happened in the first movie."

A middle-aged man leans over to talk with the person in front of him. "—so I said to my boss, 'I've been here nine years and that's the best you can do?' And you know what he had the nerve to tell me? 'Market conditions.' Whatever that means."

A man in a rumpled business suit flips through a newspaper near the front of the bus. "Gladys, I swear, if Sanjay gets that promotion over me after I covered his shifts all through October..." His wife mutters something Amy can't hear. "No, I'm not making a scene." He lowers his voice slightly. "We've been planning that vacation for months. If they pass me over again, we'll have to cancel Niagara Falls."

Amy's gaze drifts out the window, the passing storefronts and pedestrians blurring together. All these fragments of other people's lives, complaints about haircuts, family drama, workplace frustrations, ordinary problems that seem so distant from her own situation. The shrew's cry still echoes in her memory, a strange counterpoint to these mundane human concerns.

The bus lurches to a stop, and Amy nearly misses her corner. She stands quickly, swinging her bag over her shoulder, and makes her way down the aisle. As she steps off onto the sidewalk, the business man's voice fades behind her: "Just tell Bobby I'll help with his science project this weekend..."

Dusk has settled over the apartment complex, painting the shabby buildings in deceptively gentle hues of purple and gold.

She walks with purpose, eyes scanning her surroundings out of habit rather than conscious thought. Tam's card presses against her thigh through her pocket, a small talisman of possibility.

Movement across the street catches her attention. Amy recognizes him—the neighborhood fixture who sleeps behind the dumpsters and occasionally panhandles near the convenience store. The vagrant stumbles along his usual route down the sidewalk opposite the complex, his movements unsteady, gesturing animatedly at empty air.

She crosses the street, giving him wide berth, but he spots her. His eyes, bloodshot and unfocused, suddenly sharpen with unexpected clarity.

"Sarah?" His voice cracks with disbelief. "Sarah, is that you?"

Amy freezes mid-step. The vagrant lurches across the asphalt, a car honking as it swerves around him. His sunburned face contorts with desperate recognition.

"Sarah! Wait!" He stumbles over the curb, catching himself on a parking meter. His clothes, a mismatched assemblage of donations and discards, hang from his frame like forgotten laundry.

Amy's muscles tense, ready to bolt. The rational part of her brain catalogs escape routes while another part wonders who Sarah might be. A daughter? Wife? Someone lost to him?

He's closer now, close enough that she catches his smell: unwashed body, cheap alcohol, and something medicinal. His eyes, though, they're surprisingly clear, fixed on her with absolute certainty.

"They said you were gone." His voice drops to a whisper. "But I knew. I knew you'd come back."

He reaches toward her, fingers trembling. Amy steps back but doesn't run.

"I'm not Sarah," she says firmly, maintaining eye contact. "You've confused me with someone else."

His hand drops. The clarity in his eyes clouds over, replaced by confusion, then embarrassment.

"I—" He blinks rapidly. "I'm sorry. You look just like—" He shakes his head. "I'm sorry."

Before Amy can react, he lunges with surprising speed. His fingers, grimy and strong, clamp around her wrist, yanking her toward the narrow passage between buildings.

"Let go!" Amy struggles, but the man's grip tightens as he drags her behind the apartment building.

"You think you can just walk away?" His breath reeks of cheap malt liquor and decay. "After what you did? After you took everything?"

Amy's back hits the brick wall.

The man looms over her, his face contorted with rage and confusion. "Sarah, you promised. You promised we'd always be together." His voice drops to a whisper. "But you left me for him. Left me with nothing."

Something shifts in Amy's expression. The initial shock transforms into a slowly simmering pique. Her breathing steadies as she stops struggling.

"You're right," she says, her voice deliberately soft, a measured whisper that slithers between them. "I did leave you."

The man blinks, momentarily confused by her compliance. His bloodshot eyes widen with surprise, then narrow with suspicious victory. His grip loosens slightly, fingers slackening just enough around her wrist that Amy can feel the blood rushing back to her fingertips.

"I knew you'd admit it eventually," he mutters, swaying slightly on his feet. The stench of unwashed clothes and sour alcohol rolls off him in waves. "Always knew you'd come back to me. They all said you wouldn't, but I waited. I always knew."

Amy's gaze appraises him with strategic exactitude, taking in every detail: the yellowed fingernails, the patchy beard, the constellation of broken blood vessels mapping his nose and cheeks. Her expression remains carefully neutral, a mask that reveals nothing of the figuring happening behind it.

"What did Sarah take from you?" she asks, her tone almost conversational, as if they were discussing the weather rather than standing in a filthy alleyway with her back against rough brick.

"Everything!" He slams his palm against the wall beside her head with such force that bits of mortar crumble down. Spittle flies from his mouth as he leans in closer, his body trembling with rage. "My life, my dignity, my—"

Amy Elder, with her emerald eyes gleaming in the dim light of the alleyway, doesn't bother to listen to the rest of the man's rambling. She's heard enough to understand the depth of his delusion, the winding narrative he's constructed in his mind. With a haughty dispassion that belies her ten years, she readies herself, her body coiled like a spring, poised for action.

In a fluid motion, honed by experience, Amy strikes. Her knee drives upward with ruthless precision, slamming into the man's groin with a force that jolts through his body. His breath hitches in his throat, turning into a strangled gasp as he doubles over in pain. Seizing the moment, Amy wrenches her wrist free from his suddenly lax grip and uses the momentum to swing her book bag around, the sharp edge of the strap catching him squarely on the temple. The impact sends him reeling, his legs tangling as he stumbles sideways, arms windmilling for balance that eludes him. With a resounding crash, he collides into a precarious grouping of empty trashcans, sending them flying across the dirty pavement in a racket of hollow clatter.

The vagrant lies in a dazed heap, the wind knocked out of him, his body curled in a fetal position as he grapples with the pain radiating from his groin and the throbbing ache in his head. Amy stands over him, her small frame casting a long shadow in the alley's dim light.

Her voice, when she speaks, is calm and steady. "She must have had her reasons," she says, her words slicing through the man's moans. "Maybe you deserved it."

The man's eyes, clouded with pain and confusion, lock onto Amy's face. Recognition dawns, and with it, the realization that he's not dealing with the woman he thought he knew. "You're not—"

"No, I'm not Sarah," Amy confirms, her voice devoid of emotion. She bends down and picks up a brick that's fallen from the crumbling edge of the wall. She weighs it in her hand, knowing all too well its potential as a weapon, the damage it could inflict. "But I understand her."

The man recoils at the icy certainty in her voice, a primal fear flickering in his bloodshot eyes. He realizes too late the grave mistake he's made. "Please," he begs, his voice reduced to a whimper. "I made a mistake."

Amy's fingers tighten around the brick, her short nails scraping the rough surface. She imagines the satisfying crack it would make against his skull, the release of tension it would bring to the constant pressure building inside her. It would be so easy, such a rush.

But then, the sound of her name pierces the air, a voice calling from the street, cutting through the fog of violence that has enveloped her. "Amy? Amy Elder, is that you back there?"

It's Mrs. Kellerman from 3B, her head poking around the corner, her eyes squinting from behind her thick glasses to make out the figures in the dimly lit alley. "Everything okay?" she asks, her tone laced with concern.

Amy lets the brick slip from her grasp, watching dispassionately as it plunks to the pavement, coming to rest against the curb. She turns to face Mrs. Kellerman, a practiced smile spreading across her face, the mask of innocence sliding back into place with ease.

"Fine," Amy assures her, her voice light and airy, a perfect imitation of childhood innocence. "Just taking a shortcut through the alley."

The nosy neighbor eyes her for a moment longer before nodding slowly and withdrawing, leaving Amy alone once more with the man who now poses no threat at all. Amy spares him one last glance before she turns on her heel and walks away, leaving the man to his torment.

CHAPTER 33

Amy sits still in the oversized chair across from Ms. Levine's desk, hands folded in her lap, features composed carefully as neutral. The wall behind the counselor displays framed degrees and cheerful posters about self-esteem and conflict resolution. A box of tissues sits prominently on the desk corner, prepared for tears that Amy has no intention of shedding.

"How are you settling in, Amy?" Ms. Levine asks, her voice calibrated to project warmth and safety. "It's been, what, three weeks now?"

"Fine," Amy replies, the word a complete sentence.

Ms. Levine makes a note on the yellow legal pad in front of her. "Your teachers say you're very quiet in class. That you don't interact much with the other students."

Amy says nothing, merely waits for the actual question.

"Making friends can be difficult when you're new," the counselor continues, filling the silence. "Especially after experiencing trauma. It's normal to feel... disconnected."

Still, Amy offers no response beyond continued eye contact.

Ms. Levine shifts strategies. "I understand you've been through something very difficult. Losing your mother, moving to a new city, living with a grandfather you didn't know. That's a lot for anyone to handle, especially someone your age."

"I'm managing," Amy says, offering the minimum necessary to prevent any escalation of concern.

"I'm sure you are. You strike me as a very capable young lady." Ms. Levine leans forward slightly, her expression softening into professional empathy. "But everyone needs support sometimes. That's why I'm here. To help you process your feelings, to provide a safe space for you to talk about what you've experienced."

Amy studies the counselor analytically, noting the wedding ring (gold band, well-worn), the sensible shoes (practical brown loafers with minimal heel), the family photo featuring two smiling boys in Little League uniforms posed proudly with aluminum bats (against a bucolic backdrop of manicured green fields). A normal life, she concludes, untouched by the realities Amy has navigated since birth—a life of predictable weekend games and scheduled dinners, of stability and mundane concerns, so foreign to her own experience it might as well exist in another dimension.

"There's nothing to talk about," Amy says finally. "My mother died. I live with my grandfather now. I go to school. I do my homework. Everything's fine."

The woman makes another note. "Your grandfather... how is that relationship developing? Is he taking good care of you?"

The question contains layers of potential complication. Amy recognizes it as a probe for signs of neglect or abuse, a standard part of the protocol when children enter new guardianship arrangements. She calculates her response carefully.

"He works nights. I don't see him much. But there's food in the refrigerator, and I have my own room. He bought me school supplies." She recites these facts as evidence of adequacy, knowing they meet the minimum threshold for acceptable care.

"And how do you feel about him?"

Amy tilts her head slightly, as though considering the question. "I don't know him well enough to feel anything in particular."

It's a deliberate deflection, and one that the mentor clearly recognizes. Her pen pauses above her notepad. "Sometimes, when we experience loss, it's difficult to allow ourselves to form new attachments. We worry that if we get close to someone, we might lose them too."

The amateur psychology might apply to a normal child who had experienced normal trauma, but it slides off Amy like water off waxed paper. Still, she recognizes the need to provide some response that will satisfy Ms. Levine's professional obligations.

"Maybe," she concedes. "I'll think about that."

The noncommittal answer seems to satisfy Ms. Levine, who smiles encouragingly. "That's all I ask. And remember, my door is always open if you need to talk." She reaches into her desk drawer and removes a small card. "Here's my number, in case you need to reach me outside of school hours."

Amy takes the card, adding it to her growing collection of adults who believe they understand her needs. "Thank you," she says, the social nicety delivered with exemplary intonation.

"You can go back to class now. But Amy?" Ms. Levine's expression turns serious. "I'm here to help. *Really.*"

The girl nods, rising from the chair. She recognizes sincerity when she sees it. Ms. Levine genuinely believes she can help, which makes her both innocuous and irrelevant to Amy's actual situation. Another well-meaning adult whose worldview cannot comprehend the reality of her existence.

"Goodbye, Ms. Levine," she says, closing the door quietly behind her.

In the corridor outside, Amy takes a moment to reset her mental assessments. The counselor's intervention was an expected complication, but a manageable one. More concerning is the pattern developing at home—James's increasing attention to her daily life, his awkward attempts at conversation, his gradual shift from reluctant guardian to something attempting to resemble a parental figure.

Last night, he'd asked about her homework. The night before, he'd left microwave popcorn on the counter with a note: "Thought you might like this for a snack." Small gestures, insignificant in isolation, but together forming a trajectory that threatens to complicate her plans.

She needs to accelerate the timeline. Needs to move before James's tentative steps toward normalcy create complications.

That evening, Amy sits at the kitchen table completing subtraction problems while James stands at the stove, heating a can of beef stew for their dinner. His night off from the Golden Nugget has disrupted their usual routine, forcing this unwanted domestic scenario.

"Need help with that?" James asks, glancing over at her notebook.

"No," Amy replies, her pencil moving efficiently across the page. "It's simple."

James nods, stirring the stew absently. "You're good at math, then. Like your mother. She could calculate odds faster than most of the dealers I worked with." He pauses, perhaps sensing he's stepped onto uncertain conversational ground. "Not that she ever got to use it properly."

Amy looks up, suddenly alert to this unexpected opening. "What would have been proper?"

"Beauty school, maybe. Beth was smart enough, when she applied herself." James focuses intently on the stew, avoiding eye contact. "Always had her nose in some fashion magazine, before... before things got complicated."

"Complicated," Amy repeats, the word flat and impassive.

James either misses or ignores the dangerous undertone. "Yeah, well. Life happens. Makes a mess of the best intentions." He ladles stew into two bowls and brings them to the table. "Eat while it's hot."

They sipped in silence for several minutes, the only sound the occasional clink of spoons against ceramic. James seems lost in his own thoughts, perhaps regretting opening the door to the past, even slightly.

"I met Aunt Tam," Amy says suddenly, the statement calculated for maximum impact.

James chokes on a piece of potato, coughing violently before managing to catch his breath. "You what?"

"Last week. I took the bus to the Velvet Slipper Lounge."

The blood drains from James's face, leaving it ashen beneath the perpetual stubble. "What the hell were you thinking? You're ten years old. You can't just—" He stops, processing the full implications. "What did she tell you?"

"Enough," Amy replies, watching his reaction as if he were a lab rat. "About you. About my mom. About why she left."

James sets down his spoon with a trembling hand. "Listen to me very carefully, Amy. Tamerlane is a vindictive, lying bitch who'd say anything to make me look bad. Whatever she told you—"

"She didn't have to tell me anything," Amy interrupts, her voice still calm, controlled. "I found Beth's diaries. I know what you did."

The words land like an atom bomb. James recoils as though backhanded, his face cycling through shock, guilt, anger, and finally settling into a defensive air. "You don't understand anything."

"I understand everything," Amy counters, her eyes never leaving his face. "I know who I am. What I am. Where I came from... *Dad.*"

James pushes away from the table abruptly, the chair legs scraping against linoleum with a sound like fingernails on a chalkboard. He crosses to the cabinet above the refrigerator, retrieves a bottle of gin, and pours three fingers into a water glass. The clear liquid disappears in a single swallow.

"You think you know," he says finally, his back still turned to her. "But you don't. Can't. It wasn't—" He stops, shakes his head. "It doesn't matter now. What's done is done."

"Is it?" Amy asks, the question hanging between them like the blade of a guillotine.

James turns, studying her with newly wary eyes. Something in her tone, a certain knowing edge, has punctured his defensive shell. "What does that mean?"

Amy shrugs, the gesture deliberately childlike, a performance of naivety at odds with the atmosphere she's created. Her lips curve into a mirthless smile. "Nothing. Just wondering if things ever really end or if they just change shape. Like people. Like families. Like *secrets*."

The cryptic statement deepens James's unease. He pours another drink, this one sipped rather than gulped. "Stay away from Tam. She's bad news. Always has been."

"Because she tried to help Beth? Or because she knows what you did? Did you do it to her too?"

"No!" James snaps, anger breaking through his eggshell of control. "She doesn't care about you. She's using you to get at me."

"Why would she want to get at you?" Amy asks, the question innocent on its surface, but the undercurrents of suspicion swirl through her words, a murmuration of doubt staining the air.

James's mouth opens, then closes without answering. The trap is too obvious, even to him, the bait dangled too enticingly for a man who's spent his life avoiding the snare of honesty. After a moment, he drains his glass, the spirit burning a path to his belly, and sets it down with controlled precision, the clink against the coaster a stark punctuation to his departure. "I'm going out. Don't wait up."

"Where are you going?" Amy persists.

"None of your business," he retorts, the sharpness of his tone cutting through the room's tension. He grabs his keys from the hook by the door with a hand that belies his inner turmoil, the jangle of metal a harsh announcement of his imminent escape. Then he pauses, conflict visible on his face, a battlefield of emotions etched in the lines around his eyes and the set of his jaw. "And you're grounded," he adds, the words falling like a gavel, an attempt to reassert control where it has long since slipped away.

When he's gone, the apartment settling into silence broken only by the hum of the refrigerator, Amy allows herself a small smile of satisfaction. The seeds have been planted. James's guilt, his fear, his knowledge that his secrets are no longer safely buried.

Homework done and dishes washed, Amy sinks into the lumpy cushion of her bed, a sense of satisfaction spreading through her chest. The apartment breathes a sigh of relief in James's absence, the walls no longer bracing against his restless energy. Now, with the quiet, she can dive into the pages of her latest acquisitions, each one promising a portal into a world far removed from her own.

Earlier at Goodwill, she'd navigated the crowded aisles with swanning ease, her fingers grazing over the spines of discarded books, each one whispering a story of its former life. She'd found *Sybil*, the tale of multiple personalities born from trauma, a concept not entirely unfamiliar to Amy. *Helter Skelter* had beckoned next, its cover faded and corners softened from handling. The story of Charles Manson and his followers held a grim allure, the darkness within its pages reflecting the shadows in her own family history. Finally, *Looking For Mr. Goodbar*, a bleak warning about the dangers that lurk in the guise of casual encounters. Each book was a treasure, soon to be devoured and digested.

Amy had searched for *Circus Freaks* among the stacks. Though it was nowhere to be found, she felt only a twinge of disappointment. Her tastes had evolved, her mind hungry for more complex narratives that could provide context for her life.

Now, as she opens *Helter Skelter*, the musty scent of old paper fills her nostrils. She welcomes the familiar weight of the book in her hands, the texture of the pages brushing against her fingertips as she turns them. The new lamp on her nightstand casts a warm pool of light, driving back the encroaching darkness of the room, the glow a silent ally in her journey through the night.

The opening chapters of the book lay out the landscape of the late '60s, a time when the promise of peace and love gave way to something far darker. Amy reads about Manson's ability to manipulate and control, his followers' unwavering loyalty even as they committed heinous acts. A shiver of recognition travels up her spine. In her own way, she understands the allure of such power.

As she reads, Amy can't help but draw parallels between Manson's "Family" and her own fractured kin. The way James commands the space around him with his presence—or lack thereof. The way Beth had been so desperate for affection that she'd allowed herself to be ensnared by the very person who should have protected her. Amy sees the patterns, the ways in which abuse and control can twist a person's sense of self, their perception of what's normal, what's acceptable.

Her mind drifts back to nights with Beth, their motel beds like life rafts in a turbulent world. Beth's voice had been a gentle if hesitant cadence, her reading punctuated by the effort to wrangle complex words into submission. Amy had loved those moments, the comforting lilt of her mother's voice a soothing counterpoint to the chaos that often raged outside their door. Now, reading at her own rapid pace, Amy feels a pang of longing for those simpler times, even as she acknowledges that they were anything but simple.

The hours slip by unnoticed as Amy delves deeper into the book, the world outside her window fading away. The stories within its pages resonate with her, a silent acknowledgment of the darkness that lives within families, within individuals. It's a darkness she's intimately familiar with, a welcome shadow that has trailed her since birth.

When she finally sets the book aside, the first hints of dawn are creeping into the sky, painting the world in shades of soft pink and pale blue. Amy turns off the lamp, the room plunging into twilight as exhaustion tugs at her eyelids. As sleep claims her, she finds herself wondering about the nature of evil, about the thin line that separates victim from perpetrator, about the legacy of pain that passes from one generation to the next.

In the quiet of her room, with the ghosts of Manson's victims lingering in her thoughts, Amy feels a kinship with those who have been touched by tragedy. For now, she sleeps, the rhythm of her breathing a steady pulse in the silent apartment. In her dreams, she walks through the pages of her books, a specter among the tales of loss and survival, love and madness. And when she wakes, she will carry those stories with her.

The apartment is empty when Amy wakes. James hadn't been home, as far as she can tell. The stale air felt undisturbed, no fresh cigarette smell lingering, no dirty dishes in the sink. She wolfs down a quick breakfast, stale cereal with the last drops of milk from the bent carton, then reaches for the telephone, her fingers trembling slightly as they spin the rotary dial. She squints at the sloppily written numbers on the back of the card, smudged from being handled before the ink was dry, tucked carefully under her mattress until now. Three rings echo in her ear, each one stretching her nerves tighter, then Tam's gruff hello cuts through the static.

"It's me," Amy says, keeping her voice low despite the empty apartment. "We need to talk. He knows I've seen you."

"Shit." Tam's voice sharpens with alarm, the word slicing through the line. Amy can almost picture her aunt's face hardening, those assessing brown eyes narrowing. "Did he hurt you? Tell me the truth."

"No. But he might be coming your way. He left last night, totally pissed off." Amy winds the phone cord around her finger until the tip turns white. "Called you names. Then grabbed his keys and went out."

"Great. Just what I need." The sound of a cigarette being lit comes through the line—a quick flick of a lighter, the deep inhale. "Look, kid, maybe we should cool it for a while. This is too complicated. I've got enough problems."

"It was always hard," Amy counters, straightening her posture against the kitchen wall. "But now we can scare him. He's afraid of us. Don't you see? We're winning now."

"And scared men do stupid things. Dangerous things." Tam exhales audibly. "I know James Elder. When he feels cornered, he lashes out. Hard."

"I can handle him."

"You're ten, for fuck's sake. No matter how grown up you sound, no matter what you've been through, you're still a kid up against a full-grown man with rage issues."

"I'm not by myself," Amy says simply. "I have you."

The statement, delivered with such certainty, creates a long pause on the other end of the line. "Look, I feel for you. Really, I do. But I'm not gonna be your new mom."

"I don't want a mom. I want a partner."

Another long pause. "Okay, you're officially scaring me now, Amy. Whatever you're planning, whatever you think I agreed to— no. Just no. I'll help you find a better foster placement, maybe, but that's it."

"He needs to pay for what he did," Amy says, her voice getting harder. "To Beth. To you. What he might do to me."

"Yeah, well, life's not fair. Bad guys don't always get what they deserve."

"They do if someone makes them."

Tam sighs heavily, the sound traveling through the phone like a physical weight. "Jesus, kid. Listen to yourself. You're talking about what? Murder? Revenge? That's not how the real world works. That's the kind of thinking that lands people in prison, or worse."

"That's exactly how it works," Amy replies, her eyes narrowing as she grips the phone tighter. "People take stuff, hurt whoever they want, and nobody stops them unless someone makes them. The police don't help. The courts don't help. Everybody lets guys like... *him* do whatever they want. You know that better than anyone."

The certainty in her voice—cold, calculating, utterly devoid of juvenile uncertainty—creates another extended silence that stretches between them like a chasm. When Tam finally speaks, her tone has shifted from exasperation to caution, the wariness of someone who suddenly realizes they might be dealing with something dangerous.

"Who are you, Amy Elder? Really?" The question comes slowly, deliberately, as if she is afraid of the answer.

"I told you. I'm Beth's daughter. Your niece..." Amy pauses for effect before adding, "Your half-sister."

"No, there's something else." Tam's voice lowers to almost a whisper, the words emerging with reluctant curiosity. "What happened in California? What were you and Beth running from? Because normal people don't just get shot by the police. Something happened."

Amy stands perfectly still, weighing her response carefully. The truth, the actual truth, would end this fragile alliance immediately. A partial truth, however, might serve her purposes. Just enough reality to be believable, just enough omission to keep Tam engaged.

"Beth killed a man," she says finally, her voice unnervingly steady for a child discussing maternal homicide. "He tried to hurt us. She stopped him. Permanently."

"Christ." Tam's exhale is shaky, the sound of someone having their worst suspicions confirmed. "And the police shot her for it?

For defending herself and her kid? That's the kind of justice we're supposed to believe in?"

"Something like that." Amy allows a calculated pause, letting Tam fill in the blanks with her own assumptions. Her own need to see Beth as victim rather than perpetrator. To rewrite history in a way that makes sense to her moral compass. "The world isn't fair, like you said. But we can make it fair."

"Okay. Okay." She seems to be talking to herself as much as to Amy. "That explains some things. But listen to me, Amy. Whatever you're thinking, whatever Beth taught you, this isn't the way. You've got a chance at a normal life. Don't throw it away on revenge."

"What if I don't want a normal life?" Amy asks, genuine curiosity in her voice. "What if normal was never an option for me?"

"Everyone has choices."

"Even you? Even Beth?" The questions land like darts, precise and pointed. "Did you choose to let James break your jaw? Did Beth choose what he did to her?"

"That's different—"

"No. It's not." Amy's certainty brooks no argument.

Tam clears her throat. "I've got to go. Look, just... be careful. Whatever you're planning, whatever you think you know—James is dangerous. Really dangerous."

"So am I," Amy replies simply. "I'll call you tomorrow."

She cuts off before Tam can respond, the click of the receiver a period at the end of the conversation. The apartment feels different now, the air charged with possibility, with purpose. The walls that had seemed to press in on her for weeks now feel like the containing edges of a chessboard, the opening moves already played.

Amy moves to the window, drawing back the curtain slightly to study the street below. The pavement stretches empty below the harsh Nevada sun, cracked and unforgiving like everything else in this city. Empty now, but it won't remain so. James will return eventually, possibly drunk, definitely wary, his heavy footsteps telegraphing his mood long before his key scratches against the lock. The confrontation has established new parameters, new dynamics between them. He knows that she knows. Knows that his secret isn't secret anymore. The invisible barrier of ignorance that once protected him has dissolved like sugar in hot water.

Knowledge is indeed power. And power, properly applied, can be transformative.

Or destructive.

The thought brings a slight curve to Amy's lips, not quite a smile but something adjacent to satisfaction.

Amy lets the curtain fall back into place, returning the apartment to its artificial twilight, the shadows pooling in corners where dust gathers undisturbed. She crosses to the drawer where James keeps the takeout menus, the wood sticking slightly as she pulls it open. Her small fingers bypass the greasy Chinese restaurant pamphlets and pizza coupons, extracting instead a folded paper she'd hidden there days earlier. A bus schedule, with certain routes highlighted in yellow, the paper creased along precise lines. Her fingers trace the highlighted paths, calculating distances and timing, building contingencies for every possible outcome. Her eyes narrow in concentration, absorbing details that most adults would overlook.

The Golden Nugget, where James's poker deal starts at eight p.m. tomorrow, the casino's gaudy exterior hiding the desperation inside. The Velvet Slipper Lounge, where Tam works until two a.m., serving drinks to men who look at her like she's on tap too. The all-night pharmacy where James fills his ulcer medication prescription, the little white pills he depends on to counteract his excessive drinking.

All the pieces arranged on the board, waiting for the right moment, the right move. Like chess, but with real consequences, real blood.

Amy returns to the table, the laminate surface scratched from years of careless use. She methodically finishes her now-soggy few kernels of cereal, the milk turned lukewarm and gray. Waste is inefficient. Energy must be maintained. The coming days will require both physical and mental stamina. Each spoonful is consumed with deliberate purpose, fuel for what lies ahead.

The phone rings again, slicing through the stillness of the apartment. Amy glances at the screen, her finger hovering over the green button. It's the school's number. She lets it ring, letting it go to voicemail, the sound fading into silence as she turns away.

Today isn't a day for classes or lessons about long division. Today is about strategy, about planning her next move. The chair creaks under her slight weight as she settles back at the table, pushing aside her empty bowl.

She thinks of Beth's diaries tucked away in a shoebox under her bed—frayed edges and faded ink tell stories that remain just out of reach. The entries hold fragments of Beth's life before everything spiraled into chaos: dreams and fears scrawled on paper like secrets waiting to be unearthed.

Amy stands and walks down the narrow hallway, pausing at her bedroom door. She glances back toward the phone on the kitchen counter before stepping inside. Dust motes dance in the shafts of sunlight filtering through the blinds, casting a warm glow over the mess of secondhand clothes littering the floor.

Kneeling beside her bed, she pulls out the shoebox with care, its cardboard sides soft from years of handling. Dust swirls around her as she opens it, revealing notebooks stacked precariously atop one another, each filled with Beth's thoughts penned in tight loops and hurried scribbles.

She flips through them methodically, page after page revealing snippets of life that seem mundane yet profound. The pages are stained with coffee rings and smudges from greasy fingers; they hold traces of both love and loss. Amy's fingers glide over a passage about her mother's aspirations—traveling to Paris, meeting an artist—but those dreams were snuffed out long ago.

One misspelled entry catches her eye: "Trust is a frajile thing." It resonates within her, stirring something deep.

"What can I use?" she whispers to herself, scanning for clues that might serve her purpose.

There's talk of James, a brief mention about his brother, Beth, and Tam's uncle. Her heart races; this could be useful. Another possible pawn in her game, perhaps?

Amy grins slightly, tucking that information away for later use while flipping pages faster now, determined to find anything else that could tip the scales in her favor against James. But there's no greater sin than the ones she already knows about.

The phone buzzes again in the other room, but she ignores it completely, her focus unwavering as she immerses herself in Beth's world once more, feeling more empowered with each revelation uncovered in those fragile pages.

Outside and miles away, the neon lights of Las Vegas begin to flicker to life as dusk approaches, blinking and flashing, a gaudy imitation of starlight against the darkening sky. Inside, a child who has never truly been a child continues her careful plotting, her small fingers drumming briefly against the tabletop before growing still. She arranges the world according to her design—patient, methodical, and utterly without worry. In her mind, the future has already happened. All that remains is execution.

James Edison Elder moves through his apartment with the wary caution of a man navigating a minefield. Three days have passed since Amy's revelation, three days of tense silence and careful avoidance. He rises early, before she wakes for school. Returns late, after she's supposedly asleep. Maintains his distance during the transitory moments their paths unavoidably cross.

He stands now in the narrow kitchen, coffee cooling in his mug as he stares unseeing at the racing form spread across the counter. The newsprint blurs before his eyes, yesterday's winners and today's odds meaningless against the roar of his own thoughts.

She *knows*.

The uncovered secret circles his mind like a shark, relentless and hungry. Amy knows what happened between him and Beth. Knows the unforgivable truth that he's spent a decade trying to drown in booze and anonymity. And worse, much worse, Amy has brought Tam into this mess.

His fingers tighten around the coffee mug, knuckles whitening with strain. How had the kid even found Tam? How had she even gotten to the Velvet Slipper? The questions circle uselessly, irrelevant against the naked reality of his exposure.

The telephone's shrill ring shatters his reverie. James stares at it, paralyzed by sudden, irrational certainty. It's Tam, calling to threaten him. Or the police, finally connecting the dots he's spent years obscuring. Or worst of all, someone who knows what Beth really was... what Amy might be.

On the fourth ring, he forces himself to answer. "Hello?"

"Dad? It's me."

The voice from the past hits like a physical blow. James leans against the counter for support, blood rushing in his ears. "How did you get this number?"

"We need to talk."

"We have nothing to talk about." James's voice hardens with defensive anger. "Stay away from Amy. Stay away from me."

"That's not how this works, Daddy." The old name, once affectionate, now drips with contempt. "You don't get to dictate terms. Not anymore."

"What do you want? Money?" He barks a harsh laugh. "I'm broke."

"I don't want your money." Tam's voice lowers. "I want to talk about Beth. About what really happened in California."

James's blood runs to a chill. "What are you talking about?"

"The police shooting. The reason one of your daughters is dead and your granddaughter is living in your sorry excuse for a home." A pause teeming with implication.

"I don't know what you're talking about," James insists, but uncertainty creeps into his tone. The truth is, he knows almost nothing about Beth's final years, about the circumstances that led to her death. The social worker had been vague, the paperwork minimal. "Amy hasn't told me anything."

"No, I don't suppose she would." Tam's voice takes on an odd quality, something like concern along with the habitual disdain. "Look, I'm not doing this over the phone. Meet me at Casey's Diner. Three o'clock."

"I'm not—"

"Three o'clock, Dad. Don't make me come to you." The threat is implicit in her tone. "And don't bring Amy."

The line goes dead, leaving James staring at the receiver in his hand. Conflicting impulses war within him. Run, hide, confront, deny. But beneath them all, a desperate curiosity stirs. What does Tam know that he doesn't? What happened to Beth in those lost years after she left Vegas?

The questions gnaw at him, more insistent than the guilt that has become his constant companion. With shaking hands, he pours the remainder of his coffee down the sink and reaches for his keys. He needs to clear his head, needs distance from the suffocating walls of the apartment.

He scrawls a note for Amy—"Working double shift. Money for pizza on fridge. BE HOME BY DARK."—and tapes it to the refrigerator door. The lie comes easily, another in the long chain of deceptions that forms the backbone of his existence.

Casey's Diner sits on the edge of downtown, far enough from the Strip to avoid tourists but close enough to catch the spillover from casino employees seeking cheap, hearty meals between shifts. The vinyl booths are cracked from years of use, the counter's laminate surface worn smooth where countless elbows have rested. A waitress in a faded pink uniform moves between tables with adroit efficiency, coffee pot in one hand, order pad in the other.

James slides into a booth in the far corner, positioning himself to face the door. Old habits die hard—always know who's coming, always have a clear path to the exit. The smell of hamburger grease reaches his nostrils, making his stomach growl. But he can't eat. He orders coffee when the waitress approaches, ignoring her attempt at small talk. His eyes remain fixed on the entrance, muscles tensed with anticipation.

At precisely three o'clock, Tamerlane, his eldest daughter, a thorn in his side, pushes through the glass door. She doesn't look around, doesn't hesitate, moves directly toward James's booth as though guided by an internal compass calibrated to his specific frequency. She slides in across from him, her movements fluid but tense.

She says nothing, just looks at him with an expression that shows she's found him lacking.

James's fingers tighten around his coffee mug. "What do you want, Tam?"

The waitress approaches, coffeepot extended questioningly. Tam nods, waiting until her mug is filled and the waitress departs before answering.

"I want to understand what we're dealing with," she says, her voice low enough that only James can hear. "With Amy."

"Amy is fine," James replies automatically. "Getting settled. School's good. Everything's normal."

Tam's laugh holds no humor. "Normal? That kid's *not* normal."

The statement touches something raw in James's consciousness, the unease he's felt since Amy's arrival, the sense that something isn't quite right about Beth's daughter. Her stillness, her watchfulness, her complete lack of childish spontaneity. The fact that she has his bright green eyes.

"She's been through a trauma," he says, the explanation sounding hollow even to his own ears. "Her mother was killed in front of her. Of course she's not going to act like other kids."

"It's more than that." Tam leans forward, her expression grave. "Did you know Beth was caught up in a string of robbery-homicides? All across California?"

James's coffee sloshes over the rim of his mug as his hand jerks involuntarily. "That's bullshit. Beth wasn't— She wouldn't—"

"Wouldn't what? Kill? After what you did to her?" Tam's eyes harden. "You have no idea what Beth became after she left Vegas. What she had to do to survive."

"And you do?" James challenges. "You said yourself you hadn't heard from her in years."

"I have a pretty damn good idea. And I know how to use a library." Tam reaches into her purse and extracts a folded xerographic of newspaper clipping. She slides it across the table toward James. "Take a look."

The clipping, darkened slightly, bears a headline: "MOTHER-CHILD ROBBERY TEAM STRIKES AGAIN IN PANORAMA CITY." Below, a grainy security camera image shows a woman in a long, flowered dress and small child exiting a convenience store. The woman's face is partially turned away from the camera, but something in the posture, the set of the shoulders, is familiar.

"That's not Beth," James says, but uncertainty creeps into his voice. "And even if it was, that kid's too young to be Amy. It's all just coincidence."

"Is it?" Tam produces another clipping. "This one's from two years later."

The second image is a police sketch, showing a female who could be Beth, and a child of indeterminate sex wearing a hoodie that casts shadows over the face.

"Jesus," James whispers, recognition dawning. "That could be..."

"Amy," Tam finishes for him. "And Beth. The 'Bonnie Rotten and Kid Vicious' pair that terrorized the coast for the last several months. Until Beth got shot by cops during a standoff in a motel room." She stifles a sob and quickly recovers her steely resolve.

James pushes the clippings away as though they might contaminate him. "This is crazy. Beth might have been screwed up, but she wasn't a killer. And Amy's just a little girl."

"A little girl who sought me out to talk about killing you," Tam says bluntly. "A little girl who asked if I'd help her do it."

The color drains from James's face. "You're lying."

"Why would I lie about that? What could I possibly gain?"

"I don't know. Revenge? Satisfaction in seeing me squirm?" James's voice rises slightly, drawing a curious glance from a nearby diner. He lowers it again with effort. "You've hated me for years, Tam. Maybe I deserve it. But why should I believe anything you say?"

"Because regardless of what I think of you—and believe me, it's nothing good—I don't want to see that kid follow in her mother's footsteps." Tam sighs, a sound heavy with complicated emotions. "Beth was a victim who became a monster. Amy never had a chance to be anything else."

The words land with devastating precision. James stares at his coffee as though it might hold answers to questions he's afraid to ask. The dark liquid reflects his haggard face back at him, distorted and accusatory. His bloodshot eyes blink rapidly as his mind races through impossible scenarios, each worse than the last.

"What am I supposed to do with this information? Call the cops? Turn in my own... blood?" His fingers twitch against the ceramic mug, the tremor betraying decades of morning-after shakes.

Tam's laugh is a jagged cackle that cuts through the diner's ambient noise like jagged glass. "Right." Several heads turn briefly toward their booth before quickly looking away, sensing the tension. Her expression softens slightly, the hardened edges of her face yielding just enough to reveal the ghost of the hopeful young woman she once was. "I'm not saying she's beyond help. Maybe she is, maybe she isn't. But pretending she's just a normal kid who's been through a rough patch, that's a dangerous fantasy. The kind that gets people killed."

James pushes his mug away with sudden revulsion, the liquid sloshing close to the rim. "Why are you telling me this? You said yourself you hate me." He looks up, meeting her assessing gaze directly for the first time. "Why not let her do whatever she's planning? Wouldn't that be... justice, in your eyes?"

"Because I'm not you, Goddammit," Tam says, the words lanced with pain, her thin scar seeming to whiten against her skin as her jaw tightens. "I don't hurt children. I don't abandon them. And whatever Amy is, whatever she's done, she's still a child. A child who never had a chance at normal because of what *you* did to her mother. To *me*, you bastard."

The accusation reverberates through the space between them, unanswerable and absolute. James slumps in his seat, his polyester shirt bunching around his diminished frame as the consequence of decades of poor choices, selfish actions, and unforgivable cruelties presses down on him like a cancerous mass.

"What should I do?" he asks finally, the question emerging as barely more than a whisper, scraped raw from a throat tight with something that might be fear, might be shame.

"I don't know," Tam replies honestly, her dark eyes studying him with true curiosity. "But being aware is a start. Watching her. Maybe getting her some real help, not just some school counselor with a master's degree and sixty other cases, but someone who understands trauma. Deep trauma. The kind that tears from the inside out."

"She'd never go for that." James runs a weathered hand through his thinning gray hair, dislodging strands that float down onto his shoulders unnoticed.

"Then maybe you need to create a situation where she doesn't have a choice." Tam glances at her watch, the practical, sturdy timepiece at odds with her bony, tattooed wrist. "I've got to go. Afternoon shift starts in twenty."

She slides out of the booth with fluid grace, gathering her worn leather jacket. She pauses before she turns away, one hand resting on the table between them like a bridge neither can cross. "One more thing, Dad." The word sounds foreign on her tongue, as though she's speaking a language she once knew but has deliberately forgotten. "Whatever happens, don't tell Amy we met. Don't tell her we talked. She's got plans, and if she thinks I betrayed her, I don't know what she'll do. To either of us."

James nods, the movement stiff with tension. "I won't."

"Good luck," Tam says, the words holding no warmth. "You'll need it."

She walks away without looking back, leaving James alone with his cold coffee and colder revelations. The newspaper clippings lie on the table between them like physical manifestations of his sins —proof that the damage he inflicted years ago continues to ripple outward, touching lives beyond his own, beyond Beth's, beyond even Amy's.

He gathers the clippings with trembling fingers, folding them carefully before tucking them into his pants pocket. Evidence, perhaps. Or reminders of what's at stake.

The sun dips low in the western sky as James pulls into the parking lot of his apartment building. Golden light reflects off dusty windows, lending temporary beauty to the shabby structure. His footsteps echo in the empty stairwell as he climbs to the third floor, key already in hand.

The apartment door stands ajar, a thin line of light spilling into the dim corridor.

James freezes, heart suddenly thundering in his chest. He distinctly remembers locking the door when he left. Always locks the door... the habit of a lifetime spent in neighborhoods where security is a luxury purchased with deadbolts and chain locks.

"Amy?" he calls, pushing the door open with his fingertips. "You home?"

No response. The television plays at low volume. A game show, contestants cheering over the prize of a new car. A half-eaten slice of pizza lies on a paper plate on the coffee table, the cheese congealed into a rubbery mass.

"Amy?" James calls again, moving cautiously into the apartment. "You here, kiddo?"

The bathroom door is closed, a sliver of light visible underneath. James crosses to it, knuckles raised to knock, when a sound from the kitchen freezes him in place—the soft clink of ice against glass.

He turns slowly, hand dropping to his side, and sees her.

CHAPTER 36

Amy sits at the kitchen table, small hands folded before her with unnatural stillness. She wears her nightgown, the frilly collar a jarring contrast to the stoniness in her eyes. On the table beside her sits a glass filled with clear liquid. Gin, James realizes. His gin, from the bottle he keeps above the refrigerator.

"Hello, James," she says, the adult formality of the greeting raising goose bumps along his arms.

"What are you doing?" he asks, gesture encompassing both the open door and the alcohol.

"Waiting for you," Amy replies simply. "I made you a drink."

James approaches cautiously, awareness prickling along his nerve endings. The apartment feels different, the air charged with potential energy, like the moment before lightning strikes.

"That's my gin," he says, stopping several feet from the table. "You're too young to be handling alcohol."

"But not too young to be its consequence," Amy counters, the philosophical observation grotesque coming from childish lips. "Isn't that right, James?"

The use of his first name, the deliberate distancing it creates, heightens his unease. Not that she ever called him "Grandpa," of course; she never addressed him at all. "What's going on here, Amy? Why aren't you in bed? It's a school night."

"I've been thinking about parents," she says, ignoring his questions entirely. "About the things they do to protect their children. The things they should do but sometimes don't."

James shifts his weight, detecting a new tension in the room. "Beth did her best by you," he offers awkwardly. "She wasn't perfect, but she loved you."

"Did she?" Amy's head tilts slightly, a gesture reminiscent of a raptor assessing prey. "Or did she use me? Did she make me into what she needed me to be?"

The question hovers, unanswerable. James takes another step forward, close enough now to see the contents of the kitchen sink. A dinner plate soaking in sudsy water, a drinking glass beside it. Nothing unusual, nothing threatening. Yet the mundane domesticity feels like a carefully constructed façade.

"It's late," he says finally. "Whatever's bothering you, we can talk about it in the morning."

"I'd rather talk now." Amy pushes the glass toward him with a single finger. "Sit. Drink. Listen."

Despite himself, James finds his body complying. He sits across from her, the gin glass cold against his palm. He raises it to his lips automatically, then hesitates, a new wariness creeping through him.

"It's not poisoned," Amy says, reading his thoughts with disturbing accuracy. "That would be too easy. Too nice. I want you to see everything."

"Jesus Christ," James mutters, setting the glass down untouched. His fingers tremble slightly as they retreat from the tumbler. "What is this? What do you want from me?"

"The truth," she answers immediately, her eyes never leaving his face. "The real truth. All of it. About you and Beth. About what you did to her."

James's throat tightens, old guilt rising like bile. The room suddenly feels airless, as if the walls are contracting around him. "I don't know what you're talking about," he manages, the lie sticking to his tongue like tar.

"Yes, you do." Amy's voice remains perfectly level, showing no feeling, which somehow makes it more scary than if she were screaming. "Beth's diaries tell everything. All of it. Every part. You hurt her. Used her. Made her pregnant with me."

The words thrum in the air between them, naked and ugly in their baldness. James's hands twitch toward the glass, then retreat, as though even alcohol cannot provide sufficient escape from this moment. The weight of a decade-old shame presses down on his chest like a headstone.

"I was drunk," he says finally, the justification pathetic even to his own ears. His voice cracks with the admission. "After her mother died, I was a mess. Completely lost. Beth was there, and I... I made a mistake. A terrible mistake. I've regretted it every day since."

"A mistake," Amy repeats, the word flat and uninfected. Her fingers tap methodically against the kitchen table, like someone keeping time to music only she can hear. "Is that what I am? A mistake?"

"No! That's not what I meant." James runs a hand through his goatee, panic rising as if he realizes how his words sound. Sweat beads along his hairline. "Look, I can't change what happened. I've lived with it every day since she left. The guilt, the shame, it's been in my head, never letting me be. What more do you want from me?"

"Justice," Amy answers simply. "Making things even. Making things fair."

"What?" James sputters, confusion momentarily overriding

fear. The kitchen light flickers once overhead as a moth bashes into the bulb, casting strange shadows across Amy's face.

"For every thing you do, something happens back. For every bad thing, a punishment. It's like when you push something, it pushes back." Amy's gaze doesn't move, looking at him like a doctor deciding where to cut first. "You made this happen, James. You started all this. Now it's come back to you."

"I've never heard you talk so much." He chuckles, trying to lighten the tension.

"I'm going to tell you a secret," she continues, leaning forward slightly. "I've killed. More than once. And it wasn't Beth who made me do it. I wasn't following her rules or doing what she wanted for getting back at you. I think I have bad blood. Maybe I'm just bad. Maybe I got it from *you*."

James buries his head in his hands, taking all this in. His shoulders slump with the revelation, of horrors both past and present converging in this ordinary kitchen on this extraordinary night. He keeps his eyes closed as if wishing he could disappear.

A new sound breaks the tense silence—the bathroom door opening, hinges creaking slightly. James turns, expecting... what? A police officer? Tam, despite her promise not to intervene?

When he turns back, Amy is standing, the transition so silent he didn't detect her movement. In her hand gleams something metallic. A knife? No, he realizes with horror. A straight razor.

His straight razor, taken from the medicine cabinet where it's sat unused for years, a relic from his own father's meager possessions.

"Amy," he says, his voice dropping to a placating whisper. "Put that down. You don't want to do this."

"Don't I?" she asks, sounding really curious. "How would you know what I want? You've only known me for a month."

"Because you're just a kid," James insists, eyes fixed on the razor. "Whatever you think this will accomplish, it won't bring her back. It won't fix what happened."

"I'm not trying to fix anything," Amy replies. "I'm just finishing what you started. Closing the circle."

She steps toward him, the movement fluid and practiced. James rises from his chair, backing away, looking frantically for an escape route. The front door stands open behind her, but she blocks his path to it. The window leads to a three-story drop to merciless concrete.

"Amy, please." His voice breaks, terror stripping away the last vestiges of dignity. "I know I've done terrible things. I know I don't deserve forgiveness. But this—this isn't the answer."

"Then what is?" Amy asks, her voice showing she really wants to know. "Talking to doctors? Jail? Neither seems enough for what you did."

"I don't know," James admits. "But it's not this. You're better than that."

Something flickers in Amy's eyes. A momentary hesitation, perhaps. Or simply a rejiggering of odds.

"Am I?" she wonders aloud.

James sees his opening. A glimmer of uncertainty, a hairline fracture in her resolve.

"You can be," he says urgently. "Whatever you've done, you're still young. You can choose a different path."

Amy's head tilts again, that birdlike gesture that seems simultaneously childish and ancient. "That's a nice thing to say for a man who raped his daughter. Or was it 'daughters'?"

The assessment, so brutally accurate, steals James's breath. Before he can formulate a response, Amy continues.

"But maybe you're right. Maybe there are other ways to think about." She lowers the razor slightly, though not enough to suggest surrender. "What do you think we should do?"

Hope flares in James's chest—a chance, however slim, to talk his way out of this nightmare. "We could get help. Both of us. Find someone who specializes in trauma, in family reconciliation."

"Reconciliation," Amy repeats, testing the word. "That's interesting. But getting along means having something in common. Something both people care about." Her eyes, so weirdly like his own, stare at James like she can see through him. "What do we share, James? What things do we both care about that connect us?"

The question is a trap, James senses. But what choice does he have but to answer?

"Blood," he says finally. "We're family, Amy. Whatever else has happened, whatever wrongs I've committed, that fact remains. Blood ties us together."

"Blood," Amy echoes, her gaze dropping to the razor in her hand. "Yes, I guess it does."

The movement, when it comes, happens with such balletic precision that James has no time to react. One moment Amy stands three feet away, razor lowered; the next, she's beside him, the blade flashing in the kitchen's fluorescent light.

Pain blooms along the back of his hand—bright, immediate, shocking in its intensity. He looks down to see a perfect line of red opening across his skin, blood welling in its wake.

"What—?" he gasps, stumbling backward, clutching his arm. "Amy, stop!"

But she doesn't advance. Instead, she turns the razor toward her own palm and, with the same detached precision, draws the blade across her skin. Warm fluid rises from the shallow cut, pooling in the cup of her small hand.

"Blood ties," she says, extending her bleeding palm toward James. "The only real thing between us."

James stares, horror and confusion warring for dominance. "What are you doing?"

"Starting something new," Amy replies. "A promise written in the only way that matters." She steps closer, bleeding palm still extended. "Your blood. My blood. The thing that connects us, no matter how much either of us wants to break it."

Understanding dawns slowly, horribly. This isn't an attempted murder. It's something more complex, more disturbing. A ritual of Amy's own devising, a blood oath that binds rather than releases.

"I don't understand," James admits, his voice barely audible.

"You will," Amy promises. She gestures to his bleeding arm. "Finish it, James. Show you know what we are to each other."

Logic suggests refusing, running, calling for help. But something deeper than logic, some primal recognition of the moment's significance, keeps James rooted in place. With trembling fingers, he extends his bleeding arm toward Amy's outstretched hand.

Their blood mingles, warm and sticky between their palms. Amy's fingers close around his with surprising strength, the pressure both intimate and threatening.

"There," she says, satisfaction evident in her tone. "Now there's truth between us. No more lies. No more secrets."

"What does this mean?" James asks, the question emerging as barely more than a whisper.

Amy releases his hand, reaching for a kitchen towel to wrap around her palm. "It means I won't kill you today," she answers simply. "It means you get a chance to show you deserve to stay alive."

The specificity of her assessment, the calm certainty with which she pronounces his conditional reprieve, sends ice water through James's veins. Tam is right. This is no ordinary child. This is something else altogether. Something born of his sins, shaped by Beth's trauma, honed through a hell he can barely imagine.

"Okay," he says finally, the word automatic, absurd in its inadequacy.

Amy nods once, acknowledgment rather than acceptance. "Put something on your arm," she advises, practical once more. "You're getting blood on the floor."

With that, she turns and moves toward her bedroom, leaving

James standing in the kitchen, red dripping from his fingertips, the straight razor gleaming on the countertop where she placed it with delicate precision.

The front door still stands open, offering escape, freedom, the chance to run as far and fast as possible from this apartment, this child, this reckoning. James stares at it, considering possibilities, calculating odds in the manner of a lifelong gambler.

Then, with slow deliberation, he crosses to the door and closes it. Locks it. Seals himself inside with the strange, dangerous creature that is Beth's legacy and his own damnation.

Blood ties, indeed. The only ones that truly matter. The only ones that can never be outrun.

In her bedroom, Amy sits on the edge of her narrow bed, wrapping a clean tissue around her palm. The cut is shallow, precise, designed to bleed impressively without causing serious damage. She has no intention of harming herself permanently. She is far too valuable an instrument to damage carelessly.

She tears her nightgown's lace collar, carefully created to be her explanation for the razor if questions arise. Simple, plausible deniability. Another skill learned at Beth's side, watching her mother weave webs of deception with practiced ease.

She reaches under her pillow, extracting Tam's card. The number scrawled on the back represents another resource, another piece on her chessboard. Not an ally, perhaps. Tonight's exercise has confirmed her suspicion that Tam warned James, betrayed their fragile alliance. But still useful, still manipulable through guilt and shared history.

The razor was never meant to end James's life. That would be too simple, too quick, too merciful. No, Amy has different plans for her grandfather—her father—the architect of her existence. Death is momentary. Redemption, however, requires time.

Requires suffering. Requires acknowledgment of sins and genuine contrition.

Outside her window, the city of sin goes on with its perpetual striptease, indifferent to the small dramas playing out in anonymous apartments. Inside, a child who has never truly been a child contemplates her next move, the blood drying on her palm a reminder of connections that cannot be severed. Only redirected, repurposed, perhaps even redeemed.

The apartment settles into silence, broken only by the faint hum of the air conditioner and James's unsteady breathing from the living room. The clink of ice in his glass.

Amy sits cross-legged on her bed, palms upturned on her knees, eyes closed. Her cut hand has stopped bleeding, the tissue wrapped around it spotted but drying.

The air in the small bedroom thickens, growing dense with something beyond the November chill, a presence that doesn't disturb the physical space but alters it nonetheless.

In the corner, a shadow detaches itself from the darkness. It slides across the floor, taking form as it approaches, scales catching moonlight through the thin curtains, a wedge-shaped head raised in alert vigilance. The snake's tongue flickers, tasting the air, its movements deliberate and patient.

Amy doesn't open her eyes, but her lips curve in recognition.

From beneath the dresser, another shape emerges—smaller, quicker, with bright eyes and twitching whiskers. The rat scurries forward, pausing to sit on its haunches, front paws held close to its chest in a posture almost like prayer. Its naked tail curls around its feet, a question mark of caution and calculation.

The window glass ripples like disturbed water, and through it steps a coyote, lean and watchful. Its coat carries the dust of desert travels, its eyes the ancient wisdom of survival against all odds. It settles onto its haunches, muzzle pointed toward Amy, ears swiveling to catch every sound in the apartment beyond.

More of Amy's creatures crowd the space—the spider, the

crow, the giant wasp, a wriggling maggot—last comes the shrew, so small it might be overlooked, slipping through a crack in reality that seals behind it. Quick and nervous, it darts between the larger presences, bringing with it the energy of constant motion, of life lived in perpetual awareness of danger. They form a circle around the bed, these creatures of survival and adaptation. None would naturally gather together—predator and prey, hunter and scavenger—yet here they maintain perfect equilibrium, united by their connection to the child at their center.

Amy opens her eyes. "You're all here," she whispers, her voice carrying no surprise, only confirmation.

The green viper slides closer, its scales shifting in kaleidoscopes. *The blood pact is made*, it says, voice dry as desert sand. *The venom can wait.*

For now, adds the rat, whiskers twitching with nervous energy. *We remember what he did. What they all did.*

The coyote stretches, its movements fluid and deceptively casual. *Patience serves the hunt. Let him believe he's earned reprieve.*

Watch every movement, the shrew chirps, never still, circling the bed's perimeter. *Trust nothing. Prepare for betrayal.*

Amy nods, acknowledging each counsel. "I carry all of you in my heart," she says. "Your wisdom. Your instincts."

She extends her hands, and one by one, the creatures approach. The snake glides up her arm, its scales dissolving into her skin like water into sand. The crow climbs to her shoulder, pressing its beak against her neck before fading into her flesh. The coyote rests its muzzle against her knee, its form blurring, merging with her own essence. The shrew darts to her palm, vibrating with energy that flows into her bloodstream.

One by one, Amy's spirit animals merge.

With each integration, her posture shifts subtly. Her spine straightening with the snake's confidence, her eyes brightening with the rat's cunning, her shoulders setting with the coyote's endurance, her fingers flexing with the scorpion's perpetual readiness.

When the room is empty of all but herself, Amy opens her eyes again. They reflect the moonlight differently now. Not with the shine of a child's gaze but with the layered depth of something far older, far wilder.

The game, begun years ago with James's original sin, continues. The pieces are set. The board defined. And Amy Andrea Elder —daughter of Beth, granddaughter of James, child of violence and division—waits patiently to see what moves her opponent will make next.

ABOUT THE AUTHOR

Staci Layne Wilson is an L.A. native who enjoys traffic, wildfires, and earthquakes—but since her move to Las Vegas, she's learned to love 110-degree summers, drive-thru wedding chapels, and casinos that still reek of the Rat Pack's cigars. She has been a professional writer since the age of 12, when she was hired as a columnist for a national magazine. When she's not writing books, she is making movies (Cabaret of the Dead, Dark House of the Mannequins) and running the WomenInHorror.com website.

ALSO BY
STACI LAYNE WILSON

The "Nature's Nightmares" series

The "Rock & Roll Nightmares" series

"City of Devils" short story collection

"Cabaret of the Dead" film novelization